PURGATORIUM

There is no world for me...Except purgatory, torture, and hell itself.

Shakespeare
Romeo and Juliet

"A wonderfully dark and eerie collection of tales that will keep you turning the pages. If you are a fan of *Twilight Zone*, *The Outer Limits*, or *Black Mirror*, you'll love what *Purgatorium: The Element of Horror* has to offer."

Mark Leslie, Author of *I, Death* and *Tomes of Terror*

CONTENTS

Acknowledgments — I

PLAYTHINGS

Dubious Pickles
~ Kevin Craig — 1

Carousel Eyes
~ Yvonne Hess — 23

Unstrung
~ Connie Di Pietro — 57

THRESHOLDS

Blood Pies
~ Kate Arms — 79

Ivy
~ Mel E. Cober — 93

Terminal
~ Robert E. Walton — 111

Nekomata
~ A.L. Tompkins — 131

MONSTERS

Fight or Flight
~ Tobin Elliott — 173

Mule
~ Pat Flewwelling — 199

Victim of Love
~ Samantha Banik — 221

Pieces
~ Tobin Elliott & Robert E. Walton — 255

Roll Credits — 293

ACKNOWLEDGMENTS

There is something to be said for being in the right place and time. Some call it serendipitous: to come upon or find by accident; fortuitous. This was how the seed of an idea formed. That idea; a collaboration of authors and friends who came together and created this very anthology. Some of those don't even realize their involvement. Without them, the anthology would not have been possible.

At a Writers' Community of Durham Region Roundtable meeting, where speakers from the literary world entertain, educate and facilitate, author Mark Leslie Lefebvre planted inspiration. He spoke of a collaboration of his friends writing short stories and putting them together to sell, to get their names out there, and get them noticed. He used free platforms such as WATTPAD and e-published to Kindle and Kobo. I figured I was no different than he was when he first came up with the idea. I, too, have friends who write. I knew we all wanted to be published and had great stories to tell. I shared my thought with Tobin Elliott, and from there, it grew.

So for inspiring the anthology brainchild, I must give a heartfelt thank you. If it wasn't for me sitting in the audience of writers as he spoke, I wouldn't be sitting behind my computer right now acknowledging Mark Leslie Lefebvre.

➤ Connie Di Pietro

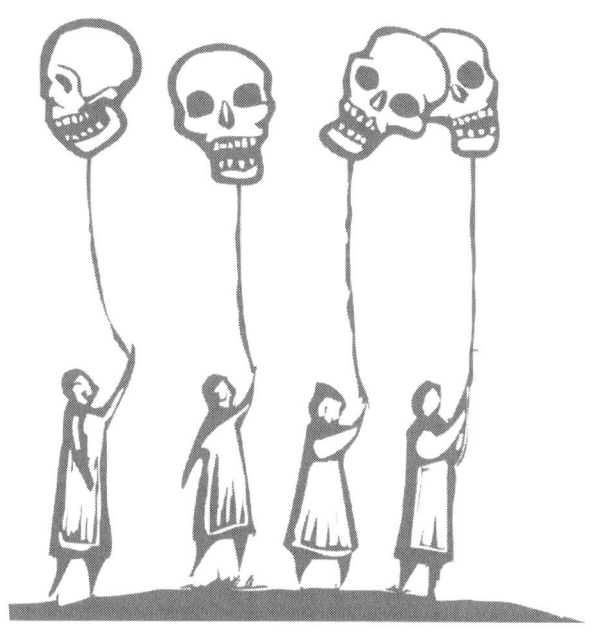

PART ONE:
PLAYTHINGS

Who buys a minute's mirth to wail a week?
Or sells eternity to get a toy?

Shakespeare
Tarquin and Lucrece

DUBIOUS PICKLES
AND THE CURIOSITY OF ARBOUR LÉVESQUE

Kevin Craig

"SOMETHING AIN'T QUITE right with Dubious Pickles," Doc Jenson said from his pulpit behind his thrift shop counter. The string of bells announcing Pickles' departure had not quite simmered to a whisper before his proclamation was out.

Doc, who wasn't really a doctor at all, spent his days passing such judgements on the few customers still brave enough to subject themselves to his ridicule.

Dubious Pickles, being of birth Paul Dubois, however, was definitely not quite right. Doc was dead on the money with that one. All the children in Dobber Corner knew this. Children are the first to know when somebody is not quite right. Children are smart that way.

Arbour Lévesque, being one of the town's brighter children, knew Doc was absolutely right. Arbour turned his gaze from the door and tried to shake the lingering shiver-creeps from his spine. He stepped up to the counter and braced himself for Doc's microscope of scrutiny.

"And to what do I owe this *honour*, my dear Master Lévesque?" Doc asked, not even attempting to hide his scorn. In his desire to needle the boy, he went as far as to pronounce the 's' in Arbour's last name. Everybody in Dobber knew the 's' was silent.

Doc's bald head glistened under the bare bulb dangling directly above him. Though the shop had air conditioning, nobody in town had ever stepped foot in the store for the sole purpose of escaping from the heat outside. Doc never actually had the air running. He glistened from May to September in his penny-pinching stubbornness.

Arbour cleared his throat and attempted to sound much older than his ten-and-three-quarters years.

"Just this here pair of boots, Doc, and…the lunchbox behind you." He pointed to a shelf behind Doc as he tossed a pair of well-scuffed size 11 cowboy boots onto the counter.

"My, what big feet you have, Master L."

Arbour, of course, blushed from tip to toe. Children do not like such things to be pointed out. Spotlights scare them almost as much as *not quite right* people like Dubious Pickles. Arbour tried his best to smile, but inside he cursed the glistening doctor.

Billy Mahone, who stood beside the counter

holding court with the good doctor, chuckled like his head would roll from his short, troll-like body. Arbour paid him no mind. Billy's nervous twitch and outhouse-dunked donkey scent scared Arbour more than just a little bit. He often wondered how a person could smell so bad and still be among the living.

"There you go, then, Arbour," Doc said, "That'll be seven-eighteen." He placed the lunchbox down beside the boots and extended his hand to receive Arbour's money.

"But the boots say two dollars?" Arbour whined, confused by Doc's tally.

"Yes. What is it with you kids, always comin' back at me with these '*but the boots say*' accusations? The boots be two dollars and the lunchbox be five-eighteen. That, Master Lévesque, comes to seven-eighteen where I come from."

Arbour lifted the lunchbox up for inspection. Beyond it, he saw Dubious' face staring in through the big front window of the store. *Like a little boy*, Arbour thought. But Dubious was a man. Very much *not* a boy.

The mere presence of Dubious Pickles had terrorized the minds of children in Dobber Corner for decades. His tentacles of auburn hair sprayed away from his deformed face in a way to suggest it, too, wanted nothing to do with its proximity. His features seemed to fall away from where they rightly belonged, making it appear as though you were always seeing him through a rain-soaked window. Arbour now stared at that tortured face in wonder.

Dubious had cupped his hands around his eyes

to block out the glare so he could see inside the shop. Arbour accidentally made eye contact. Dubious smiled, his crooked mouth looking like a frenzy of hostility. Arbour couldn't tell if it was an *I'm gonna eat you* smile or a *nice to meet you* smile. While he was deciding, Dubious did something else. Something that took Arbour's breath away.

With his hands cupped tight to the window, Dubious stared directly at Arbour as four Indian rubber balls juggled through the air above his head. Arbour's eyes went to the balls, then back to Dubious' cupped face. Dubious raised his eyes, as if to look at the balls dancing above his head, then winked at Arbour through the glass. Arbour watched as, one by one, the balls began to drop from sight.

Dubious' head shivered impossibly, as though it were a jackhammer on full throttle. His features blurred to nothing more than a wild smudge of auburn as everything winked out but the wild bush of hair atop his spasming head.

"Earth to Arbour," Doc said, noting what had stolen Arbour's attentions. "You in there, sonny boy? You pay no never mind to that Pickles character, hear? That's a curiosity that'll getcha trouble you can't pay for."

Dubious' head slowly stopped its wild impossible frenzy and came to a simmering rest on his shoulders once again, unseen by all but Arbour.

The lunchbox rattled ever so slightly in Arbour's hands. Unable to figure out Dubious' hands-free juggling trick, or the earthquaking head trick that followed it, Arbour forced himself to return his gaze to the doctor.

"The tag says three-seventy. That's five-seventy all together, Doc."

Billy bawled another stink-filled stream of open-mouthed laughter. Again, Arbour ignored him.

"Well. I'll be bashed in sideways," Doc said. "You're right, there, ain'tcha Arbour? I suppose — but just for today, mind you — I can let the works go for five-seventy. Don't you go tellin' anyone you got a deal, though, hear?"

"But it's not a deal if—"

"You take your kit and go now, Arbour. Before I change my mind and shake ya backwards for the other dollar forty-eight."

Arbour was more interested in getting outside than arguing with the cantankerous Doc. His sights were now set on Dubious, who had moved away from the window. Arbour gave Doc his money and grabbed the boots up off the counter. As he ran for the door, he heard Doc mumble something. He smiled as the bells cut off the good doctor's parting words.

Like most kids, Arbour was over-curious of the comings and goings of Dubious Pickles. Unlike most kids, Arbour almost always followed his curiosity wherever it took him. Outside the store, he looked in all directions. When he didn't see Dubious, he picked up his Windmaker 900 — *the bike that outbikes all bikes* — confident he would catch up with Dubious before he made it back to the Dubois mansion. This wasn't because he had the bike that *outbikes all bikes*. Not completely. Arbour's brother Newton had modified his Windmaker. Newton, who was four years older than Arbour, was a bona fide genius. He was, in fact, a card-carrying member of a real-life society for geniuses. Newton's modifications to Arbour's Windmaker made his bike run just about 38% faster than the bike that already *outbikes all bikes*. This made Arbour the envy of all of his friends.

If Arbour had taken his skateboard to *Doc's Emporium of All Things Fantastical*, he would have had an easier time of things. As it was, he had to hold his new boots in one hand, his lunchbox in the other, and his handlebars in both. If you had seen Arbour speeding down the sidewalk trying to catch up with Dubious Pickles, you would have half-expected to see him going ass over tea kettle. Or, at the very least, head over handlebars.

But Arbour was an excellent cyclist. He was off Main Street in no time, and heading up the hill in the direction of the Dubois mansion.

Up ahead, Dubious was turning off the sidewalk and into his driveway. Poor Arbour. Even with his tricked-out Windmaker, he was not a match for a man who could hands-free juggle and move his head at a speed faster than the human eye can see. He was not going to make it anywhere near Dubious before he disappeared back into the darkness of his crooked little mansion.

As Arbour neared the top of the hill, he suddenly forgot all about the now-vanished Dubious Pickles. What with the hundreds of dark pink Indian rubber balls that rolled and bounced down the hill toward him, it was all Arbour could do just to keep his Windmaker upright. Dubious Pickles was the least of his worries.

Arbour knew how bad it hurt when an Indian rubber ball hit flesh. This is a thing that boys do to each other when recess is drawing to an end and they have run out of things to do. During that last minute before the bell rings, that's the time when balls are thrown and bruises form on the skinny little arms of the boys who are not quick enough to jump out of way of incoming artillery.

To avoid the barrage of balls assaulting him, Arbour steered his bike to the opposite side of the street. But he didn't give up on his quest. Once he got to the top of the hill and faced the bulging Dubois mansion, he stopped.

Off his bike, he took a deep gulp of air, relieved to have been missed by most of the balls that were identical to the ones that had hovered over Dubious' head earlier in the window of Doc's place. Arbour convinced himself this was all he needed to summon the courage to cross the street. Just a simple deep gulp of air. Surely, that was enough.

Setting his new purchases and his bike down in the grass beside the curb, Arbour began the last leg of his journey. He would get to the bottom of this Dubious thing if it killed him, but he wouldn't bring his bike any closer to the Dubois house. He knew that if anything were to happen with his Windmaker, Newton would lay a hefty beating on him when Arbour finally made it home. Newton was very protective of all his inventions. It wouldn't do to bring the Windmaker home if anything bad were to become of it. Newton would clean his clock and kick his butt into next Tuesday and back. The family genius was high-strung and short-fused.

Arbour paused for a moment with his feet on

the yellow line in the middle of the road. He was about to step into the world most feared by the children of Dobber Corner. Once he crossed that line, he knew he would be in Dubious Pickles territory. The mansion itself lurched forward toward that very line, as if reaching out for any child foolish enough to come this far. But Arbour had to do it.

He looked up the street. Nothing. He looked down the street. He could still see the last of the Indian rubber balls making their way to the bottom of the hill and into town. There was nobody else around.

Arbour placed the toe of one shoe gently down on the pavement on the other side of the yellow line. It reminded him of testing the water at the local swimming hole. When nothing horrible happened at that first touch, he considered it safe to step down into the forbidden land of Dubious Pickles.

After peering into the basement window of the Dubois mansion for several minutes, Arbour realized he had to do *something*. He couldn't just lie there in the grass staring into the emptiness hoping for something to happen.

What he wanted to do was call his best friend, Woodrow Thompson, on his cellphone. The reason he didn't do this right away was because of the threat that loomed over his head regarding the use of said cellphone. His mother had threatened him many times not to use his cell minutes unless it was an emergency, and Arbour had a hard time deciding what was and was not an emergency. According to his mother, Arbour was batting oh-for-seventeen so far. Hence, his reluctance to call Woodrow.

Once Arbour made a decision, though, it was pretty hard for him to unmake it. He would stay a while longer and continue his vigil at the basement window. He was just deciding how many Mississippis he would count out before calling it a day when the light went on in the room he was peering into.

But it was not Dubious Pickles who walked into the room. Arbour pulled himself back from the window. He rubbed his eyes. He returned to the window and peered in. He couldn't decide if he was actually seeing what he was seeing or not. And rubbing his eyes had not helped him to unsee what he had seen.

Arbour knew he couldn't explain to his mother why he was certain this was an emergency. He decided he would take his chances. He dialled Woodrow's number.

"Hello?"

"It's me," Arbour whispered into his cell. "You have to come to the Dubois place, man. Pronto."

"What's that? Arbour? Is that you? I can't hear you. What'd you say?"

"Dubious Pickles. Come to the weirdo's house. Hurry!"

"You're either crazy or crazy, Arb," Woodrow said. He whistled into the phone. "Ain't no way in hell's bells I'm going there. If you're there, you shouldn't be. You know that's the place where every dog and cat in town go to die. What the hell, Arbour?"

"Come. Now." Arbour disconnected and returned his cell to his pocket. Only, he was too busy watching old Miss Laroche walking in a circle in the middle of the room to notice that the cell didn't quite make it to his pocket. It parked itself in the grass beside his pocket, instead. The cellphone cannot be blamed for this. The misdirection, of course, was all on Arbour.

Old Miss Laroche was a teacher at Trudeau Elementary when Arbour's parents went there, maybe even when his parents' parents went there. The rumours of her incredible and mythical longevity were epic. Until she had died three weeks earlier, there had been talk of having a plaque erected at the edge of town beside the one announcing the town name. *Dobber Corner ~ Home of Hélène Laroche, Canada's Oldest Old Bag!* Or something like that.

Arbour wished he was one of those kids who could walk away from questions unanswered. But he wasn't. Between the furiously shaking head, the juggling balls, and the dead old lady walking, he was hooked. Hoping that Woodrow would eventually show, but positive he wouldn't, Arbour made his way to the back of the Dubois mansion in search of a way in.

Arbour only had to wade through a handful of Indian rubber balls at the top of the stairs that led to the cellar door to know they weren't there by accident. To a boy who read all the Edgar Allan Poe he could get his hands on, he knew before he even took the eight steps down to the door that it would be unlocked. When he reached for the knob, the door creaked a breath forward to invite him inside.

As someone who often listened late into the night for signs of a tell-tale heart beating somewhere deep within his own house, Arbour knew this was a little too easy. He knew that when a kid followed the town weirdo home—the same weirdo who just happened to be hosting the town's latest octogenarian to have passed on to the other side—that kid was in for a heap of trouble and chaos.

Arbour also knew that when you found an unlocked door in the Dubois mansion—practically inviting you inside—you should run like hell, get the hell on your Windmaker 900, and head for the hills. Or, at the very least, head for home.

Arbour pushed the door in and stepped inside.

He could hear the shuffling footsteps of his old teacher in the distant room, so he decided to steer clear of that particular direction.

"This isn't happening," Arbour near-whispered. In the old cellar that felt recently dug out of the earthy soil it still reeked of, his words bounced around and got louder as they crawled deeper into the darkness beyond him. He imagined old Miss Laroche's head swivelling in his direction as she heard him speak. Before he gave himself time to contemplate whether or not the dead were capable of hearing, Arbour made a quick beeline for the stairs. He hoped they led to the main floor of the Dubois house.

Surely it would be better upstairs where the amount of walking dead might be slightly fewer. Whatever he found up there surely had to be better than old Miss Laroche wandering aimlessly in a dark, dank cellar that stunk of earth and rot…and maybe a little like old Miss Laroche herself.

Even Arbour Lévesque knew it would be better to dance with the dead than to come face to face with Dubious Pickles. As he approached the top of the stairs, he slowed his pace and tried to think about what his brother Newton would do. Being a genius, Newton would probably not go anywhere near the crooked old Dubois mansion.

At the top of the stairs, Arbour opened the door and came into a large room that felt bigger than the outside of the house should allow it to be. His eye was immediately drawn to the grand staircase in the centre, leading to the top floor. It was a staircase that went off in two directions about halfway up.

Arbour knew instantly which of the two forks to take when an Indian rubber ball began a slow descent down the left side case. One stair at a time. Newton would tell Arbour that physics would not allow for an Indian rubber ball to descend a flight of stairs in this manner; calmly and decisively, like a Slinky.

Having more curiosity than common sense, Arbour took to the stairs. Halfway up, he scooped up the descending ball. He held it at the ready, should he need to whip it at someone.

As Arbour went to place his lead foot down on the upstairs landing, it came down on the first step back at the bottom of the staircase. Just like that. The adrenaline this caused was enough to make him flee the house screaming. But as nothing catastrophic followed the impossible feat of finding himself back at the bottom of the staircase, he made the climb again. *Second verse*, thought Arbour, *same as the first*. Again, he grabbed the slow, meticulously bouncing ball on his way up. Now he had two weapons, should he need to take someone out at the shins.

The second time he planted his lead foot on the landing, that is exactly where it fell. Perhaps it was just a case of it being a staircase that did everything twice.

At the top of the stairs, Arbour found a long hallway that went madly off in both directions. He knew the shell of this house could not possibly fit its contents. He didn't need his card-carrying genius brother to tell him this. The Dubois mansion definitely defied physics.

When he noticed the two Indian rubber balls floating at the end of the hallway on the left-hand side, he knew he should run like hell and not look back until he was down the hill and back in the safety of the town's main strip. He also knew this was the direction he would take. The balls had, after all, lead him every step of the way so far.

As he approached a door, the balls dropped to the carpeted floor with nary a thump. They did not bounce.

Arbour grabbed the doorknob. His premonition told him this was the point of no return. If he crossed the threshold of the room behind this door, there was no turning back. Dubious Pickles juggling without hands, Dubious Pickles making his head spasm faster than the speed of light, old Miss Laroche dead and walking in the cellar, Indian rubber balls defying gravity at every turn, and a staircase doing everything twice. These things did not stop him, but also did not mark any paths of no return. But behind door number one? Oh, he just knew this was it.

Without a sign of Woodrow's approach or the comfort that the reinforcement would give him, Arbour turned the knob and stepped inside.

Dubious Pickles stood in the centre of the cavernous ballroom. A chandelier the size of a small planet spun above his head, much like the balls had done earlier. The scream of spinning crystal shards and icicles clanging against one another in such an impossible display of centrifugal force brought Arbour immediately to his knees.

Arbour, on his knees and covering his ears as much as he could with a ball in each hand, was a pitiful sight. His muffled yell of, "Too loud!" was barely audible above the racket of the chandelier.

This made Dubious laugh. As Arbour covered his ears ever tighter to escape the chandelier's scream, Dubious bent in laughter. Dubious rose back up to a full standing position, a good three feet taller than he had been back at the store window, and pointed at the careening chandelier.

Arbour, never for a moment taking his eyes off Dubious, noted how the finger controlled the chandelier's movement. At its whim, the motion stopped, the scream became a whisper…almost a remembrance of noise. The way the world goes hum-silent in a snowfall.

Arbour removed his hands from his ears and breathed a sigh of relief. The scream of glass and crystal had filled his universe. He stood up, looked at Dubious, and waited for his hearing to come back to normal.

Before it did, Dubious began to walk across the floor in Arbour's direction. Arbour tried to move, but couldn't. His feet were no longer his to control.

The smile that cracked across the long and twisted face of Dubious Pickles was the smile a thousand freak show aficionados would pay to see. It was an angry knife slice of a wound, from ear to ear. The more Dubious smiled, the more his face slit open. His gums were as visible as his teeth. His uvula dangled menacingly like a pendulum, keeping time with the footfalls of his approach.

What would Newton do? What would Newton do? It was a mantra in Arbour's brain as he tried with every cell in his body not to scream.

Before Dubious quite made it to Arbour, though, the room filled with a sharp tinkle, tinkle, tinkle. He knew that sound from the approximately eight-hundred and forty-nine times Newton had dropped a scattering of ball-bearings across their shared bedroom floor.

While Arbour was lulled by the memory of those falling ball-bearings and the safety of being in his bedroom with his brother, the floor at his feet began to fill with what looked like pearls.

He opened his mouth to say something, but no words came out. By the time the pearls had reached the height of his ankles, Dubious stood before him…mere inches from his face.

Arbour attempted to hold his breath. He needed to keep the dank swampy earthiness of Dubious' breath from entering his lungs. From the gashed-mouth trick, which was now in full-swing, Dubious' breathing was made sickly. Arbour tried to keep the wet flapping sound of the raspy inhale-exhale rhythm from entering his brain, but he couldn't. The sound filled his head just as the pearls appeared to be filling the impossibly vast ballroom. They were now up to his knees. He was finding it difficult to keep his focus, what with the unending chorus of swirling pearls and raw wet rhythmic breathing coming from Dubious.

When Arbour attempted to step back from Dubious, he found he could move again, and it was relatively easy to navigate through the waist-deep pearls. Despite the bloody gash on the face of the maniac in front of him, the demeanour of Dubious Pickles was one of playfulness. Perhaps he was not yet quite ready to eat Arbour.

In fact, Arbour thought maybe the man wanted to play with him. But that couldn't possibly be the case. Could it?

No words had been uttered by either party.

Arbour knew none of the other children of Dobber Corner had ever heard so much as a peep out of Dubious Pickles. In fact, the rumours were that if you did hear Paul Dubois speak, it would be the last thing you ever heard.

Though the sound of the pearls swirling together like an ocean of glass and tinkling gritty sand was almost enough to drive Arbour insane, it was still a comfort to him that Dubious had thus far refrained from speaking.

Arbour remembered the balls he had kept carrying. Two. That he had at one time considered them weapons now seemed silly. With Dubious in front of him, his bloody maw of a grin slicing his face in half, Arbour knew there was nothing in this world he could possibly do to hurt him.

With the pearls now up to his chest, Arbour needed to act or drown in the sea of pearls that was now threatening to swallow both him and Dubious Pickles whole.

Just as Arbour was finding his bearings in the impossibility of his predicament, Dubious extended a hand for him to take. A hand as hideous as the open gash of a smile he also extended freely in Arbour's direction.

With his nails long and jagged and filled with earth and stench, Arbour could only assume Dubious had dug out old Miss Laroche with his own bare hands. A flap of skin fell free of Dubious' extended index finger and came to rest upon the one below it as he shivered his hand a bit, urging Arbour to take hold.

Seeing no alternative, Arbour reached through the pearls that now swallowed up everything but his shoulders and head. Swimming his hand up through the pearls was easier than he thought it should be. They gave way to his movements where he thought they would cement him in place.

Dubious, being inexplicably taller — and quite possibly still growing — Arbour had to reach to slide his hand into the rank and bloody one being proffered. But Arbour was also pretty sure his feet had left the floor a while back.

Once the two held hands, Arbour's fear redoubled. The grip was not something he would ever be able to break free of, should it come to needing to. Holding Dubious Pickles' hand could very well be the last thing Arbour ever did.

The pearls now threatened to fill in the rest of

the room. Dubious gave a tug on Arbour's hand and up they swam, rising to the ceiling on the momentum of the pearls quickly filling in all the spaces behind them. As they reached a vent near the ceiling, Dubious opened the little grate covering it and began to swim inside.

As the vent hole widened to allow both of them to enter together, Arbour swam in alongside the town monster. *Two peas in a pod*, Arbour thought, with not a little internal scream popping off inside his vast cavernous panicky mind.

Dubious let go of Arbour's hand long enough to reach behind him and close the grate. Arbour's last glimpse of the grand ballroom showed him just how bereft it was of pearls of any kind. Were it not for the few fallen pearls about them in the tiny shaft in which he was now trapped, the last few minutes of noise and pearl-ness would be a mere dream of improbability.

Arbour didn't have to ask himself what Newton would do if he found himself stuck inside a vent shaft in the Dubois mansion nestled in beside Dubious Pickles. It simply wouldn't happen.

Dubious reattached himself to Arbour's hand and began to drag them both through the over-warm shaft. Arbour could see, not five feet ahead of them, a light bright enough to blind. He prayed it would lead to a happy place, but the closer they crawled to it, the worse the smell that engulfed them became.

Once at the end of the shaft, a mere twenty feet from where they had begun, Dubious spilled himself out onto the floor beyond. He helped Arbour out of the shaft, handling him as though he were nothing but a bag of rice.

When he plopped the boy onto the dank cellar floor, Arbour made a noise much like a rabbit in a snare. It was nothing like the noise a little boy should be capable of making. Before his mind could make the calculation of impossibility that brought him from the third floor to the cellar in a short crawl, Arbour heard the scratching, dragging feet of the dead making their way in an ever-widening circle of pointlessness on the other side of the room he had just been delivered into.

"Oh my god, oh my god, oh my god," Arbour said to no one. He could feel his sanity shaking his insides, much like Dubious' head had shaken earlier. Back at the store when Arbour still had a chance to walk away with his cowboy boots and lunchbox.

"Arbour. Play." Dubious was apparently incapable of stringing together a sentence. He was more a man of single solitary words stitched together between intakes and outtakes of breath. Words you held your own breath to hear, to piece together, to fathom. "Arbour. Play. Miss. Laroche. Sing. Song. Arbour. Play.

"Play," Dubious repeated as he pushed the boy toward his former teacher. "Arbour. Play."

Dubious Pickles laughed and clapped his hands in eager anticipation, hopeful for a day of fun with his newfound friends.

Arbour stumbled ever closer to his teacher as Dubious began a shove, clap, shove, clap shuffle across the room. "Arbour. Play."

"Newton," Arbour whispered in a final plea to be saved by the only genius he ever knew. The genius who had helped him out of so many predicaments in the past. But Newton, he knew, would not be able to help him out of this one. He tried, with everything he had, to hold on to the final tendrils of sanity he felt escaping him.

As he heard a sudden thumping coming from above, he knew one thing for sure: hearing Dubious Pickles speak was not necessarily the last thing a child would ever hear. As Arbour felt himself blink out of existence and into insanity, it was the voice of Woodrow Thompson that was the last thing his mind registered before leaving him.

As he was pushed up against his rotting, scurrying former teacher by the persistent Dubious Pickles, Arbour heard his name being called by Woodrow. "Arbour? Arbour Lévesque? You in here?"

But Arbour Lévesque was suddenly nowhere to be found inside the head of Arbour Lévesque. Arbour Lévesque was gone.

KEVIN CRAIG IS the author of young adult novels (*Summer on Fire*, *Burn Baby Burn Baby*, and, *Half Dead & Fully Broken*) and adult-themed novels featuring young narrators (*Sebastian's Poet* and *The Reasons*). He is a five-time winner of the Muskoka Novel Marathon's Best Novel Award. His poetry, fiction, and memoir have been published internationally. He has had ten short plays produced for the stage. Kevin is a member of the Writers' Community of Durham Region and the Canadian Authors Association. He was also a founding member on the Board of Directors for the Ontario Writers' Conference. Kevin is represented by Stacey Donaghy of Donaghy Literary Group.

CAROUSEL EYES

Yvonne Hess

MERRI-LEE PRESSED HER chin down, clutching her coat at the neck to block the chilly October wind. Six slabs on the sidewalk, and she would pass it. Although weeds choked out the stone walkway and climbed the walls, she loved the old house, with its graceful arched front door and the scrolling gingerbread trim around the half caved-in porch roof. It was her favourite, and the only house like it on the street. The rest were clusters of cheap, compact townhomes like the one her family rented.

No one moved in or out of the old house, yet it was never torn down. Little Eddie's house was beautiful, and its infamous past made it even more interesting, but not a place where she wanted to linger.

The legend went that Little Eddie – an odd,

musical prodigy – had no friends, and in his loneliness had jumped from the roof one night in the glow of the full moon. In the wake of the disappearance of several children over the years, the legend grew that Eddie's ghost sought revenge on kids, as they had shunned him. Generations of kids since would wait until the moon was glowing, then run as close to the front door as they dared, calling, "Little Eddie, Little Eddie, come play with me," to see if he would come and snatch them up. It was a cruel taunt as much as one filled with fear.

One slab to go and she'd be clear…

"Go on, Merri-Lee, I dare you to call Little Eddie out."

Merri-Lee turned to see a gang of eighth graders in the middle of the road, snickering and pointing. They were only a year ahead of her, but thought they ruled the neighbourhood.

Merri-Lee rolled her eyes. "It's just a dumb story."

"If it's so dumb, go ahead and do it, then."

Merri-Lee glanced at the door but did not move. Whether she believed it or not, she didn't know for sure; she just knew the story was ingrained in her.

"She's a chicken. Let's go. We're wasting our time." The group walked on, leaving a wide arc between themselves and the sidewalk.

They're afraid to come too close. She chuckled to herself.

Once again alone, she heard a faint sound just under the rustle of leaves, so soft she held her breath, straining to hear. People claimed to hear his music – the tinkling of a piano, a symphony, or strains of a single violin. The strangest was the cheery *oompah-pah* chugging of an organ, like circus music, they said. It was a piano…was the sound inside her head?

She held her breath. There it was again. *It's the piece I have been practicing*, she thought…

"Practice!" Merri-Lee found her legs and ran, her backpack thumping behind her.

She was late. Her mother would be steaming and The Hagatha (a.k.a. the piano teacher) would have her mouth in a sour pucker. Merri-Lee hopped the low picket gate and flung open the door, slamming it shut behind her.

"Where have you been?" her mother shouted. "That deranged maniac might have got you. How would we know?"

While the spirit of Little Eddie was said to snatch up children, the reality was that there were ten bronze plaques bolted to the wall inside the church niche. One for each of the missing girls. Their names were carefully etched into the bronze. No bodies had ever been recovered. Beneath the names, ten devotional candles were kept constantly lit. Those little girls were taken, her mother constantly reminded her. *Don't talk to strangers. They could be that deranged maniac!* had been drilled into her head.

Merri-Lee sat and ran through the scales to warm up her fingers, while The Hagatha paced behind, her footsteps keeping time.

"Extraordinary." The teacher sniffed, tapping the antique maple wood baton against her hip. "Your mother spends good money on you. Again!" she snapped.

Merri-Lee's knuckles stung as the stick cracked

down. *Don't you cry.* She refused to let the tears escape. No, she would learn it even if her hands were bruised and swollen. She would learn it and be the best. They would see. She squeezed her eyes shut and sent her sore fingers fluttering up and down the keys, over and over.

THE DRIED LEAVES of autumn gave way to blowing snow. The gutters became grey slushy troughs against the cheery, colourful lights outlining windows and roofs up and down the street. Merri-Lee's fingers worked inside her mittens, rehearsing the music for the Conservatory grading the next day. Speeding up as she passed Little Eddie's house, her foot thumped against something and made her stumble.

A boy looked up at her from where he sat on the curb. His dark brown hair was cut short and neatly combed. He wore no coat, just a shirt and a pair of brown shorts. His brown leather shoes splashed in the icy muck.

"Aren't you cold?" Merri-Lee asked.

He stood up. His eyes were blue, the same colour as a bit of sea-glass she once found among broken shells and sand at the shore.

"Gurlitt's *Little Flower*," he said.

Merri-Lee blinked. "What?" She pulled out one earbud.

"You were humming it."

Had she been humming it out loud? She was listening to the music on her iPod, working her fingers over the keys in her mind, but she was sure it hadn't been loud enough for him to hear.

"Would you like to come in and see my piano? We could play a duet. Mother will give us tea and cakes."

Tea and cakes? He spoke proper, like children she'd seen in British movies.

"Um, maybe." She shrugged, but secretly her heart thumped. It would be nice to have a friend who loved music the way she did and, if she didn't look at his weird outfit, he did have a very cute face.

"Where do you live?" Merri-Lee asked.

He pointed. "Right here."

Eddie's house? "But no one…" Her skin prickled. "Are you sure?" She stared at him.

"What a strange question." He laughed. "I'm quite sure."

He seemed real, not a ghost at all…

What am I thinking? It's not Little Eddie. Eddie had lived, and died, years before, she reminded herself.

"Ma-maybe another time," Merri-Lee stammered and hurried away.

She went to sleep early, her hands stinging and throbbing from hours of practice. Hagatha hadn't come but the memory of the crack of her stick still stung. Merri-Lee would not fail her father.

DESPITE PASSING HER grade three level that morning, lessons continued. The boy she had talked to, now stood on the sidewalk, watching her through the front window. Large white snowflakes fell around him, but did not seem to land on or disturb him at all. He smiled and waved.

"Do you see that boy?" Merri-Lee asked her teacher. *A ghost doesn't sit on the curb or stand out front of your house.*

The Hagatha didn't turn her head, but instead answered with a slap of the stick that made Merri-Lee's knuckles throb.

"No, no, no!" the teacher yelled. "Again." She snapped her notebook shut and marched off, her heels clicking on the kitchen linoleum floor.

Distracted by his unexpected appearance, the whole lesson had been a disaster.

Merri-Lee's mother shot into the room.

"I'm sorry, Mother. It's just…" Merri-Lee pointed outside. "He keeps looking at me."

"Who?" Her mother pushed the sheers aside.

He was gone.

"You ungrateful girl! Your father works himself to the bone to pay for these lessons." Her face flushed with anger. "Go to your room."

Merri-Lee stretched out on her bed and rubbed at her aching knuckles. Her father was the black sheep in a family of professional musicians and yet happy with his lot in life, swinging a hammer and twisting wrenches to fix other people's broken-down things. They did not live in luxury or travel to exotic places, but there was always enough, and some for her lessons. He couldn't make heads or tails of the notes, he would say with a shrug. She heard her father's voice: "It's your way out of this crummy place."

She was grateful for the break, but was filled with guilt that the cost of the lesson had been wasted. Merri-Lee knew what her playing meant to her father.

She remembered the recital hall in September. She had wiped her hands when her turn came and her breathing only calmed when she saw her father sitting in his usual place – front centre. A grease spot marked his smiling face. She knew he had stolen away from work to watch her as he always did. The pride in his eyes when she finished meant more than any qualification. She would not disappoint him.

But she had disappointed him today. It was that boy.

Was he Little Eddie? Was it possible? She laughed it off. *Of course not.* It was more than creepy, though, the way he appeared and just stood there on the sidewalk, watching her. She decided she would take a different route home from school for the rest of the year, even if it took longer.

"Hello, Merri-Lee."

Cherry Popsicle melted down her hand under the searing July sun. She'd avoided the corner house during the year but had become distracted on her way back from the variety store.

"You know my name?" she asked.

He laughed.

She tossed the stick and wiped her hands on the grass. "You're him," she ventured to say, standing back up. "Little Eddie."

"Edwin!" he snapped, his black eyes narrowed. "I hate that stupid nickname."

Merri-Lee stumbled back as if she'd been given

a jolt in her gut. Her legs wobbled.

"Forgive me," he said with a nod of his head, his features softening once again. "I'm Edwin Herbert. Will you come inside? I will get you a drink of water or lemonade."

He put his arm firmly around her waist. She felt herself effortlessly guided through the low gate and along the crumbling path, as though her feet were floating over the ground.

"It can't be you," she mumbled.

He said nothing as they passed waist-high thorny nettles and weeds on either side. It reeked of decay. They climbed the three rotted steps. The grey front door (perhaps once blue?) was faded, the paint cracked and peeling. The ornate brass knob was dark and squeaked as Edwin twisted it.

"No…wait," Merri-Lee protested, but they were already inside.

The dizziness cleared. She inhaled the lemony-scented air. The floors gleamed. The dark wood furniture was polished, and prim lace doilies sat under lamps and porcelain figurines. In the centre of the space was a deep red velvet sofa and two matching high-back chairs.

"You haven't tracked mud on my clean floors, have you?" A short, plump woman appeared. Her hair was piled on top of her head in a bun. She wore a high-necked blouse with a silver filigree broach pinned at the throat, and a long plain skirt to just above her ankles.

"No, Mother."

"Oh, how nice. You've brought a little friend."

Edwin blushed. "This is Merri-Lee. She's come to play."

"Hello, my dear."

"Hi."

Merri-Lee looked around. Everything looked old-fashioned and yet like new. Merri-Lee thought Edwin's mother looked like someone from an old Western movie. It was also quiet in the house, she realized. No hum of a television or rattle of air conditioning stuffed in a window that ran night and day, like at her own house. Despite the stifling heat outside, it was the perfect temperature in the cozy living room.

"Come on," he said.

"You haven't tracked mud on my clean floors, have you?" Merri-Lee looked back as she climbed the stairs after Edwin. Edwin's mother stared up at them and blinked. "Oh, how nice. You've brought a little friend."

Strange how she'd said both of those things already. Merri-Lee wanted to ask if she was all right but thought it would be too rude, having just met them.

The room they went into was scattered with toys. In the middle was a child-sized table and four chairs.

"We can listen to some music." Edwin flipped through a stack of thick records. They were old, she knew, but much larger than the ones her father had in old milk crates in the basement. He chose one, placed it on the Victrola and wound a crank on the side of the wooden box and placed a large arm down. The speaker hissed and spat, then a horn blasted, as though being played in a tunnel. The music was pretty, a little haunting, coming out of the huge cone.

"No iPod, I guess?" she asked.

"A what?" He shook his head and sat on the floor.

Merri-Lee looked around and sat across from him. There was nothing electronic at all, she noticed. No computer, no clock radio. "Are you guys one of those eco-families or something?"

"Let's play," he said.

They built a tower of blocks and turned the keys on his collection of metal cars, watching them spin crazily on the floor. They set up blue and grey painted soldiers in rows facing one another on the braided rug battlefield. She had packed her own toys away when she turned ten, two years ago, and she felt embarrassed that playing was fun.

After several rounds of checkers, Merri-Lee stood up when her cellphone alarm beeped. "I have to go now."

"Can't you stay a little longer?" he begged.

"Lessons."

"But I want you to play my piano." He reached for her hand. The warm eyes swirled like a raging blue and grey storm at sea. She was mesmerized by the pop-star handsome face only inches from hers. "You don't need lessons from that…that hag." The walls seemed to vibrate from the rumble of his voice.

"I—I have to go." She snapped out of the trance-like state. "Bye, Edwin." She stumbled back, ran down the stairs, and out the door.

Back out in the sunshine, she felt her heart racing and adrenaline pumping. She glanced around quickly, praying no one had seen her coming out. She glimpsed back at the decrepit house, trying to reconcile how it did not reveal a hint of the pristine interior.

HER MOTHER STOOD in her bedroom doorway, turning an envelope in her hands. "This came for you."

Merri-Lee took the envelope. She hardly ever got any real mail. Even her grandmother had started to email her instead. The thick paper was the colour of French vanilla ice cream. The writing was like the calligraphy font on her computer, only perfectly penned in real black ink.

"Well, who is it from?"

"Mom! It's my personal mail. Geez."

Her mother frowned, and rolled slowly out of the doorway. "Maybe this is how that lunatic lured those poor girls."

"It's not." Merri-Lee closed the door, glad to be rid of her. She carefully lifted the flap of the envelope and pulled out the thick sheet of paper. The writing was meticulous, black scrolling loops on perfectly straight, but invisible, lines.

Merri-Lee,

> *I hope you are not angry with me from the other day. I didn't mean what I said about your teacher. Would you please come for a visit today? I would like to show you my piano.*

Yours,
Edwin.

Merri-Lee hesitated just for an instant before walking up the stone path. She hadn't cared a wit about Eddie calling her teacher a hag. She did wonder, though, how much trouble she would be in later for ditching lessons. Something she'd never done before.

The bushes had been trimmed and a warm yellow light glowed dimly through the lacy front window curtains. The door was not grey but a soft blue, and the brass knob had been polished. It was embossed with tiny lions and tigers. She knocked. What harm was one more visit? Didn't her father tell her she should make new friends? So there she was, but it was the piano she itched to see.

Eddie opened the door. "You came."

She could not hold back the smile that came to her mouth. She swallowed back the bitter taste of guilt. He took her hand, and she stepped inside.

She followed him into a room at the back of the house where a wall of windows looked out over the green, trim grass. Several green velvet chairs were placed next to stands holding sheets of music. Instruments were everywhere. A cello leaned against the wall. A violin sat in red velvet in a case on the floor. In the centre of it all, a Steinway Grand; the ebony finish gleamed under a sparkling crystal chandelier.

"Can you play all of these?" she asked.

"Yes," he said with a shrug.

"Do you want to see my last recital?" She took out her cellphone. "My dad puts everything on YouTube. It's so embarrassing." She waved it around. "Hmm, no signal."

He patted the place next to him on the bench.

"Sit here by me." Edwin stared up at her as though she had not spoken.

Merri-Lee sat down. Edwin closed his eyes. His hands flew across the keys, his leg shifting slightly as his feet worked the pedals. The song, one she didn't know, filled the room. She sat perfectly still, unable to twitch even a finger, holding her breath while the music rose to a heartbreaking crescendo. She exhaled as the notes slowed to a deep tone, finishing with a soft chord that faded into silence. Edwin lifted his hands, clasped his fingers together, and slowly opened his eyes.

"That was amazing," Merri-Lee whispered, her throat tight with tears.

"Let's play together. Mozart's *Sonata*?"

She shook her head. "I can't."

He picked up her hand, delicately placing her fingers down on the correct keys.

"It's much too difficult--"

"Shhh," he whispered.

A tingling began in her finger tips and climbed through her arms. It felt as though her skin buzzed but there was no sound. Her fingers pressed down and she played, hearing every note of hers as well as Edwin's. Merri-Lee had never played without sheet music. She felt Edwin's pull on her, drawing the music from her as they played in harmony side-by-side.

When it ended, Merri-Lee looked at him. "How?"

He smiled, got up, and picked up the violin. Pressing it to his shoulder, he played. The music sped up, his fingers flew over the neck, and the bow strained as he swiped it back and forth. It ended abruptly with a final pull of the bow.

"You choose the next piece." He placed the violin back on the stand.

"I've always wanted to play Chopin's *Nocturne Opus 9, Number 1*, but – "

"Excellent choice." He sat down.

They finished and quickly started the next, and then another. Merri-Lee was dazed, nearly breathless when she saw Edwin's mother standing in the room holding a silver tray.

"Oh, how nice. You've brought a little friend."

"Yes, Mother. This is Merri-Lee, remember?"

"Hello, dear. Welcome." She blinked several times.

"Hi," Merri-Lee replied with a shiver. The woman seemed to be out in space. *Maybe she's sick and on some kind of drugs*, Merri-Lee thought.

"We will go outside for our drink." Edwin took the tray holding a sweating jug of lemonade with fresh slices of lemon floating on top.

They went outside through the French doors leading to the yard. There were orange smudges left on the horizon; somehow the whole afternoon had passed. They sat at a table beneath the covered veranda. On either side of the door was a trellis where red roses climbed. Their fragrance wafted heavily in the air. He poured the lemonade, and they ate crescent-shaped cookies decorated with pink sparkles, and squares of cake covered in smooth, white and mint green icing, topped with tiny pink rosettes. Everything tasted exquisite. At home, powdered crystal drinks and boxed cakes were only brought out for birthdays and occasions.

"I have something special to show you," Eddie

said.

"Something else? This day has already been special."

He smiled at her and whistled as he walked through the garden, his hands tucked into his pockets. Merri-Lee could see nothing through the high, thick shrubs surrounding the perimeter of the yard, which felt impossibly larger than it looked from the outside.

"Will you get mad if I ask you something?" Merri-Lee asked.

"Of course not. We're friends," Edwin replied.

Merri-Lee cleared her throat. The rumours couldn't be true. "What happened to you? Did you really jump from the roof?"

His face grew dark red and his chest pumped in and out as he puffed deep like a dragon. "No! It was an accident. I fell, I tell you!"

"Take it easy! It was just a question."

His shoulders fell instantly, his face drained of colour. "I don't want to talk about it."

"Okay." Merri-Lee shrugged, feigning disinterest, but inside, her heart raced. For a second, she thought he was going to pounce on her. Something had obviously happened, but what, she couldn't say. And she would perhaps never know since Edwin's mood turned so easily; one minute happy, and the next raging as though his head would explode.

"I wish you would never, ever leave, Merri-Lee." He took her hand, and they ran past manicured flowerbeds blooming with flowers. "We're almost there."

They rounded a cluster of birch trees, and Merri-

Lee gasped. "It's not possible."

The carousel glowed with the globe lights all around the top where it rose into a point. Mirrors reflected the lights in endless circles. Mythical creatures – unicorns, great majestic birds with gold wings, dragons, and mermaids with glittering green scales – stood on poles, wrapped in colourful ribbons. Each creature wore a bridle and saddle of real leather, tooled with intricate designs and gilded in silver and gold. Their eyes were polished glass orbs. Blue, green, and amber irises bloomed in the centres. Merri-Lee stared into their eyes. They seemed to be staring back with pained expressions…

Pained? What am I thinking?

She took Edwin's hand and stepped up. A unicorn stood next to her in a graceful pose. Its head held a twisted horn, and one front leg bent as though ready to prance away. Its mane and tail hung in frizzy tatters, and the white body was chipped in spots, the eyes merely faded paint. So unlike the others.

"Poor thing. Why is this one all worn out?" Merri-Lee asked. "Are you fixing it up?"

"Yes. Get on," Edwin said.

"You mean it actually works?" Merri-Lee slipped her foot into the stirrup, settled into the leather saddle, and picked up the reins.

"Of course it works." Eddie weaved across to the other side. He sat on a stool in front of a massive pipe organ and flipped a switch. The beast beneath her jolted slightly, and then the carousel began to move. Merri-Lee giggled as it went round. The unicorn rose up and went down as she threw her head back and laughed.

"It's magical!" she shouted.

The music wheezed out of the organ, faster and faster, going up and down in rhythm with the bobbing animals. There was nothing but the music and the breeze. She passed Eddie in a blur, round and round. It slowed and stopped. Eddie now sat beside her on a gold-beaked gryphon with shiny copper and white feathers. Its wings were up as though it was taking off. She could have sworn he had been at the organ only a second before.

"We are true friends forever, aren't we?"

Merri-Lee nodded and found she meant it this time. She reached shyly for his fingers. "Yes. I want us to be friends."

It was dark and the carousel lights dimmed the stars overhead. "It must be getting late. I should go." Merri-Lee slid off the unicorn and patted his ratty mane. "My mother is going to freak. She's always going on about the kid-killer around here."

Eddie sprang from the gryphon, landing in the grass. "No! Wait, you can't leave!" he thundered.

"My father will kill me if I get home too late."

"You don't need him!"

Merri-Lee turned on her heel and walked away, shouting, "You don't get to tell me what to do, Eddie!"

BIRDS CHIRPED FAINTLY over the sounds of waves in Merri-Lee's earbuds. She took a few deep cleansing breaths where she lay stretched out on the yoga mat. Meditation calmed her nerves and centred her as she ran through the program in her mind.

As the last wave faded away, music began, soft strains at first. Merri-Lee frowned. Where was it coming from? She knew this sequence off by heart and this…*Chopin.*

"We will be true friends forever…"

Merri-Lee sat up, heart pumping and pulled the earbuds from her ears. She looked around. No one was in the room, but she knew that voice. *Edwin.* Sometimes she dreamed of him and woke with a weight of guilt on her chest. She hadn't seen him again after that ride on his strange carousel.

"I must have fallen asleep."

Usually she spent ten or fifteen minutes in quiet preparation, but this night was special. This was Carnegie Hall, and she needed to be perfect, so she had taken more time than usual. Now she was rattled. Why had Edwin appeared, tonight of all nights?

There was a knock at the door, and a young woman wearing a headset peeked in. "Five minutes, Merri-Lee."

Merri-Lee swallowed, pressing her shaking hands down on the floor. "Thanks, Gwen." Her assistant was a godsend.

"Knock, knock." A man stepped through doorway.

"Oh my, a secret admirer." She smiled, relieved to see her fiancé and noting he had worn his favourite navy suit.

"Admirer yes, secret, hardly." He put the roses down and leaned in, pecking her on the cheek. "Break a leg, darling."

She moved in closer to hug him. "Thank you,

Richard."

He held her back. "Darling, my Armani."

"Right, of course." She watched him smooth the already perfect jacket lapels.

"I'll see you after." He blew her a kiss and left to find his seat.

They had met at a coffee shop eight years before, when Merri-Lee was at Juilliard and Richard at NYU. She knocked her coffee cup and he was there, wiping the spill, and she stared at him, completely speechless. He had proposed at Christmas, and the wedding the following June was going to be a glittering social affair that made Merri-Lee more than woozy at the thought. That was Richard's world, not hers, but somehow she would manage it; had to, if she was going to fit in.

The high black curtain waved where she waited in the wings. She glimpsed the audience. Carnegie Hall, the pinnacle of success, but it was the chair front centre that held her gaze. Her father sat proudly looking forward, a beaming smile on his face.

The applause began. She stepped out into the bright white lights, blurring out all thought. She sat down and stared at the Steinway. A flare of anger rose in her. *Where is my goddamned Bösendorfer?* It was the kind she had learned to play on and the type she needed for such an important night. Not this yard sale Steinway! Her eyes met Gwen's with the question where she stood just off stage. Gwen shook her head.

As dead quiet fell in the hall, she ran her hand across the unusual ornate music board of the glossy black grand that somehow seemed familiar.

Returning her focus to the music, she began to play.

Backstage exploded when she returned. Cheers and applause greeted her, and Merri-Lee couldn't help the flow of tears when her father hugged her tight. Gwen, her manager, Richard, and so many other faces congratulated her that she could not take them all in. Champagne corks popped, hitting the ceiling. She took a long drink and swallowed, desperate to embed every moment of this celebration into her memory.

"I'm sorry about the Steinway," Gwen said. "The promoters said – "

"Don't even think about it!" Merri-Lee was high on the moment. The piano didn't even matter. "In fact, it actually felt good." She shrugged, too happy to ask herself why.

The good news continued when new offers came in, talk of global performances, and Merri-Lee knew she had finally made it.

They returned to their apartment in New York the next night, and she savoured two days of floating from the rave reviews of her Carnegie performance before her joy crashed at her feet. Her mother called and broke the news that her father had died. Just natural causes, they told her. Fell asleep and never woke up. Merri-Lee felt in her bones it was all some kind of terrible lie.

She watched Richard pack. Her own suitcase stood beside his.

"I wish you were coming with me," she sighed. "You know how hard this is going to be."

"I know, darling, but Hong Kong can't wait. I'm sorry."

Not even for my father's funeral? she wondered again. But he was focused on a big deal that couldn't wait, and it would be useless to try and talk him out of going.

THE TAXICAB IDLED at the curb out front of her childhood home. It seemed so much smaller. The mortar in the red brick had receded, the fake shutters had faded to a dull grey, and the shrubs, overgrown with weeds. It was sad, as though the house, too, was in mourning.

Inside, she watched her mother pace from the kitchen to the front room. She'd taken up smoking again. "We couldn't afford for both of us to go to your fancy show in New York."

"I know, Mom. It's okay. Daddy told me."

They could have both come if they would have taken the plane tickets she offered, but, stubborn as they were, they would not. So only her father had come to Carnegie.

"It's him you wanted there anyway," her mother said.

"I wanted both of you there."

Her mother lit another cigarette with the tip of the finished one. "You always were a daddy's girl."

Merri-Lee left her mother to smoke and put her

bags into her old bedroom. The pop-star posters and pictures of friends were gone, but it was essentially the same, except it, too, seemed to have shrunk.

Merri-Lee joined her mother in the living room. She found comfort sitting in her father's old chair, which still carried a hint of his citrus cologne scent. Or at least, she imagined it did. Still, the sun would come up, and her father's funeral would take place.

"Another girl went missing about a month ago," her mother said.

"Oh? I never heard."

"Well, you wouldn't, would you? Another name plate in the church." Her mother clucked her tongue.

Merri-Lee reached out for her mother's hand. "You always kept me safe."

"Well, of course, I worried myself sick. You taking off here and there. You didn't understand the danger."

"I'm okay now, Mom."

"Yes, yes." She wiped at her eyes and stood up.

"Can you tell me what happened to Daddy?" Merri-Lee asked.

"One minute he was fine. Then he went out for a walk, which was not like him. He came back, went straight to bed, and never woke up."

Merri-Lee bit her lip trying to gather her composure. "Where did he go?"

"Down toward the Little Eddie house. Lord knows why he went that way."

Merri-Lee felt a cold stab through her stomach. "Did he say anything about hearing strange music? Seeing any odd people?"

Her mother shook her head. "I don't know. I can't remember. It was all so…"

"It's okay, Mom. You don't have to think of it now."

"I'm worn out. I'm going to bed. Long day tomorrow, I suppose."

Merri-Lee spied her grandmother's Bösendorfer piano, in its place of honour in the front window and went to it.

"Hello, old friend."

She sat down and played softly, staring out the window. There had been snow falling, and a boy outside…

Merri-Lee heard a knocking on the front door. It was just past nine, but odd that someone would come at this hour. It was not like New York, where people were just getting home and out to dinner at nine p.m.

A man stood there. His dark hair was a little long, curled around his ears. His eyes smiled first, followed by a wide smile that spread across his mouth and that lit up those ocean-blue eyes outlined by dark lashes. Merri-Lee felt a little skip in her stomach. His were the kind of looks seen in sexy designer underwear advertisements. She blushed, thankful he couldn't see her imagining the six-pack that was most definitely under his shirt.

He tipped his head once. "Hello, Merri-Lee."

"You know me?" A little breathless, she sighed. "I'm so sorry, I don't remember you." She really was sorry she didn't remember this gorgeous man.

"Well, then I am the one who should be embarrassed. Edwin Herbert, at your service." He bowed.

Their eyes locked. "Edwin?" she whispered, pressing her hand against her chest.

The memories unwound like bursts of light, one after the other: the toy room, the piano, the carousel. That magical ride! How wonderful it had been. Edwin…the boy down the street.

"Wow, you've grown up," she said. Little Eddie. Silly childhood fancies. Ghosts, as far as she knew, didn't grow up into gorgeous men.

"As have you, Merri-Lee."

His voice still had the proper English lilt he had as a child, only now with a man's deep tone. She twirled a lock of hair around her finger, feeling like a self-conscious teenager.

"Will you come for a walk with me? It's a lovely evening."

"Well…"

"Your fiancé wouldn't mind, I don't think…You and I being old friends."

It was her attraction to him that made her hesitate, not Richard's potential jealousy.

"No, of course he wouldn't," Merri-Lee agreed. "He's not here anyway." *Why did I say that?* "Wait, how did you know I was engaged?"

"May I say, your ring is very impressive." He reached up and ran a finger down her cheek. "You don't expect me to not be envious, do you?"

His touch felt like fire. She could not step away. Her mouth went dry. Envious? He was envious?

"Will you walk with me? If you're comfortable, of course."

"Sure. All right." *What harm would a walk do?* She grabbed a sweater and threw it over her shoulders. He held out his arm, waiting until she nervously tucked hers through. It seemed too intimate, but she remembered that Edwin had been raised in a home with old-fashioned ways. His strait-laced mother had probably told him it was the proper way to stroll with a lady.

"You've done well. I've watched your career with much interest," he said as he led her, veering left and walking down the street.

"Well, thank you. That's kind." She blinked.

"Of course."

They had been friends as children. The little boy outside her house in the snow. That had been him. The memories flooded back; his music room, the pieces she had been able to play without quite comprehending how. It had felt so good, as though her blood coursed with his knowledge somehow, and she hadn't wanted to question it. She could feel the same intoxicating feeling gripping her now, walking with her arm tucked into his.

It was his incredible talent that had astounded her. Surely, he must have done something with it, but she had never run into him on the circuit or even heard the buzz of his name among colleagues.

"And what are you doing these days? Do you still play?"

"I keep busy," he said. "I play, of course, but for my own enjoyment."

"I could set up an appointment with my manager. She would go crazy for you."

"Did you enjoy Carnegie?" he asked, ignoring her comment, his voice smooth in the quiet street.

"It was incredible." The Steinway. Now she remembered. It was very much like his, the one they had played together as children.

Walking slowly, Merri-Lee became absorbed in taking in all the familiar sights of the neighbourhood. The sidewalks were new and the road recently re-paved. The shabby little houses looked cozy in the dark, lit within the cones of light from the street lamps. She jerked out of her thoughts, realizing they had stopped walked. They stood in front of his house. Brambles and weeds stood waist high and the roof was still half-cracked, always on the verge of falling in.

"Will you come in?" he asked. "For tea? Or perhaps you prefer something stronger. Wine, or brandy?"

"I shouldn't…." It was one thing to walk and talk, catch up with a childhood friend, and quite another to go in for a drink.

"Please. I will be very offended if you say no." There was a glimmer of a smile in his eyes.

Merri-Lee sighed, her shoulders relaxed. "Oh…well…all right."

He pressed his hand lightly on the small of her back, and she felt propelled, as though merely floating over the cracked stone path. She was sure the doorknob had once been polished to a shine, and the blue paint of the door, smooth and bright, and the roof had been fixed. Why had he let it fall into such disrepair? It was a shame. It had always been her favourite house.

Just one quick drink, she thought. Among the other memories, his temper too came to mind. It seemed unlikely that the man he was now could still be the once-volatile lonely little boy. They walked through the front door together. Inside, it was exactly as it had been. Despite the years that had passed, nothing looked worn or aged, and there was not a speck of dust.

"Is your mother here?"

"My mother?" he chuckled. "No, she has been gone many years."

"I just lost my father."

He went to the sideboard, picked up a crystal decanter, and poured two glasses of clear liquid. "Yes, I know." He handed her a glass.

She sniffed. It burned inside her nostrils and smelled of fermented fruit. She drank the whole shot, feeling the alcohol numb her tongue.

"Why did you leave me? You were different, special. It killed *him* to let you go, too."

A sound caught in her throat. "Killed who?" Merri-Lee fell back, leaning against a wall.

"Your father, of course."

Her glass slipped from her fingers and shattered around her feet. "How dare you say that!"

Edwin grabbed her wrist.

"Let go of me!"

He leaned in close, whispered in her ear, "You were never supposed to go. I thought you would be different. You meant something. The others…they meant nothing. I wanted you, needed you…"

Their eyes locked. *He needed me? For what?* she wondered. What did he want? She was unable to look away from the liquid fury of the ocean swirling of his eyes. His hand released the vice-like grip, and he turned away.

Her heart raced. She needed to get out of here. "We were children. It was just a childhood crush."

"I became desperate. You must understand. It

was a mistake to let you go. I thought…hoped…if something happened to him, you would come back."

Desperate. He had been desperate to see her? Merri-Lee was so startled, she simply stood frozen in place. "Did you…oh God…did you do something to my father?"

Edwin smiled without humour. "Don't you see? I needed you. You promised you would stay!"

"You're crazy!" she screamed. She started to back away. Her foot crunched on the broken glass at her feet. The alcohol had gone to her head, and the floor tilted and her balance faltered.

His face softened. He looked at her with a shy smile. "I want to play something for you."

"What?" Christ, he was out of his mind. "No. I want to leave." Jesus, how could he speak of playing now? She just wanted out of there.

"I'm afraid not. Besides, it would be rude wouldn't it? Your bitch of a mother must have taught you at least basic manners."

She tried to get past him. "Move out of my way."

"Enough! The others thought they were so much better than me, too. Well, now they are names on plaques in some ridiculous nave." His smile was thin and evil.

The volatile child had grown into a dangerous man. *That deranged maniac*, she heard her mother's voice say, and Merri-Lee's heart sank into her stomach. *The others? Oh god, the plaques. The missing girls.*

"It was you?" Her voice was a strangled whisper. How was she going to get out of there?

She needed to keep calm and wait for the swimming in her head to clear. But the first little girl had gone missing in the 1920s sometime. "How could that be?"

"I was a weak child, who loved music. My sister hated that my mother favoured me. She pushed me from the roof. I became a cripple, a recluse. My father couldn't bear the shame. He shot my mother, my sister Charlotte, then me, before himself."

"Oh my god, Edwin. But when was that?"

"Oh a long time ago. Let's see…I was born in 1814 – "

"What are you saying? That you've been alive – no, dead – for over two hundred years?" This was insane. Panic took over. Merri-Lee searched for a way out. His arm gripped hers. He was not going to let her go yet.

He pulled her, and she had no choice but to follow. They entered the music room. He pushed her to sit next to him on the bench facing the piano; the glossy black Steinway with the ornate music board.

Now she knew why the one at Carnegie had been so familiar. "It was you," she said in a strangled whisper. "But how – " Tears rolled down her cheeks. He had nearly sabotaged her performance, killed her father, and now was probably going to kill her. *That deranged maniac. Oh Mom, you were more right than you knew. I'm sorry.*

"Shhhh." He took a breath. A single note rang out, then the song rose in a complex composition. It rose, the music gentle and rich, yet, despite the horrific situation, she was rooted to the seat. Tears flowed as she silently sobbed. The sound slowly spiralled down, becoming softer. Her eyes closed. She felt as if she could see the notes. The song was so tender, so heartbreaking, and then it slowed until it was only that single note once more.

"That is what you are to me," he said.

Merri-Lee opened her eyes, blinking away the wetness on her lashes. She could only stare back into his face as he took her hand gently.

"I wrote it for you." He pressed her fingers to his lips.

Every part of her pulsed. An impish grin replaced his sultry stare. He took her hand and pulled her through the French doors. "Come."

The fresh air did little to clear her head. There was something she needed to do, something important, but what?

Fragrant flowers bloomed, and she felt like a child again, transported to a secret garden. The tickly wet of the dew on the grass clung to her ankles.

The carousel. The lights turned on with a *pop-pop*! The mirrors reflected a thousand watts of light. As a child, she had squealed with excitement, looking through wide eyes at the fun. Now she saw every delicate detail of the mystical creatures on their poles, waiting for riders.

"Surely you must remember," he said.

"Of course I do."

She felt him behind her. He swept her hair to one side, his lips glided over her neck, leaving her skin shivering, then he lifted her onto the platform as though she were weightless. Her fingers slid through the wispy hair of the mane and she looked into the chipped, painted eye.

A small smile came to her face. "My unicorn." She giggled and felt like a young girl again as she climbed into the saddle, taking up the reins. "Poor thing. He's still shabby."

"Riding the carousel was the only time I felt normal again," Edwin said.

"But you've worked so hard. So many are finished. It's just this one creature left."

Edwin stepped in close, pushing her chin up to meet his gaze. "Yes. The others worked perfectly, but no jewel could match the brilliance of your emerald eyes. It's been waiting for you. You are the finale."

The cold leather reins tightened around her wrists. The straps squeezed as they wrapped themselves up and around her arms.

"What's going on? Edwin?"

Her head began to clear. The drunken feeling lifted. *This was for me? The others...* An amber-eyed mermaid looked back at her. She heard the voices: "Get out! Go! Help us!"

"The children! This is what you've done to them." She choked between terrified sobs.

He took her face in his hands, kissed her hard on the mouth, then turned and walked toward the organ. "We are going to be together forever, just as we promised."

"Wait! Help me! What's happening?" she screamed as her legs pressed into the unicorn's flanks as though it melted around her skin.

Her arms thrashed, trying to unwind the straps. Blood seeped where the leather cut deep into her skin. The carousel began to turn. The organ wheezed to life, growing louder and louder, drowning out her screams. The other creatures bucked and reared on their poles. They made no sound, but somehow she sensed their eternal, mournful cries.

Her vision began to blur, the lights and colours turned to streaks going round and round.

"No! Edwin…please!"

A RIDERLESS SKATEBOARD zoomed off the sidewalk, landing face up in the gutter, the wheels spinning.

A boy in a knitted sweater-vest and tweed shorts picked it up, studying the scratched up bottom. "Is this yours?"

Her knees were scabbed beneath long, black shorts, and her t-shirt was emblazoned with a pink, sparkly skull. "I'm the only one here, aren't I?"

He handed it to her. "Of course."

"I'm Olivia. I prefer to be called Oli. Get it?" she nudged his arm.

He stared blankly back at her.

"No?" Her eyes looked him up and down. "I guess you're a little too nerdy. It's a skateboard word – ollie. Oh, forget it."

"I'm Edwin."

"I just moved here and heard the story about this creepy old house. You wanna run up to the door and try?"

"Try what?" he asked.

"You must have heard it. If you call Little Eddie, his ghost will come and get you." She wiggled her fingers and bugged out her eyes. "Hey wait, your name is Ed too. You're not related, are you?"

"Not related, no." Edwin turned and opened the small garden gate. "Come on."

"You think we should?" Oli asked.

"Sure," Edwin said with a shrug, and started up the walkway.

"Cool." Oli followed behind through the thick thorny bushes that grew wild, obscuring most of the path.

Edwin twisted the knob of the front door and flung it open.

"What the…?" Her crystal blue eyes widened. "You live here?"

"Yes." He took her hand and led her inside, through the back door, and out into the back garden, stopping where the wisteria hung down through the slats of the portico.

"Dude, is this some kind of museum?" Oli asked, her eyes wide with wonder.

"Olivia, your eyes are like sapphires."

She gave him a backhand on the arm. "Ew, gross." The pink flush on her cheeks belied her disgusted tone. "Where are we going anyway?"

"Come and see." He broke into a run, and she quickly caught up.

They rounded the cluster of birch trees. She stopped dead. Her mouth hung open.

"It's nicer in the evening."

Suddenly, it was as though the sun had been blotted out. The birds stopped chirping and the *cree-cree* of the crickets began. The globe lights popped on, one after the other, until the whole top was lit and glittering in endless reflection.

"Wow!"

Oli climbed up onto the platform, weaving

between the rows of creatures. She stopped at the majestic unicorn. Bright green glassy eyes stared back at her.

"Freaky. It's like it's looking right at me."

"She's very special." Edwin ran his fingers through the thick, white, silky mane.

Oli got on the back of a green-scaled dragon and wrapped the leather reins around her hands. "Eddie, this poor dude needs a paint job. And new eyes like the others."

He hurried across and flicked the switch. The carousel jerked and started to turn. He sat at the organ, and the music poured out. "You're quite right. I thought bright blue might be nice."

Yvonne has been writing for over twenty years and is passionate about stories steeped in history and romance. Her short fiction has won awards and been published in <u>Surfacing</u> magazine. She has completed several full-length manuscripts and hopes to have her novel published in the near future.

UNSTRUNG

Connie Di Pietro

THIS WAS THE fifth town in two years. Stewart hoped this would be the last move. He had received the key to the new home later than he had anticipated and moving in the dark was never ideal, but it would afford him fewer nosey neighbours. He had had his share of intrusive people in the past.

"Port Salerno it is, Tom," Stewart said. "I have a good feeling about this place." He glanced briefly at his best friend. Stewart didn't want to take his eyes off the road for too long and miss the street.

Tom kept his face turned to the window.

"Don't be like that. I know you miss her. I do too." Stewart reached to rest his hand on Tom's shoulder. "I have a surprise for you. You'll see. We'll be a happy family again. I promise."

Stewart slowed the large truck, turning onto

Camino Street and scanning the numbers over the garage doors. Every house looked the same, and the steep Home Owners' Association fees ensured no one deviated from the beige stucco walls and orange shutters that matched the terracotta roof tiles. The numbers 5468 let him know he had found the right place.

"Here we are," Stewart said. "Don't you love it!"

The front window of his neighbour's house glowed with the light of a television.

Stewart jumped out and went around to the back of the van, lifted the rolling door, then pulled out the ramp. Boxes of all sizes filled the cube van completely. His brain buzzed with the sheer and inescapable amount of work ahead of him. He wanted to get it all done in one night so he could return the rental van without late fees. He lifted two of the boxes and stumbled under the weight, set both back down, and decided to carry one at a time.

The rubber soles of his sneakers smacked against the tar driveway and gave a beat to the rhythm of palms swaying in the breeze.

A woman's silhouette stood in the corner of his neighbour's window. Breasts sat high on a long torso which narrowed to a small waist. Dormant yellow jackets awoke and began to crawl with their tiny feet along the walls of his stomach and toward his groin. He closed his eyes for a moment and took a breath.

"Do you see her?" Tom hadn't moved from the passenger side of the cube van.

"Yes," Stewart hissed out in a whisper before he disappeared into the house. He returned empty-handed.

"Well, forget it," Tom said when Stewart had reached the van.

Stewart narrowed his eyes at his friend.

"She's not for us. You can't do anything this time," Tom said.

Stewart tried to ignore Tom, but he continued.

"Not if we want to stay here longer than three months."

Stewart lifted a wardrobe box with the help of a dolly. He shifted the box, careful not to drop it. 'Fragile' was scrawled in large black letters over all four sides of the box. Once he knew it was centred properly, he rolled down the truck's ramp.

Tom rattled on. "We have enough to worry about…"

His voice followed Stewart to the house.

"Always complaining about something," Stewart muttered under his breath. He released a heavy sigh and enjoyed the silence within the walls of the house. He wheeled the large box into the master bedroom. With careful back and forth movements, he shimmied the box off the lip of the dolly, and then headed back to Tom, who he knew would pick up right where he had left off.

"…I can tell you're not listening to a thing I'm saying." Tom looked at Stewart with raised brows, a wide smile, and a twinkle in his eye, emphasized by the street lamp reflecting in the side view mirror.

"Don't give me that look. I'm just trying to get all of this done before midnight." Stewart grabbed another wardrobe box and wheeled it out. "It's not like you're any help."

He turned his back on Tom and went inside, knowing he'd hear about that jab as soon as he returned. The halls in this house were wide enough for him to wheel boxes around without worrying if he'd scrape the walls. After he put this box down beside the other, he rested his elbow on the dolly's red metal handle and looked around the empty bedroom.

"This is a nice house. I think we're really going to like it here." He scuffed the heel of his sneaker over the white tiles that ran through the entire home. "Easy to clean. Quiet neighbourhood. What else could we ask for?" With a nod and a smile he took hold of the dolly and went back to get more boxes.

The black wheels squeaked in time with his heartbeat; each rotation a cry for oil. A warm breeze wafted through the open door, and Stewart inhaled the fresh air.

An ear-splitting scream stole his breath.

He ran outside, and stopped short.

EARLIER THAT EVENING, Leah picked up her cellphone for a fourth time, checked her messages, and tossed it back on the sofa beside her. She strangled the bowl of her wine glass, took a mouthful of Shiraz, and allowed the peppery notes to swish around her tongue before letting it slide down her throat. A dribble streaked down the side of the glass and landed on Charlie, the white Persian lounging on her lap. The red sank into the cat's fur.

"Shit." Leah wiped at the drop of wine. After she cleaned the cat and checked her cell again, she picked up the remote and flipped through different reality shows, landing on one about a wedding planner.

"Don't fucking do it," she said to the screen where a handsome couple stood on a beach and talked about their expectations for their special day. Naïve smiles spread across both of their faces. "Two years in and you'll be drinking a bottle of wine alone, while dinner sits cold on the table and your husband is more than three fucking hours late. Again."

During the commercial break, Leah slid Charlie off her lap, got up, took the wine bottle from the dining table back to the couch, and poured herself another glass.

The bride-to-be choked up when she saw herself in the wedding dress for the first time. Hot tears pricked at the corners of Leah's eyes. She stroked Charlie, raising wisps of fur around her. The cat vibrated under her touch. She picked up her cell again. The last five texts to her husband were still unanswered. *I'm going to kill him.*

-MIKE?- she typed again. Her finger hovered over the Send button. "Maybe I'm being paranoid." Every Friday for the past month he had come home late.

It was always the same excuses; *"Out for drinks with the guys"; "stuck under a mountain of paperwork"; "boss needed the proposal done before the weekend".*

They all seemed plausible. So, why not answer a simple text? She hit Send.

Leah downed her wine and emptied the last of

the bottle into her glass. She shed a tear as the TV bride walked down the aisle, oblivious to the life that awaited her after the altar. Leah sniffed and wiped her nose with the heel of her palm.

Headlights streaked across the walls of the living room through the curtains, and Leah rose, pushing Charlie off the sofa, and went to the window. Her heart sank when she didn't see the gunmetal-grey Porsche. The lights came from a cube van that had pulled into the neighbour's driveway. The house had been vacant since April.

"Wonder who our new neighbours are, Charlie," Leah said as she watched a man carry boxes from the van. "It'd be neighbourly to say hello, don't you think?"

Charlie meowed, stretched, and flopped on the floor at Leah's feet. She ran her toes over the length of his side. She sipped at her wine, an alcohol fog filling her head as she thought of what to say to the stranger. The tip of her nose and cheeks tingled and courage bubbled inside her. "I'm going to say hello." She looked around the room. "I should bring something."

Leah walked past the dining room table where dinner for two sat untouched. Beside the table stood a small bar cart filled with wine bottles. She surveyed the brands, then chose her favourite. With the neck of the bottle grasped tight in one hand and a half-emptied glass in the other, she walked out of the house, barefoot.

Damp grass tickled the edges of her feet as she staggered across her front lawn to the neighbour's driveway. Palm leaves rustled in the hot breeze. She didn't see the man who had been carrying the boxes, but noticed someone sitting in the passenger side of the cab.

"Hello?" she said as she approached the passenger door. Her toe banged into the metal sprinkler head at the edge of the lawn and driveway and she crunched over in pain, spilling some of her wine. Gathering herself, she licked the dribble off the side of her glass and looked into the cab. Her eyes widened. The wine glass fell from her hand and smashed into shards around her bare feet.

A painted white face with a wide red smile and violet glass eyes stared back at her through the truck's open window. Her scream pierced the night air.

IT WAS HER. The silhouette from the window.

Stewart contemplated his approach and cautiously walked from the house around the back of the van and waited before he went to her. Long taut legs like a gazelle. A golden tan bathed in the street lamp's light. Round bottom, tight shorts. Muscles flexed over lanky arms. A Superman emblem stretched over breasts high and firm, unsullied by age or gravity. Blonde hair ran in waves down her back. A perfect specimen.

Stewart realized what had made her scream, and he ran to her.

Glass shards lay scattered over the driveway around her feet and beneath the truck.

"Hello," Stewart said.

She jumped and turned to face him. Bright green

eyes widened further as she looked at Stewart. "Oh my god." She placed her hand over her heart and took a deep breath. "That fucking doll scared the living shit out of me." She began to laugh.

Stewart cleared his throat and clenched his jaw. "Marionette."

"Pardon me?" she said as she wiped tears from her eyes.

"He's a marionette, not a doll." He took great care with how he delivered the words, and pushed the building anger away.

"Oh. Sorry," she said. "I'm your next door neighbour." She pointed to the house with the television light glowing in the window, shuffled the bottle of wine from one hand to the other, and held out her right. Her long, pink nails matched her toenails. "My name's Leah."

"Stewart." He shook her hand. Her warmth raced through him and chased away his anger.

"This is for you," she said, holding out the bottle of wine.

He looked at the bottle and the red wine stain down her thigh, then to the broken glass by her bare feet. "Let me clean this up first before you hurt yourself. Don't move," he said and bent to pick up the glass around her.

Car lights moved around them, brightening up her smooth legs. Stewart's eyes traced the tight lines of her muscles and settled on the spot where the frayed white threads from her cut-offs tickled the tops of her thighs.

A piece of glass sliced the pad of his thumb. Blood surfaced. He pressed his thumb onto his jeans.

"Mike," Leah said. She bounded toward the car turning into her driveway, stopped short, and ran back to Stewart.

His heart hastened.

"Almost forgot." She leaned over and placed the bottle of wine beside him and ran back to the car.

"Slut," Tom said once she was out of earshot.

"Don't talk about her like that." Stewart kept his eyes on Leah as she jumped on the man coming out of the car. Her long arms wrapped around his neck as she kissed him. The man pushed her away and Leah stumbled backward.

Leah shook her head and paused, aghast, at his reaction toward her. She crossed her arms over her chest. "Why are you so late? Where have you been?" Her voice chased him into the house. "Don't ignore me," she said, following him.

"How could any man walk away from her?" Stewart said.

"She's a drunk slut."

Stewart picked up the last of the glass and stood at Tom's window. "How can you say that? You don't even know her. Besides, I like her. She seems nice."

"You said the same thing about Clair," Tom said.

"And I was right."

"Clair was a slut, too."

Stewart clenched his jaw again. "Not anymore."

"Just because this chick gets your dick hard doesn't mean you're her Mr. Right," Tom said.

"Shut up!" Stewart punched the cab door sending a stab of pain to his thumb. He turned to the blue illuminated window, where Leah and the man continued to argue.

ON MIKE'S DRIVE home from the office, he flipped through different stations on the car radio trying to find anything other than country music. And anything to take his mind off what he was going home to. His thoughts drifted to the Ferguson account and Natalie, the intern who was helping him close the file. He could still smell her on him.

He pictured the dinner Leah would have prepared – the empty bottle of wine, the only thing she would have touched of the meal. He knew her anger would be ripe, fueled with alcohol, but he didn't care. He was tired of Leah's shit. Two long years of the same thing every day; her telling him about the clients she was training and their progress, wanting to show him a new squat that promised to give you a yoga butt. Then dinner; quinoa and chicken salad with organic peppers and non-dairy feta. He just wanted a fucking burger made with beef. He didn't care if it had by-products. He didn't give a shit if the chicken was happy when it was alive or if the cow ate grass or corn. And he wanted his goddamn cheese to come from milk, without Leah's diatribe of conscious eating and the fucking footprint they were going to leave behind for the kids he didn't even want to have.

He didn't need food. He didn't want Leah. He wanted to be ramming Natalie on the couch in his office while the cleaning lady vacuumed dangerously close to the office door. He got hard just thinking about how many times they had almost been caught.

Leah, too, had loved risqué sex. Between that killer body and her unquenchable sex drive, he couldn't control the words that tumbled from him, the day he asked her to marry him. She used sexual adventure to trap him and his money. Too bad she was such a good fuck. If only she'd learn to keep her mouth shut.

A headache pulsed at his temples thinking of her nagging voice. If only she'd simply disappear, life would be much easier.

His grip tightened around the steering wheel. He needed to be rid of Leah, in a way that wouldn't cost him a small fortune each month.

Mike pulled on to Camino and his stomach became a pit of molasses.

The lights from his Porsche shone against a white cube van backed into the driveway beside his house.

New neighbours. Hope they're quiet. Last thing I want, to have to be social with some guy every time I step out the fucking door.

He pulled into the driveway. The glow from their television washed the window in shades of blue. Mike hoped Leah had fallen asleep waiting for him so he could sneak in unnoticed.

As he climbed out of the car, Leah jumped from out of nowhere and threw her arms around his neck. Her mouth pressed over his. The sweet scent of wine and rose perfume came at him. The world was closing in on him and he had to get away.

"Let me get in the fucking house, will ya?" he said and pushed her aside.

Her voice scratched at the inside of his head, as she rattled on with question after question. He rubbed his forehead. The headache worsened. His chest felt like drying cement. He dropped his briefcase beside the couch and walked to the kitchen table as he continued to ignore her.

Quinoa and chicken, surprise, surprise. Empty wine bottle on the coffee table. No glass? Interesting, maybe she's graduated to straight from the bottle.

He picked up the remote and Leah grabbed it from his hand. His eyes burned as he glared at her. "What the fuck!"

Hands on her hips, she narrowed her eyes at him. "Tell me where you've been. Why haven't you answered my texts?"

"What the fuck do you want from me? I've been working." His arms swung in the air as he spoke. "How else do you think you can live here? Your personal training gig would never afford this lifestyle."

"I contribute too, you know," Leah said.

"Whatever."

"Don't 'whatever' me, I want answers. Who is she?" Leah's face reddened.

Mike crossed his arms over his chest and shook his head. He was so done with her shit and tempted to tell her the truth. Natalie didn't ask stupid questions. She didn't want to talk about his feelings or know what he was thinking. And he never had to explain himself to her.

"I don't know what you're talking about," Mike said.

"I can smell her on you."

"I'm tired. I'm going to take a shower." He pointed to the table as he walked past it. "And clean this shit up."

"Fucking jerk!" Leah threw the remote after Mike as he left the room. It hit the door frame and bounced onto the table, landing in the bowl of quinoa.

She flopped on the couch. Tears rolled over the bridge of her nose and into the other eye, joining the other tears before they dropped onto the sofa. She watched Charlie rub his head into the corner of Mike's briefcase, covering it in stray white hair. His cellphone poked out of the front flap.

She had never snooped before. But the draw to alleviate her suspicions was too strong. She could hear the shower still running. Leah crept to the briefcase. Behind the phone sat a torn open envelope with figures scribbled on the outside. Kramer Insurance stamped on the corner. Their life insurance policy. She peeked into the open envelope, fingered through the folded papers, and made a mental note to give them a call the next morning.

She then pulled out the phone and turned it on. *Password?* Her mind went through the various possibilities but she knew she'd only have a couple of tries before the phone disabled any chance of her opening it.

Her fingers hovered over the keypad. L E A H, she punched in.

Try again.

Why would he use my name? He doesn't even call out my name anymore on the rare occasions we make love. She thought again. Company name? Too long. Birthdate? Too obvious. Anniversary date? Wishful thinking.

His mother's birthday. Leah got excited with that thought. He was a real Momma's boy. How naïve she had been to think he would treat her with that same kindness.

Her heart pounded against her ribcage. One try remained and then the phone would be disabled. *He'd know it was me going through his phone. He'll kill me for sure.* Plus, there would be no going back once she unlocked on the phone. She wouldn't be able to un-see whatever she found. And then what? What would she do with this information? *What if there's nothing in there? Maybe he's telling the truth. Maybe he is working late all the time because he's trying to provide me with a better life.* She'd be the one driving him to be disrespectful.

Her distrust could even send him into another woman's arms.

Leah stared at the darkened screen. She pushed the button and slid the screen to enter the passcode. The numbers framed in circles stared back at her. She pressed cancel and put the phone back in his briefcase without trying to unlock it again.

Her shoulders slumped as she walked to the window. Arms crossed over her chest, she watched Stewart continue to move boxes into his house.

Soft footfalls padded behind her. The smell of grapefruit soap filled the air. Mike's strong arms wrapped around her waist, pulling her in close. Heat from the shower emanated off his bare chest.

He nuzzled his chin into the crook of her shoulder and neck. The scruff of his unshaven beard scratched lightly over her skin, raising gooseflesh over her body. His lips opened and closed, moving up toward the back of her ear. Leah shivered as the butterflies alighted in her stomach.

"I'm sorry babe," he breathed into her ear. His hands roamed and pushed up beneath her tank top. "Hard day at work." His other hand went past her belly button, the tips of his fingers sliding beneath the waistband of her shorts. "Forgive me?"

Anger melted into a puddle at her feet and condensed into lust. Leah turned to face him, her hands cupped his bottom, and she crushed her mouth against his.

"Do you think she'll be okay?" Stewart asked Tom as Leah threw the remote across her living room. Her husband – or whatever he was – easily had a foot on Stewart. But Stewart knew if he saw this man strike her, he'd be able to take the jerk out.

"Tone it down, lover boy," Tom said. "She doesn't need a hero. She needs a pot of coffee."

Stewart picked up the bottle of wine she had given him and held it tight to his chest. It smelled of grass and roses. He brought the bottle to his nose and breathed in her scent as he closed his eyes, imagining her there with him now.

"Look, Mr. Casanova, we don't want things to get messy again. It always gets so messy," Tom said.

Stewart watched Leah's posture sag as she stood

alone. "She deserves better than him."

"Just finish unpacking. We don't have all night," Tom said.

Stewart stared at Tom, shook his head, and went to grab more boxes.

After the last of the boxes had been brought in, all that remained to bring in the house was Tom. Stewart slid the ramp back in place and closed the gate on the back of the truck and moved to Tom's side of the cab. He took one last look at Leah's house. She stood at the window watching him. Stewart didn't want to make it look as though he noticed her staring, but he couldn't tear his eyes from her. The man returned. He wrapped her in his arms, kissed the side of her neck. Stewart's chest collapsed. *She can't. She won't.*

"Looks like she's got things under control," Tom said.

Stewart closed his eyes and turned back to Tom.

Tom remained silent. Stewart opened the cab door and lifted Tom out, cradling him over one arm. With his knee, he closed the door and then turned back to Leah's house.

She was locked in the man's arms, her mouth accepting his.

Stewart tensed his muscles and squeezed his eyes shut.

"Ouch!" Tom said. "Loosen up, Rambo."

"Sorry," Stewart said, messing Tom's moppy hair as they made their way up the front walkway.

He closed the door to their new home, clicked the lock, and fastened the deadbolt. Boxes lined one side of the hallway leading through the house. Each room held a number of cardboard boxes.

Stewart went into the kitchen at the back of the house and set Tom down on the chair.

"You're better off without her," Tom said. "We can't have what happened in Texas happen here, too."

Stewart peered at Tom through narrow eyes and went to the box closest to the fridge. He ran a knife across the top, slicing the taped seam open. As he peeled the flaps back, Stewart looked over his shoulder at Tom. "Not like *you* didn't get anything out of it," he said and pulled out another marionette.

He clasped her body. Long arms made of basswood flopped back and forth. Delicate hands with long fingers swung in their place. Pink, pouty lips and blue, glass eyes contrasted against the dark-toned face. Black hair in a long bob framed the soft angles of her jaw. She was a masterpiece. Tom had said as much on numerous occasions. Long lashes made of real mink fur gave her a human-like appearance. The deep neckline of her red sequined evening gown revealed an appreciable amount of cleavage. She was one of Stewart's greatest creations. But not the best.

Tom growled. "How can anyone complain about *her*? I'd like to take her to my new bedroom and give her some wood."

Stewart smiled. "Yes, well, we both have our own bedrooms now, so you'll have all the privacy you need." He placed the marionette on the chair next to Tom and then left the kitchen.

Stewart twisted the knob of the last door on the left and went in, flicked on the light, and closed the door behind him. Four wardrobe boxes lined the wall. He walked to the large window facing the side yard. A chain-link fence separated his property from Leah's, bordered with flowering oleander. He could see right into the bedroom where she and that guy were having sex with the blinds open.

He yanked the blackout shade down and went to one of the wardrobe boxes marked 'fragile'. "This place is almost too perfect. Tom's right. I can't worry about Leah. I can't save everyone." He ran his hand over the front of the box, then pulled the knife from his back pocket.

"We'll be happy here." He slid the knife over the taped seam and then placed the knife back in his pocket. "Clair will be happy here, too." Stewart pulled the two box flaps open. "Won't you?"

A full-sized marionette hung from the wardrobe box's cross bar. Twenty-gauge metal wire looped over the bar and in through the marionette's hand. The flesh pulled away from the bones because of the weight of the arms. Her head flopped to the side. Blue eyes, wide with love, looked back at Stewart. He stroked the side of her face. She was his greatest creation.

He examined the scalpel marks made around her lips. The scars had healed well. She now resembled the wooden marionettes and puppets he created. He was impressed with his workmanship on this puppet. He climbed up on a stool and checked out the threading of wire going through her head. It was the one spot he had worried about most; it had taken days for the bleeding to stop. Now a thick, encrusted scab sat over her red hair. He'd wait a few more days before he'd remove that to ensure it wouldn't start to bleed again.

"Don't worry Clair, that horrible man you were married to can't hurt you anymore."

Clair moaned.

"I saved you. Freed you." His fingers traced her neck and down toward her breast. The muscles flinched under his hand. "I'll save Leah too, if I have to. Then you'll have a friend."

CONNIE DI PIETRO lives the small village life in Brooklin, Ontario, with her husband, four kids, a barn cat, and an Old English sheepdog named Odin, the dog of dogs. Though she writes horror, and has been dubbed the 'Queen of Macabre', Connie's also known to dabble in the historical, romance, and fantasy realms. Represented by The Right's Factory, Connie is an award-winning author and slam poet. A long-time member of the WCDR, she makes time to pursue her passion for writing by contributing to three regular writers' circles. Connie takes great pleasure in editing other writer's work, and believes it strengthens her own writing chops. You are most likely to find Connie behind a computer, typing furiously, in a room surrounded by books, or writing and editing in her backyard oasis. For more information on Connie Di Pietro, please visit, www.conniedipietro.com or follow her on Twitter, @scribescribbles and Facebook.

CONNIE DI PIETRO

PART TWO:
THRESHOLDS

Golden lads and girls all must,
As chimney-sweepers, come to dust.

Shakespeare
Cymbeline

BLOOD PIES

Kate Arms

Victoro Sanchez was ready to go home, or he would have been ready to go home if there was any comfort to be found there. He yearned to lie down beside his sleeping wife, wrap his arms around her enormous belly, and feel the baby kick him. Those kicks reminded him why he had taken this crappy second job, working delivery for Tito's Pizzeria. But all that waited for him at the apartment tonight was an empty bassinet, rocking mercilessly in the closet where he had hidden it after Estella disappeared.

He shuffled into Tito's through the back door after the regular Friday night delivery to Zeta Psi, with enough time left on his shift to do one more run. He stepped into the storage room to avoid Billy, rushing through the narrow corridor with a pile of empty boxes so high he couldn't see Victoro over them.

"Two large with extra sauce," the new guy on the cash register called to the kitchen.

"Two blood pies," Jason, the chef, corrected him.

Victoro hadn't been around long, but he had already picked up some of the kitchen slang: flyers, screamers, and green slime instead of pepperoni, mushrooms, and green pepper. He still wasn't sure what Edgar Allen Poe or bondage pies were, but it didn't matter. He was just the delivery guy.

Before Victoro reached the counter to pack the boxes for his next run, his manager, Matteo, stepped in front of him, whispered, "Outside," and pointed to the back door. The look on his face said ask no questions, so Victoro didn't.

He waited in the humid shadows in the alley, fingers drumming on his hips, mind racing. One of two things was happening and they were both bad. Either Matteo had finally noticed that the inventory in the cleaning supplies closet was dropping faster than usual, or he was testing him for inclusion in the more profitable side of the pizza business. The illegal part of the business. He had promised her he wouldn't get involved. *Does that promise matter anymore?*

Estella had pleaded with him not to take this job. Tito scared her. Her cousin, Eduardo, said the business was a front for drug distribution and that people who messed with Tito disappeared. Victoro hadn't listened. He needed the money and none of the other jobs he applied for would work around his schedule at the building site. But he had promised Estella he would quit once they had saved up enough for a two-bedroom place.

Waiting in the alley, he wondered if taking the job had been a mistake. *Has Tito done something to Estella?* Drugs flowed like water through the nightclub where Eduardo worked as a bouncer. Eduardo knew things. Victoro would never forgive himself if Tito had stolen his wife as punishment for some stolen bleach.

Victoro hadn't planned on stealing from Tito. But the stuff Estella wanted for the baby wasn't cheap, and he couldn't bear to see her go without.

Three doors down, the scrawny, blonde girl working the night shift at the bakery blew smoke rings. Victoro imagined the aroma that didn't quite reach his nose. It triggered the craving he feared would never leave him. *Will Matteo be long enough for me to bum a hit off the kid? Better not. Plus Estella would kill me if she ever found out.* Victoro turned away. No point torturing himself with the reminder of yet another thing he had done for the baby.

The door opened. Matteo stepped into the alley with two of the largest delivery bags, one in each hand. Followed by Tito.

Shit. Victoro's stomach fell. Tito never came in unless there was a problem. Victoro summoned his *cojones*, cocked his head, and looked at his boss. "What's up?"

"Special delivery for a friend of mine." Tito was all business. "Roselawn Cemetery."

A cemetery? Fuck. This friend is gonna shoot me.

"You take Matteo's car."

"Don't touch nothing in it." Matteo glowered. Victoro tried not to react, but he felt the gulp in his throat.

"GPS is programmed. Payment's taken care of." Tito continued as though he hadn't been interrupted. "You don't talk to the customer. You don't tell nobody what you see. You don't come back here. You get a $500 tip when you show up for work tomorrow. *Capiche?*"

$500? Holy Mary, mother of God, I could use that kind of money. If Estella ever shows up again.

Ten minutes later, he was driving Matteo's black Impala through the city, half listening to English talk radio, to deliver two bags of what he hoped were pies to Roselawn Cemetery. And he still had no idea whether this was his lucky night, or the end of the line.

At the building site, the danger of working on the high girders forced him to focus, and he could forget about Estella while working. Here in the car, even with the radio on, he couldn't avoid his thoughts. *Where is she? Is she alive? What about the baby?*

"So, you think she had it coming, then?" The talk show host attacked his caller.

I should have looked. Victoro turned his eyes to the bags beside him. *Did it really matter?* If it was drugs, he was dead. If he was being set up, he was dead. And if it was just pies in the bags, Estella was still gone. It didn't matter.

As he drove along 15th Avenue into the industrial district of West Harwood, a police siren wailed.

Great, he thought. *Just what I need. Pigs in the area, and I still don't know what's in those bags.*

"Of course not." A woman with a high, breathy voice replied to the radio host. "No one deserves to be shot for loving the wrong person."

Mierda, Victoro thought. *When would people shut up about Justine Summerall?* He gripped the steering wheel tighter. *Focus on your driving. Where's that cop?*

The police car was behind him, coming up fast in the left lane. Victoro pulled right with the rest of the north-bound traffic, and breathed a sigh of relief as the cop sped past.

His fingers shook on the wheel as he pulled back out into the left lane and continued into the community of Ashland: medium-sized brick buildings with small yards, good for raising a family, the sort of neighbourhood he and Estella dreamed about.

He only ever drove this carefully with Estella or his mama in the car, but he couldn't afford trouble if those bags really did contain drugs. If he made it through to the end of tonight, he wanted tomorrow not to be worse than today.

"That DJ Dante collected the life insurance, right?" Another woman caller. "She got killed 'cause she was with him. And it turns out she had that new life insurance. Like she knew she was gonna die."

"You think Dante killed her for the money?"

"No way. With all that stuff happening at the house that week and Dante off in Japan? Her daddy paid some Mexican who's gonna take the fall."

Victoro turned the radio off. Delivering pizza to a cemetery was creepy enough. Delivering a pizza to Roselawn and listening to people talk about that stuck-up bitch was unbearable. He had ignored the radio and TV all day yesterday to avoid news of the funeral. Not that there would have been any coverage of the two cleaning women who had disappeared on their way to work at the Summerall house two days before the murder. Just all those sob stories of how Justine's promise had been cut short and how tragic it was for the family. *What about my family? What about Estella and her sister, Teresa? What about my baby?*

His woman was gone, probably dead. And the pigs and the press didn't give a damn about two Latina nobodies.

Rosedale Heights was a different world: huge mansions secluded behind fences and security cameras. Sometimes he had walked with Estella as she went to work in these houses, the two of them laughing together as she shared stories of the bizarre things people did with too much space. *Would she have made it to work that day if I had walked with her?* The thought tormented him.

Roselawn Cemetery filled the northwest corner of Rosedale. The entrance was marked by ornate, wrought-iron gates that had been left open, waiting for him.

He stopped the car, just inside the gates, long enough to swipe his sweaty palms on his jeans. The GPS wasn't going to be much help for the rest of the journey. A location within the cemetery was marked, but the map showed no roads between the gate and the marker. *Exploring in a fucking cemetery after dark. Just like a horror movie.* Home was more appealing all the time, even without Estella waiting for him.

Beyond the gates, the road curved left into

darkness beyond his headlights. The GPS marker was ahead and to his right. He turned his high beams on, wiggled his fingers, and grasped the wheel again.

He inched through the small patch of road lit by his headlights, his eyes bouncing from the GPS to the road and back again. He struggled to pay attention both to the road and where he was trying to get to. Lights danced around him as his headlights reflected off wisps of mist drifting among headstones. He turned right, but the road veered left again and the GPS marker drifted further from his heading.

The mist thickened. His high beams blinded him. Victoro flicked them off, realizing almost too late that he was driving past a right hand turn. He swerved hard, missing the road as he turned. His left front wheel slowed through soft grass and then bumped over a flat gravestone. An extra yank on the steering wheel kept his rear wheel off the grave marker at least.

He pulled back onto the road and stopped the car.

"Sorry." He looked up as he crossed himself.

According to the GPS, he was heading in the right direction now. He looked ahead to where the delivery location should be. A dark shape moved in the mist at the edge of the light, low to the ground, and then was gone. Victoro's hands trembled on the wheel.

Time to finish this. He inched the car forward, eyes shifting between the edge of the road near the car and his target.

He saw movement ahead and slammed on the

brakes. The car shuddered to a stop. A coyote ran across the road at the edge of the light. Victoro heard himself yelp. He closed his eyes, put a hand on his sternum, and pressed hard against his throbbing chest. His other hand squeezed the wheel so hard it hurt.

With a few forced exhalations, he stilled the worst of his panic.

When he opened his eyes, he saw it. Just where the GPS indicated he was going. Light gleamed in front of a large mausoleum at the back of a field of gravestones.

Shadows reached toward him from the tombstones between him and his destination. And from two large piles of dirt. Two figures moved through the light, one much taller than the other. Two people and two full delivery bags. *Not good. This isn't a party.*

Victoro got out of the car slowly. If they were going to kill him and bury him here, he wasn't going to help them by walking to his own grave.

The hum of a generator whirred in the air.

The larger figure, a man, came toward the car. A dark hood pulled forward hid his face. Victoro tried to look calm as he got the insulated bags from the passenger seat. His hands shook. He held the bags out toward the man approaching him. Gloved hands reached out and grabbed the bags. Without a glance at Victoro, the man walked back toward the light.

Two tripods between the mounds of dirt held yellow caged work lights. The smaller figure, a woman perhaps, was low to the ground, shivering.

Victoro turned to leave. A prickle ran up his

spine. *This is when I get shot in the back.* He put his hand in his pocket, grasping his phone. *Is there anyone to call? Tell them where I am? In time to help? Should I take a picture of one of the tombstones? Send it to someone? Who's up? Nobody. Nobody who won't just laugh at me – a sissy, scared in a graveyard.*

"Babe," the man's husky voice broke the silence. "Food's here."

Is that code? Victoro's eyes scanned the area. All of the gravestones along this path were Summeralls. *What the hell?*

When he reached the driver's side of the car, he fumbled for the door. *Mierda.* Tears welled in his eyes. He was going to lose control, and he wanted to get home first, so he could crawl into bed with a bottle and drown his grief. The police said he had to stay calm to help them find Estella. He had to get in the car and drive off. He had to. He gathered his focus, grabbed the door handle, and wrenched the door open with a scream. Not his scream. A woman's.

Get out of here. Now. Victoro threw himself into the car, and was pulling the door closed when the next scream came.

"Noooooo. Help me!" He knew that voice, would know it anywhere.

She's alive.

He was out of the car in an instant, running toward the screaming.

The man and the woman he had seen earlier were dragging a heavily pregnant woman away from him. *Estella.*

"Miss Summerall, please. Don't hurt my baby," Estella pleaded.

Miss Summerall? Not possible.

His foot caught and he stumbled, landing with his knees on something soft. His wrists buckled under him. He held still, holding the cry of pain in his mouth, forcing himself to be silent.

"I got this, Justine. You need to eat," said the man.

"We gotta bring our baby back, too, Dante. We just gotta," said Justine.

Baby? There had been nothing on the news about a baby.

Victoro looked around for something he could use as a weapon. *The lights. If I can get to them. Or the pizza bags. But shit, they're heavy.* Not great ideas, but he didn't see anything else.

He pushed himself to his knees. His foot was caught in a strap. A purse, mocking him, reflections from the work lights glinting off a T of pink sequins. He pulled the strap off his ankle and stood.

"I need your baby," Justine croaked. She grabbed her belly and slumped forward with a weak sob.

"Eat, babe." Dante commanded. "You've been dead for a week. You need to eat."

Dead for a week? What?

"You gotta bring our baby back."

Victoro stepped carefully around the purse. His ankle screamed and gave under him. *Damn.* He couldn't run. *Time for a new plan.*

Estella was straining against Dante, but without success. Her arms were bound by her side. *Pinche cable ties!*

"I brought you back, didn't I? And I got the

money. Just like you planned," said Dante. "You eat for the baby. I'll start the ritual."

Justine shuffled away into the darkness. Victoro heard the zipper of a delivery bag, followed by a box being opened, and then the grunts and slurping of someone eating too fast. *It really was pizza in the bags.* Victoro didn't have time to be relieved. He had to get Estella.

As he inched closer, he could see piles of loose dirt around the grave. It had been dug up. If he could have read the headstone, he knew what it would say. Justine Summerall's coffin was in there, open, and missing a body. He was sure of it.

That bitch zombie wants Estella's baby – my baby – to bring Justine's unborn baby back to life. ¡Ni verga!

"Get down, there," Dante growled, pushing Estella toward the open grave.

"Noooooo," she cried. She was trying to kick him, but he was holding her tight. She couldn't get her belly around his body to get a good angle.

Victoro scanned the area. *Yes.* On the ground between him and the open grave was a shovel. Victoro staggered, ignoring the pain. He grabbed the handle with both hands and lifted the shovel to swing like a bat as he charged at Dante.

"Toro!"

Estella pushed back against Dante so hard she knocked him flat to the ground. Top-heavy with the baby and unable to extend her arms for balance, she fell on him. Dante gasped for breath, winded and trapped under Estella's weight.

"No!" Justine ran toward them, tomato sauce dripping from the corners of her mouth like blood.

Victoro struggled past Estella and Dante. He

swung the shovel at Justine, connecting solidly with her head. She dropped to the ground. Victoro shook as he turned to help Estella.

"Lean back," he shouted at her, raising the shovel over his head. She looked up, then did what he asked. The shovel struck Dante's windpipe with a crunch. Dante's head lolled to one side. Blood sprayed like he had hit a water main. Victoro dropped the shovel.

He grabbed Estella under the armpits and helped her up, guiding her as she stepped over Dante's lifeless body. He squeezed her, feeling the baby between them as they whimpered together.

"I need to get you free." He pressed his hands lightly over the cable ties binding her wrists to her thighs.

"What about them?" Estella asked, tilting her head toward Dante then looking at Justine.

"I'll take care of it." Victoro helped Estella to the ground and kissed her on the forehead. *I'll always take care of it.*

Dante wouldn't be getting up. Justine was the question. She lay on the ground where she had fallen, her eyes dull and lifeless. She looked dead, but Victoro wasn't sure that meant anything. She had been dead before.

At least I can put her back in her coffin, he thought.

Victoro took the gloves Dante had been wearing and put them on. He grabbed Justine by the ankles and dragged her across the ground, so she was lying next to the open grave. Kneeling beside her, he put her hands on her hips and pushed. She tumbled over the edge and landed with a thud.

Victoro peered into the grave. He needed to

know the fall hadn't woken her up. His stomach lurched with an upward heave. Staring up at him from between Justine's feet was a face covered in congealed blood. He gagged. And then he froze. He knew the face. *Teresa.*

His body trembled.

"You okay?" Estella's voice broke through his shock.

"Yeah," he lied. He willed himself to a false composure and turned back toward her. "Just never killed a dead person before." He tried to laugh, but what came out was half-strangled.

Robot-like, he dragged Dante's body to the grave and pushed it on top of the two women already lying there, without looking into the abyss. He pushed several small piles of loose dirt back into the grave before turning back to Estella. He wasn't going to tell her he had found what was left of Teresa in the empty grave, or what had been done to her.

Together, they hobbled to the car. Victoro found a knife in the glove compartment to cut the cable ties and freed Estella. He helped her into the car, then went back to the gravesite for the pizza bags. He would worry about what to do with the bags and the car and the fact that he had killed Tito's friend tomorrow. Tonight, he was taking his wife home and he was going to sleep with his arms around her. And try not to dream about anything except a healthy baby.

KATE ARMS

KATE ARMS IS an award-winning freelance writer, theatre director, and Leadership and Creativity Coach. Writing about other people's lives keeps her sane in the face of her own life with four kids, including a set of triplets; a needy black cat; and four rats. Her fiction ranges from YA urban fantasy to adult literary fiction, and she is the author of *Unblock: Writing Prompts for Works in Progress*. Kate has written for *The Creativity Post, The Artist's Road*, and *An Intense Life*. Kate's short stories and poetry have appeared in *Renaissance* and *Word Weaver*. Her novel, *The Lighthouse Keeper's Daughter* received honourable mention in the 2014 Muskoka Novel Marathon Best Novel (Young Adult/Juvenile) category.

IVY

Mel E. Cober

THE INFERNO ENGULFED the old wooden house at an alarming rate. Smoke billowed up through the dense pine branches, almost blotting out the full moon's glow. The intense heat blew out the windows, shattering glass, and the crackle of flames replaced the normal forest sounds.

"Ivy! Hang on to me!" Jason yelled over the pandemonium. With the child in his arms, he coughed hard as they raced out of the house.

The fire wasn't quiet, as she had imagined. The pops and crackles as the fire consumed their home seemed to bounce off the trees, amplifying the sounds. Ivy stared at the flames in amazement. She never felt hot or cold, so she didn't fully grasp her father and sisters' panic. Her father was sweating lots; something she knew meant he was hot. The fire had licked at the hem of her dress as her father carried her out of the house, but Ivy was unharmed.

"Daddy! Daddy! Come back. I'm stuck!" Cara screamed from inside the tiny home.

Jason shoved Ivy onto the old wooden swing. His youngest grabbed at his shirt, trying to keep him away from the house.

Fear crossed her father's face and, for a second, he stared at Ivy.

"What did you do?" he asked her, untangling himself from her grip.

"They wouldn't play with me," Ivy said, her eyes never leaving the fiery house.

A crash from the house made her father's head turn sharply. He raced back into the ravaged house. Ivy clenched her eyes shut tight.

"DADDY!" Cara shrieked.

There was a crash, louder than any thunderstorm. When Ivy opened her eyes, the roof was inside the house and the yelling had stopped.

"You weren't supposed to take my daddy!" she screamed at the fire. "That's not what you said."

IVY SAT ON the old wooden swing, gripping tightly onto the worn, grey ropes. She stared straight ahead, her left foot skimming the dirt with her toes when the occasional breeze caused the swing to move.

"Daddy?" she repeated for hours, until her voice was scratchy. There was no reply except the wind; even the *Bad Voice* was quiet.

IVY

The fire had died down. It had consumed the tiny house in a fraction of the time it had taken her father to build it. The full moon shone brighter now that the wind had carried away the smoke, illuminating what remained of their isolated home. The blackened stone foundation and piles of ash and glass shards were all that remained.

Ivy's blue dress, trimmed in white lace, faded from many washes, now smelled of smoke. The hem had long ago come undone, and a small, scorched piece of lace drifted in the breeze at her ankles. Her filthy feet dragged along the dirt rut below the swing.

The wind picked up, dispersing the ash like a January snowfall, allowing the full moon to shine on Ivy in the clearing. She knew the smell of charred wood and bodies would remain for a long time.

The heat from the fire had singed the grass nearly all the way out to where Ivy sat on the swing.

Ivy stayed there for hours after the roof caved in. Her backside was numb, her legs as well, but still she sat.

Alone, in the woods where she had remained since her daddy had brought them to this isolated home, after she had gotten mad at the nanny.

No birds or forest animals ever ventured near Ivy. They knew she wasn't like other children. They feared her.

The woods couldn't protect them. Not from Ivy, nor her anger.

◄ ✧ ►

Ivy had been told about her mother many times by her daddy. Even in death, her daddy still loved her mother more. Ivy had destroyed most of the photos of her, one at a time, over the years.

She had only been little when her Mom had died, but she still remembered all the details. Ivy never forgot anything. Or forgave anyone.

"I can't believe we're going to have another baby!" Jillian Bayne had said into the phone. She had thought she was alone, chatting with her friend, but Ivy was always listening. She could not allow another baby. Her daddy didn't spend enough time with her as it was. The *Bad Voice* stirred inside her.

Four-year-old Ivy threw herself out of her bedroom so fast her mother didn't even see her coming. Her rounded belly and the basket of laundry she carried made her lose her balance even faster. The fall down the front stairs was incredibly loud, Jillian bounced off the railing, and her feet went up in the air. She may have been able to right herself, but she tumbled over the laundry basket, scattering the pastel clothing down the staircase.

Ivy was right behind her mother as she fell, and gave her that last shove that made her neck snap.

"Ivy," Jillian had whispered, staring into the cold eyes of her youngest daughter. Blood trickled out of the corner of her mother's mouth. Ivy stood perfectly still, staring at the woman who had given birth to her. Watching someone die was fascinating to the child, and the thrill as her mother's breathing grew laboured was unlike anything she'd ever experienced.

IVY

"Good job, Ivy," the *Bad Voice* said.

As Jillian Bayne took her last breath, Ivy noticed her mother's swollen belly move.

WHEN JASON BAYNE returned from work that evening, he found his wife of ten years dead in the front hall. Before Jason could even process the scene in front of him, Ivy came bouncing down the stairs.

"Hi Daddy!" Ivy said, stepping over her mother's body as if it were nothing. "I missed you!"

The coroner deemed Jillian's death an accident – an expectant mother simply tripped when carrying a basket of laundry down the stairs.

What was most disturbing was the fact that Jillian's belly had been covered in what appeared to be tiny handprints. Hundreds of tiny, hand-shaped bruises on her belly. The coroner's office failed to determine a cause, but did rule the pregnancy likely terminated due to the trauma sustained by the mysterious bruises.

SEVERAL NANNIES CAME and abruptly left the household, each staying a shorter time than the one before. The second last one called Ivy's father at work.

"Mr. Bayne? This is Maria. You need to come home – it's Ivy."

"Is she hurt?" Jason Bayne had asked, but in his

heart he knew.

"Mr. Bayne. I cannot work for you anymore. That child. She's the devil. I must leave. Today. Now."

Every nanny Jason had hired since his wife passed said they couldn't handle Ivy. Two had said they were afraid of her.

Windows had shattered for what seemed like no reason at all when she was angry. All of the neighbours' cats and dogs had mysteriously vanished or died, except for the dirty orange tabby kitten that had showed up on the front porch. That cat had rushed past Jason when he'd come home from work one day and refused to leave. It was a nasty thing, with a crooked tail and one ear grossly tattered. But it somehow seemed to lessen Ivy's fits, and slept with her every night. It made life slightly easier, so Jason wasn't about to get rid of the cat Ivy called Cinnamon.

None of the neighbourhood children would play with the little girl, and the adults all hurried by the Bayne house. Jason felt like everyone was talking about his family, and the few neighbours he had once been friends with had moved away. Ivy herself was always cold to the touch, although she never gave any sign of being cold. Or hot.

Cara and Alice never played with their youngest sister, and Ivy was very jealous if Jason paid attention to her sisters.

"I'll be home by 6 p.m. at the latest," Jason had told Becky, the twenty-year-old nanny the agency had sent over. He'd had to change agencies after complaints from previous nannies about Ivy.

"Not a problem, Mr. Bayne," the cheery blonde said. "I'll take them to the park today and we'll have fun, won't we girls?" Cara and Alice nodded in unison. Jason glanced up the stairs then, his hand on the front door knob.

Ivy stood motionless, staring at Becky.

I don't like her, the *Bad Voice* hissed in Ivy's head.

She clutched a headless doll in her hands, dirty stuffing poking out from where the head had been before Ivy tore it to shreds in one of her too-frequent fits. Ivy loved the headless doll and refused to ever put it down.

In the last two months, she had grown overly attached to the dismembered doll. Jason hated to go back to work, but his boss had insisted he couldn't keep working from home.

"Goodbye, my girls," he said, opening the door. Ivy was no longer at the top of the stairs. Jason tried to tell himself everything would be okay, and headed off to the office.

BY THE TIME Jason got home, the police and an ambulance were at the house. Cara was crying. She had been the one to find the new nanny's body.

"It's going to be okay," he told his oldest, but even he didn't believe his words. The police tried to take Cara's statement, but Cara wouldn't, or couldn't tell them how the nanny had fallen down the basement stairs.

"I don't get it," the officer said. "That woman

looks like she was in a car crash, not a stair fall, but there are no signs of forced entry, and the alarm system has been engaged since this morning. Are you certain no one else had access to your home, Mr. Bayne?"

Jason shook his head. "I don't know either," he lied. "Must have been just the way she fell, I guess. Just a freak accident."

"Did your wife not die from a stair fall just a few months ago?" the officer asked, lowering his voice. A shadow moved at the top of the stairs. "How many children do you have, Mr. Bayne? I've only seen one other. Alice is it?"

"Yes, that would be Alice. Ivy is – well, she's shy and she's only four. She hides when strangers come in. Don't worry about Ivy, I know where to find her."

"I'm afraid I'll need to see your other daughter as well, just to be sure she's okay," the officer insisted.

"Fine. Follow me."

Jason found Ivy upstairs, right where he expected her to be. She was staring at the static-filled television, rocking back and forth, and clutching her horrible doll.

"Ivy?" he said. "This police officer would like to talk to you."

"No," Ivy replied, her gaze never moving from the television.

"Daddy?" Alice called from downstairs.

"Excuse me," Jason said to the police officer, as he went to check on Alice.

"Hello there, I'm Officer Fuller. I'm sorry about what happened to your nanny—" Ivy's whole body turned around to face the officer. Her eyes. There was something unnatural about them. The way she stared right through him made him uneasy. He took a step back.

"Leave us alone."

A low growl filled the small room. It seemed to be coming from the little girl. An orange cat Officer Fuller had not noticed before, hissed from the corner, arching its back. The temperature dropped, and a wind whipped around the room, causing Ivy's hair to fly about her face. The bedroom door slammed closed.

Get out.

The voice was deep, too deep for a child. The hairs on the back of Officer Fuller's neck stood erect. Ivy began breathing heavily, still not blinking. The child's lips hadn't moved. It was as if the voice was inside Officer Fuller's head.

The officer clutched his head, a painful migraine suddenly starting.

"I've seen enough. Thank you," Officer Fuller said, nearly colliding with Jason on the stairs as he made a fast exit.

"WHAT DID YOU do, Ivy?" Jason asked his youngest child.

"He won't be back," Ivy whispered, staring back at the TV, and petting her now-purring cat.

Jason Bayne decided then that something had to change. The police officer could easily report him to Children's Aid.

Jason walked away from his job that day. He

emptied the savings accounts, and vanished with his children before the sun rose the following morning. Jason moved his children miles from any city, deep in the woods. No more TVs for Ivy to stare at, and he made sure Ivy's creepy doll got lost in the hasty move. He hoped it would be enough.

A MEOW SOUNDED from behind her, and Ivy turned to see her orange tabby cat at the edge of the woods.

"Cinnamon!" she called to the cat, thrilled he had been spared.

The cat meowed again as though it was calling her to follow.

Ivy finally released her tight grip on the aging ropes of the old swing and pushed herself to the ground. The dead pine needles poked at her feet, but she didn't notice. Ivy had never felt pain.

Ivy followed her cat along the well-worn path to the river. The forest around her was silent except for the sound of her bare feet crunching on the pine needles and dead leaves. Fall was fast approaching.

Cinnamon finally paused long enough for her to catch up. He flicked his tail impatiently. Ivy crouched to pet her only friend, the cat with the tattered ear and soot-covered tail.

"Where are we going?" Ivy asked.

She scratched under his chin, and he began to purr. She noticed how short his whiskers were now, and blackened at the ends.

"Did you use up another life?" she whispered to the cat. The cat was one of the few she would speak

IVY

to. Her daddy and the *Bad Voice* were the only others. The cat purred in response, rubbing against her bare legs.

The cat led Ivy to the clearing by the river. The light was much brighter here, as the canopy of trees opened up above them. She knelt by the river, cupping water into her mouth with her hand, as the cat lapped at the cool water next to her.

The silence of the forest surrounded them. She had never been past the river without her daddy, and those trips were infrequent.

The cat was the only animal that had ever gone near Ivy. Even deep in the forest, it was rare they heard birds or saw wildlife of any kind. It was as if the other animals could sense Ivy wasn't like other children.

"What are we going to do?" she asked her cat. Ivy sat down on a stump. The cat wound around her legs, as if trying to warm her. They needed to get to the bunker her daddy had built. There was food and water there. She was so thirsty; her throat was raw from all the smoke last night. The drink from the river seemed to have only made her want more water.

Daddy always worried about keeping all of their food and water in one place, so he built a small shelter out by the river. He was constantly afraid they'd be discovered out in the woods, and Ivy would be taken from him. The bunker was his back-up plan, as it was well hidden. They could live there for several days if needed. He'd told his girls before, if anyone came to their isolated house, run to the bunker.

He called the small shed-like structure covered

in tin "the bunker", but she never knew why. If only she could remember which way it was down the river.

Ivy had walked down to the bunker just a few times since they'd moved to the forest, but she had never been inside. Alice and Cara had helped daddy bring items like blankets, bottled water, and cans of food inside, but Ivy was never asked to help.

Ivy hated to help out with anything, and her fits of rage were bad enough that Jason stopped requesting her help long ago. It was Alice and Cara who did most of the cooking and cleaning, while Ivy wandered around the edges of the woods, carrying on a conversation with the cat. Ivy wouldn't come in until Jason went outside and led her in each night. She much preferred the outdoors, and was miserable on stormy days when Jason had to keep her indoors.

"Come on, Cinnamon," the child told her companion. "Let's find daddy's bunker."

A journey down the river to the north soon convinced her she had turned the wrong way. The trees here didn't look familiar at all, and the river took a sharp turn. This was wrong; she'd have to turn back.

She stood for a minute, staring at the river. The current here was much stronger. Her daddy had always warned them not to venture too far down the river, as it grew wide, fast, and dangerous the further they strayed. The cat pawed at her leg, reminding her she needed to find the bunker before night came.

Walking faster this time, the little girl headed

IVY

back the way she had come. The cat took the lead, seeming to understand the urgency to find their way before the rain fell. They passed where they had begun the search for the bunker, and headed up the river the opposite way. They travelled for a time until they came to a lofty hill in the vast woods.

The little girl recognized the place at once. She followed the base of the steep hill around the corner and away from the river. An overgrown bramble of bushes daddy had transplanted here camouflaged the little tin building built into the side of the hill.

She pulled back the bushes, and her heart nearly dropped when she spotted the padlock on the tin-covered door.

The wind whipped up, causing her dress to rise in the breeze. She remembered her daddy kept a key under the rock by the big pine tree only a few feet away.

Cinnamon meowed at her, warning her of the encroaching darkness. She raced to the big pine, and shoved the stone off the key.

Ivy found it hard to get the key into the lock with her cold hands. She didn't feel the cold, but her hands still reacted as though they were numb. The padlock finally popped open. She tugged on the heavy door, which gave way with a loud groan, just enough to allow Cinnamon and Ivy to slip inside. An old, greying peach basket sat just inside the door. Crank flashlights were kept there.

She pulled one from the basket, pulled its handle out and began cranking the noisy flashlight as she had been taught.

After a couple minutes of charging the flashlight, the sound bouncing off the bunker walls, she was able to turn the light on and see the inside of the bunker for the first time. It was not as shallow and tiny as she'd imagined it was from the outside. Rather, the shed was merely an entranceway into a cavernous room built into the side of the forest hill.

"Wow," she whispered. The cat's green eyes glowed in the dim light. "This place is giant!" The beam of the flashlight didn't even reach all the way to the back. Ivy was truly amazed, something she had never felt in her short, sheltered life.

"I wonder what this place was before daddy found it? There's no way he could have built this himself."

The wind whipped up again, out in the darkness behind her, slamming the door, closing it tight.

The child jumped at the sound, but was relieved at how much quieter it was here out of the wind. She shone her flashlight further into the room, checking out all the supplies in the cavernous space. Shelves lined the walls, loaded with can after can of food and bottles of water. She moved over to a large, plastic box marked 'blankets' and dragged it out from under the shelf.

She pulled a fuzzy green blanket out, and wrapped it around her shoulders, covering her scrawny arms. She was hungry from having gone all day without food, but she knew from experience she couldn't open canned food without help.

She was happy to find cases of bottled water against one wall, something she had only seen a few times in her life before. Her daddy had always

IVY

said he didn't believe in bottled water, but occasionally she had found a bottle or two along the river bank over the years that he had allowed her to keep and carry water in.

She dug at the plastic wrappings covering the water bottles, suddenly very thirsty. The lids on the bottles however, wouldn't unscrew for her.

After about twenty minutes, Ivy figured out how to stab the top of a water bottle with a screwdriver she'd found in the bunker.

Ivy drank the water greedily, letting the room-temperature water flow down her throat.

Cinnamon pawed at her, as if asking for a drink as well. She cupped her hand, and poured some water into her palm, giggling at the tickling sensation from the cat lapping at the water. Ivy and her friend settled in for the night.

IVY'S HUNGER GREW. The rows upon rows of canned food made her angry, as she couldn't operate the can opener with her tiny hands. At some point, her father had put a case of foil cat food pouches in the bunker. Those, she could open. Cinnamon gobbled down each meal, while Ivy's tummy growled.

The greedy cat seemed to smile at Ivy as he washed himself after finishing yet another meal in front of her.

"Stupid cat!" Ivy said, trying to keep her temper under control. She knew what happened when she got angry. She'd heard her sisters whispering about how she had killed their mother with her powers.

She had only been little then, but her mommy had tried to have a new baby. She couldn't let that happen. The *Bad Voice* had warned her if her mommy had a new baby, the baby would get more attention than Ivy.

The nanny had spanked her. Spanked her! Ivy had always hated to be held or even touched. Her family knew better than to interfere when she was in one of her moods. It wasn't her fault she had trashed the kitchen that day. Sometimes, the sound of the smashing dishes and emptying all the cupboards and fridge onto the floor was the only thing that could calm the *Bad Voice* that lived in Ivy's head.

She only recently discovered she could start fires with her mind. At first, she had started tiny fires in the woods. Her daddy caught her one day, and told her she would burn down the entire forest if she wasn't careful. She hated when her daddy scolded her.

SHE HADN'T MEANT to burn down the house, but sometimes the *Bad Voice* took over. It always told her it wouldn't hurt her daddy, though. The voice had lied to her.

Thinking about her daddy, her sisters, and her empty stomach angered Ivy further. She clenched her eyes tight, but the *Bad Voice* kept mocking her, telling her it was all her fault.

You lost control. You killed your daddy.

"Shut up! You said I had to teach my sisters a lesson!"

IVY

They are all dead. Your entire family.

"Why aren't you helping me?" she yelled. But the *Bad Voice* was silent. It had always come and gone as it pleased, which made Ivy more distressed.

She spun around, focusing on the rows of canned foods. They flew off the shelves and against the walls. Their tops bulged, but still she could not open them. The walls seemed to pulsate.

"Open, dammit!" Ivy yelled, her face getting red.

A case of bottled water shook violently. Cinnamon yowled at the door, and began to scratch at it, wild to get out. The entire case of water exploded, the steam making the bunker instantly humid. A second and third case exploded close to Ivy. Red welts appeared on her flesh, but she didn't notice.

Ivy yanked open the big wooden door to the bunker and stepped out into the cold autumn wind. Cinnamon charged out of the door as soon as it opened. The cat never looked back as it ran hard and fast into the woods, and that enraged Ivy.

A massive pine cracked. Flames acted like lightning and tore through its trunk. The tree crashed to the ground. Another burst into flames – and another. Ivy had never been this anxious or alone. She couldn't stop.

The flames consumed the forest. The *Bad Voice* laughed inside of Ivy's head.

It's time you learned who's in control here, it hissed. *Who's always been in control.*

Ivy was not afraid. She had never been afraid. Instead, she stepped forward into the flames, her arms outstretched.

"You don't control me anymore," Ivy whispered.

Mel E. Cober is also known as Melly Loves Orange. She's a writer of humour, real-life, and darker works, and has a slightly unhealthy obsession with the colour orange.

Mel has had various blogs published for BOOM 97.3, and others. She's also been published in *Hamlet Life*, *Word Weaver*, and *Surfacing Magazine*.

Mel has lived in Durham Region for well over a decade now, but is originally from Tillsonburg, Ontario.

TERMINAL

Robert E. Walton

PAUL STOOD IN the silent terminal and stared out the window at the plane. Shiny and sleek, it simply hung in the air mid-takeoff. One minute it was roaring skyward, and in the next heartbeat, it stopped.

He blinked, rubbed his eyes and blinked again. The plane still hadn't moved. Paul pressed his face to the window. His forehead squeaked against the cool surface as he looked from side to side. Not only was the plane not moving, but the luggage trains weren't either. As far as he could see, everything was frozen in place.

Paul pushed back from the window. He laughed a quick nervous bark as he tried the wipe his face smudges off the glass. "It's amazing what they can do with flat screens these days. It looks so real." Paul examined the frame around the window. Cold aluminum, nothing else.

He turned to seek reassurance from the crowd that mingled in the departure lounge. A sea of frozen expressions stared back at him. The second hands on the bank of clocks showing the times in various zones didn't move. 8:05 a.m. was the local time. Everyone had stopped.

Paul was sure he had caught them in between tics and that a crowd that size couldn't hold their ruse for very long. He stared defiantly at them waiting for someone to blink, to break. He counted to one hundred.

Nothing.

Fed up with waiting, Paul approached the nearest person in the terminal, a woman with a severe ponytail, business jacket and matching skirt, and black framed glasses. If they weren't going to move, then by God, he'd make them move. He waved his hand in front of her face. "Excuse me, miss?" No response, not even a twitch.

Paul glanced nervously around the terminal, swallowed loudly and dried his sweaty palms on his pant legs. If this didn't elicit a response – a slap at the very least as payment for his forwardness – he didn't know what would. He touched her cheek with a tentative finger.

He flinched back in anticipation of a blow that never came.

Still nothing.

He reached out, more boldly, and touched the woman's cheek again. This time he let his finger linger. Her cheek felt warm and supple, lifelike even, not hard and cold like he expected. His hand dropped to his side as he looked around the terminal at the crowd of what he considered zombies that surrounded him.

"Hello?" Paul called out. "What's going on? Is this some kind of joke?"

Instead of an echo, his voice fell flat. The ominous silence of the terminal pressed on his ears. It drowned the nervous laughter bubbling in his chest as he waited for someone to let him in on the prank.

"This isn't funny anymore," he shouted at the silent crowd as he moved from person to person, waving his hand in front of each of their faces.

He stalked to the boarding podium and reached over the counter, past a clerk as maddeningly still as everyone else. He grabbed the loudspeaker mic, and barked into it, "I don't know how or why you are doing this, but it's not goddamned funny."

He listened as his voice fell from the speaker. The lack of echo made his ears hurt, like he needed to pop them but couldn't, no matter how hard he tried. Like a warehouse full of mannequins, the crowd in the terminal offered no response or reaction. Their frozen faces and unseeing eyes that followed his every move made the hair on the back of his neck prickle. Anger filled him, temporarily pushing away the growing unease that gripped his chest. "I said, cut it out, dammit!"

Paul turned and eyed the male boarding agent. He had never bothered to learn the man's name when they passed through this gate earlier. Never paid much attention to him. But now Paul studied him. Looking for the chink in the façade. Artfully dishevelled hair, a smug leer, a uniform as rumpled as he could get away with without violating the dress code, and a brass name plate that proclaimed, 'Hi, my name is Mark'. Paul gritted his teeth as Mark stared smugly back at him.

"I said, stop it." Paul reached across the podium and shoved him.

Mark fell backward. It wasn't a slow motion fall like in the movies. He didn't do anything to stop his descent. He just fell. His head made a sickening crack when it bounced off the floor. He lay still, his expression unchanged.

Paul skirted the podium and crouched next to the fallen agent. "Oh my God, are you all right? I'm so sorry."

A pool of blood grew around Mark's head, but he continued to lay there unblinking, his hand still poised to receive the ticket from the next passenger. Panicked, Paul bent and put his ear first to Mark's mouth and then on his chest. Neither breath nor heartbeats were evident.

"Oh my God, oh my God. C'mon, buddy, stay with me." Paul jumped up and shouted into the mic. "Help! Somebody, help."

That weird soundproof room type pressure deadened his call. Not a person moved.

Paul looked back down at Mark. The puddle around his head had grown to look like a grotesque thought balloon. Mark still wore the same expression.

Paul crouched and straightened Mark's arm, expecting it to be stiff, but to his surprise it straightened easily. He arranged Mark in what he thought was a more comfortable position, stood, and looked around the terminal again. Nothing had changed. The clock still read 8:05 a.m.

What the hell was going on here?

Paul tried to remember what had happened. He'd been standing at the window waving as the plane carrying both his wife and daughter winged its way out East to visit his wife's parents. He remembered a burst of light, like a camera flash had gone off, but one so powerful that it washed the world in blinding white. When it cleared, everyone was frozen. Everyone except him.

Why am I the only one still able to move?

Paul felt light-headed. "You won't help yourself? Then fuck you, Mark, you're on your own. I need some fresh air." He slammed through the terminal doors and stepped outside. Even here, everywhere he looked, people and cars were in various states of stopped movement: drivers hanging out of their windows, frozen mid-wave or mid-rude gesture, people grouped together loading suitcases or greeting each other with a hug. As inside, everything was still, not even a hint of a breeze.

Paul ran a shaky hand through his hair. *I gotta get home.*

As he weaved his way through the forest of stalled bodies, Paul felt like something was off, besides the fact that everyone was stopped. He was actually becoming accustomed to the lack of movement. Well, as accustomed as one could get in a situation like that. No, there was something else. Was it a noise? A movement? He stopped and looked around, listening intently and as he scanned the crowd, the thing that was off became blood-chillingly clear. These people had no faces.

Everywhere he looked, blank faces, devoid of

features stared back at him. Even without eyes, he felt them looking at him.

Jesus Christ in Heaven, I'm going crazy!

Paul took a step backward. Before, he wanted someone to move; now, he was afraid they would. With hands outstretched, reaching, groping, faceless faces moaning. He flinched as a drop of cold sweat crawled down his neck. At the same moment, something touched his shoulder.

Paul spun around, arms flailing, a strangled cry in his throat.

One of the faceless tottered toward him, arms wide. Paul scrambled backward, right into another faceless. The impact jostled a cry from his throat and past his lips. He dodged into the street, head on a swivel, heart hammering.

Don't look back, that's how they get you!

He ran to the parking garage, found his car and pressed the unlock button on his key fob. The clunk of the doors unlocking startled him. He had expected there to be no response. Never had he been so relieved to hear the sound. He put his hand on the door handle and pulled. The door opened smoothly, like it had thousands of times before. Paul threw himself into the car, then slammed and locked the door behind him.

He scanned the parking lot for any movement, but there was none. He could see back to the terminal. No movement there either, just a pile of bodies on the sidewalk.

As his breath rasped in his ears, the rational part of his brain took over. He must have backed into one of the frozen people and knocked them over, and in doing so, caused a chain reaction. The rest fell like bowling pins.

Yeah, that's it. They weren't moving, just falling, and they aren't faceless, it's just masks. Yeah, that's it.

Paul rested his head on the steering wheel and willed his breathing to slow.

I gotta get home. Something is wrong with me. I have to be hallucinating, like that time I mixed cold meds with alcohol.

Paul sat up, put the key in the ignition and turned it. The engine rumbled to life. The car filled with white noise, and it took Paul a minute to realize it was the radio. He thumbed through his station presets, each time rewarded with more static. He switched to CD, and The Rolling Stones' *Paint It Black* poured out of the speakers.

Paul put the car in gear and pulled out of the parking space only to find his way blocked by cars frozen in the process of parking, leaving, or just cruising for a spot.

"You've got to be kidding me," Paul yelled at the roof of his car. "You. Have. Got. To. Be. Fucking. Kidding me." He punched the horn, and then held it down as he screamed along with the noise.

Not a single person in the garage flinched.

Paul leaned forward and lightly banged his head on the steering wheel in time with the song. As the last notes faded, he peeked up again, hoping for movement. Anything. A bird, a dog, anything. But nothing had changed. Not even a piece of litter blown on the wind.

The CD slipped into the next song, and the bonging intro to AC/DC's *Hell's Bells* blared out of his speakers. It felt like the world flexed in time with each peal of the bell and contracted as the note faded. Paul could almost see it happen outside as much as he felt it inside. The sound rattled in his chest.

Paul shook his head as the bells dissipated and the guitars took over. The world outside was still once again.

He jammed the shifter into Park, threw open his door and stepped out. Paul leaned into the car to turn it off and take the keys out, but stopped with his hand on the mini-flashlight keychain.

Who's going to steal it?

Instead, he ratcheted the key back into the ignition, flipped it to Accessory, and cranked the stereo for maximum Angus.

He straightened up. The music bounced off the walls and the people. He looked down at his car. The black Charger gleamed back at him.

This might just bring someone out of hiding, he thought and walked away from the car. If this was a game, he could play it too. He even allowed himself a laugh as he walked, one that quickly grew. He dodged among the cars lined up to leave the garage, but never would. They'd be like some child who outgrew his Hot Wheels and left them trapped in a box in the back of a closet. That thought sent him into spasms of laughter.

At the pay booth, he stopped and eyed the attendant. She was tiny and wrinkled with a sour look on her face, the world's meanest Cabbage Patch doll. He remembered her from earlier. Her personality matched her appearance. But at least she had a face. Her hand reached for the money from the driver of the car in front of her booth.

Paul snatched the money from the driver's hand. "Down low, too slow." He flapped the cash in the attendant's face. She stared from under the black, shiny bill of her hat. Stale cigarette smoke wafted back at him. Paul snatched the hat off her head and threw the money in the booth. He jammed the hat on his head.

"It's mine now, Captain SmokesTooMuch. If you want it, come and get it." He danced away from the booth and giggled at her. "What's that?" He cupped a hand behind his ear. "I can have it? It looks much better on me? Why, thank you."

Paul stood for a moment sniffing the air, "Ewww. On second thought, you can keep it, but you gotta go catch it." He tossed the attendant's hat toward the street. It spun like a Frisbee through the air. As it reached the top of its flight path, Paul noticed the other planes hanging motionless in the air. They looked like models hung on fishing line from a child's bedroom ceiling.

He shifted his attention back to the hat in time to watch it land in the intersection, then his laugh died in his throat. Everything beyond the intersection was gone. Not a building, a car, a pedestrian, nothing. A wall of black occupied the space, like the physical division between day and night.

AC/DC gave way to R.E.M. *It's the End of the World as We Know It*. Michael Stipe's voice followed Paul to the street. He scooped up the attendant's hat as he passed it, and he stopped an arm's distance from the black wall. He looked up. The blackness stretched as high as he could see, but it curved in toward him as it extended to either side.

He turned around and looked past the airport. There, on the other side, was the same black wall. It encircled the area completely.

Paul had seen enough horror movies to know better than to reach out and touch it. He threw the hat, half expecting it to bounce off, but instead it disappeared into the blackness. No noise, no explosions, no growls. Nothing. He'd seen frozen planes, frozen people. Hell, he'd probably killed a guy. He'd abandoned his car and called a lady a Cabbage Patch doll. Now, he was staring into the Void. A black nothingness created by whatever fueled these hallucinations and he was afraid of it. To top it all off, he wasn't sure if the Void stared back at him. So he did the only logical thing one would do in a situation like this: he looked for a stick or something long to poke it with.

A faceless man standing on the corner had an umbrella looped over one arm. Paul didn't even stop to wonder why the man had it. It was a stick with a handle. He plucked it off the man's arm and ran back to the black wall. He hefted the umbrella, testing its weight and balance, adopted a fencer's pose and jabbed at the Void with the umbrella's tip, yelling, "Ha!"

There was no resistance. It was like poking at air. He pulled the umbrella back and promptly dropped it like he had been stung. The part that had pierced the Void was gone. He hadn't felt anything cut it or chew it or pull it. It just wasn't there anymore. There were no cut marks or burns. No marks of any kind. It was like it never was whole in the first place. It was just a collection of shortened spokes and a band of flapping material hanging loosely from the end of a stick. It no longer resembled an umbrella.

Back in the parking garage, the intro to *Hell's Bells* rang out again as the CD player started the disc over. Paul wondered how he could hear it all the way outside and yet those bells vibrated in his feet and rattled in his chest like he was standing right beside it. The world flexed again. This time Paul saw the blackness move away from him and fall back in. On the outward flex, he could see the tip of the umbrella lying on the road, intact. The black fell back in but instead of stopping where it had been, it moved closer.

With each peal of the bell in the song, the black retreated and advanced, eating up more space every time. It was like it pulsed in time with Paul's heartbeat. Could the Void have been waiting for him to notice it before starting to move? Or had the bells from the song triggered its movement?

Had it picked up on me because I got too close? Or is it because I'm the only person moving around? The only one living?

He stood, frozen like the people around him, watching, as the blackness took bites out of the scenery. A taxi in the intersection lost its mirror. Again, no noise. One moment, it was there, the next, it was gone. When the black flexed out, the mirror lay on the ground beside the car, like it had been bitten off and spat out.

He watched as the black took the passenger side off the cab.

A sudden thought occurred to Paul. *What will it do when it encounters a human being? Chew me up and spit me out, too?* He didn't want to find out. He ran to the cab and jerked open the driver's door. The cab driver sat, featureless head looking straight forward. Paul didn't care. Face or no face, he was still human.

"C'mon, get out of there!"

The driver, like everyone before him, didn't move or flinch. Paul grabbed him by the front of his shirt and pulled. The man slid toward Paul but stopped before he cleared the car.

Shit, the seatbelt. Who wears seatbelts?

The black pulsed in and back. The car tilted, taking the taxi driver with it. Half the car was gone. Thankfully, there were no passengers. Paul reached in and jabbed at the release. The belt popped free, but the driver remained stuck, his fingers wrapped around the steering wheel. Paul pulled. The black pulsed. And suddenly the driver was free. Paul collapsed in a heap with the driver on top of him.

The smell of gas filled the air.

"All right, enough is enough." Paul pushed the cab driver off and stood. "We gotta go..." He backed away, mouth gaping. The driver's hands were missing. The left hand, which had been furthest from the Void was missing at the wrist, while the right arm was missing from the elbow down. As with his hands, where his feet had been, there were only fleshed-over stumps, like he had never had the appendages to begin with.

He had an image then. If that wall pulsed out far enough, he'd see the man's feet, his left hand, his right forearm and hand, scattered on the ground. Like the umbrella. Like the mirror.

The black pulsed again and the cab was gone. Paul backed toward the garage, afraid to take his eyes off the advancing Void. He abandoned any idea of going to his car. He thought about moving the people away, but where would he put them, and how would he move all of them?

What about the others that had been beyond…Oh my god! Karen and Amy!

Paul ran back toward the terminal. He didn't care if he knocked anyone over in his haste. He slammed through the doors and skidded across the tile, past Mark, and went straight to the window. The plane his wife and daughter were in still hung in the air over the runway. The black wall loomed at its wingtip.

Paul vaulted the turnstiles and bolted past security. The alarms screamed as he ran through, down the boarding ramp and out onto the tarmac. Off to one side he spotted an emergency truck with boarding stairs on it. He ran to it and threw a silent "thank you" toward the heavens when he found the keys in the ignition. The truck roared to life. Paul sped across the runways, bumping and bouncing as he crossed the grass medians. The plane was just barely off the ground. He hoped the stairs could still reach the door. He brought the truck to a screeching halt and was out of the cab before it had stopped rocking. It took him a moment of wobbling the stairs up and down until he could figure out the controls. He extended them out as far as they could go and ran up the steps. The plane hung in the air, yet the engine wasn't running. Like all the other machinery he had encountered, it was immobile, but Paul still was sure at any moment those massive turbines would start spinning and fry him where he stood. He bolted up the stairs past the engine and stood trembling at the rear emergency door. The release handle wouldn't budge. His fingers groped around the door, looking for purchase, another release, anything. Desperate, Paul looked through the windows. The people inside the plane sat frozen but he couldn't see his wife and daughter over the seat backs. Through the windows on the opposite side of the plane, he could see the wall of black already halfway along the wing.

He pounded on the windows. Nothing.

Paul slid down the stairs and ran to the cab of the truck.

I'll smash it open.

He backed the truck up, stopped and stared at the plane as he built up his nerve. Knuckles white from gripping the steering wheel, Paul watched the Void flex. He revved the engine and popped it into gear. The tires chirped on the asphalt as he streaked toward the plane.

As the ladder collided with the side of the plane, the nose of the truck became momentarily airborne. The engine roared, the shriek of metal on metal filled the air, and then the ladder tore right off. As the vehicle slammed back onto the runway, the driver's door popped open and Paul was almost thrown out. The truck slewed to one side under the plane, screaming hot rubber on asphalt. The black wall loomed in the passenger side window.

No, I'm not going out like this.

With the speed bleeding off the truck, Paul was able to pull himself back upright and find the brakes. The truck shuddered to a stop and Paul slumped over the wheel. When he could breathe normally again, he swung the ruined machine around and drove back to the plane.

The side of the plane was scratched and the door was dented in, but still intact. And now he had no way to reach it. He watched in helpless horror as the black wall swallowed the wing six inches at a time. When it reached the body of the plane and pulsed back, various bodies and limbs lay scattered on the tarmac amongst the pieces of the fuselage. Paul could not bear the thought of finding his wife or his daughter amongst the bodies.

He turned away, refusing to watch.

PAUL STOOD WITH his forehead pressed to the terminal window, smearing his previous smudge and not caring. The encroaching Void had swallowed the plane. The only remaining area of brightness was the terminal in which he stood. He knew. He had checked it twice. On his second circuit, the music from his car had mercifully ended Terry Jacks' syrupy ode to sentimentality, *Seasons in the Sun*, when the black took it too.

Why the hell did I even have that song on a CD? I hate that damn song.

Now, as the cool window soothed his headache, he wondered what came next. His eyes ached from crying, his throat hurt from screaming, but nothing he did changed anything. The horror of the body pieces falling from the plane had left him unable to blink, to breathe. And even though he couldn't hear it, he flinched with every imagined smack of flesh hitting asphalt. He'd read somewhere that when catastrophic grief hit, the human mind did one of two things to protect itself: it lapsed into madness, or it became numb. He wondered, with a strangely frantic calm, if it was possible to experience both at once.

Paul pushed away from the window and the undulating darkness beyond its pane. He moved across the floor to where Mark lay, crouched next to him and looked around the waiting area at his handiwork. In between frenzied bouts of grief and anger, he had made himself busy. At the window, his mind had been numb. Earlier, he was sure, he'd been mad.

He had removed the bindings holding the business woman's ponytail and let her hair fall to her shoulders. He had then taken off her jacket and shirt—which, if he was honest, and really, why shouldn't he, he'd had some palpitations and some guilt at the sight of her freed and available bosom— and dressed her in a Superman t-shirt he found in the gift shop. He then put her jacket back on but left it unbuttoned, and arranged her in the classic Clark Kent pose. The whole process was surprisingly easy as her limbs were bendable, unlike the mannequins at the department store. His final touch, one that made him laugh, was to arrange several of the men from the waiting room around her, all on their knees reaching out to her.

Paul turned his attention to the benches where he staged the family of fighting, screaming kids into a scene right out of *The Sound of Music*. They all now sat around their mother and father who held books in their hands like they were reading aloud.

Considering the two scenes now, he wondered if

the Supergirl pose was a tribute to his wife, and the family scene a tribute to his family.

Or maybe he was just, in the words of Freddie Mercury, going slightly mad.

He sighed and patted Mark's shoulder. "You know Mark, I think we're friends now. I feel I can tell you things. Turns out, you're a good listener, so brace yourself." Paul peered around the terminal conspiratorially, as though worried someone might be listening. Then he leaned in closer, a friendly hand still on the agent's shoulder, and said, "I think God was trying to talk to me through my car radio."

Paul nodded at Mark's silence. "I know! Freaky, isn't it? But if this is the end of the world as we know it, like the song said, it's not how I thought it would happen, you know? I was expecting fire and brimstone."

He leaned in a bit closer, cupping his hand to his ear. "What's that, Mark?" He looked down at Mark who stared back at him. "Hordes of locusts too? Good catch."

Paul paused and glanced around. "I guess the other signs were all there, if you looked for them. Famine in the third world countries, the world moving toward religious strife, wars..." Paul dipped and raised his arm in an exaggerated motion. "Check, check, and check." He looked down at Mark again and knocked on his forehead. He immediately regretted the action. "I bet that hurt, didn't it? No? Okay, maybe not. Are you going through your own personal end in there? Some place where *I'm* the one stopped with the rest of them while you rattle around in this airport?"

He looked at the blackness outside the window and then cast a sidelong glance at Mark. "You...didn't happen to knock me over and crack open my coconut, did you? 'Cuz that was an accident, and I've apologized."

Paul waited. "You don't have to answer that. Your end would be different than mine, wouldn't it? You'd probably be all wild and crazy, stripping all the people down to their civvies, burning stuff, getting drunk or high, like you hipsters do.

"What's that? That's what I should do? Have sex with Supergirl? No, I couldn't." Paul arranged his jacket under Mark's bloody head. "Yes, she's good-looking, but, no, no I couldn't. Everyone should go out with dignity." He briefly considered how dignified it was to have a crazy man replace your business wear with a superhero shirt while getting your ta-tas ogled, but pushed it aside. That was a question for a wiser man than he.

"I mean," he said, "if this is the end, and God closes the book on humans like He's turning out the lights, what's the point?"

As he watched, the darkness seeped under the doors. It pressed against the large windows and oozed around the frames.

This is new.

Paul didn't like this change. It reminded him of Steve McQueen's movie, *The Blob* and just as that movie had scared his 10-year-old self, this new development inspired that same fear to bubble inside him again.

Paul backed away, only to find himself in the exact spot he had been standing in this morning when everything had stopped. The darkness tightened around him. Mark was gone now, along with Supergirl and the Von Trapps. Thankfully, there was no sound, just his breathing. No horrible smack of limbs falling to the ground on the out pulse of the Void as before. Just its silent, inevitable creep.

No, that wasn't entirely true. There was a noise. He could barely hear it, but it was there. A drawn-out drone like a dial tone but higher pitched, more like a smoke detector. The harder he concentrated on it, the louder it became, until it filled the darkened terminal. The black encircled him, tightening its radius until the only light in his little circle was like a spotlight on a darkened stage.

Beeeeeeeeeeeeeeee

He sat on the floor, his face cradled in his hands. The fear in his heart gave way to grief. His wife and daughter were gone. Everyone was gone. Was this how it was to end? As the black engulfed him, the dial tone rose in volume until it shrilled from every pore of Paul's being; fluttered in his chest.

He made one last silent plea: *Please, I don't want to go.*

eeeeeeeeeeeeeeeee

"Time of death, 8:06 a.m., Tuesday, June 24, 2013."

eeeeeeeeeeeeeeeee

"Cardiac Arrest. Poor guy was dead before he hit the floor."

eeeeeeeeeeeeeeeee
No. Non022ono.
eeeeeep…
NO!
…Beep.

Beep.
Beep.

ROBERT E. WALTON always has a story on the go. From reanimated stories of folklore and Christmas ghosts to monsters and ghouls who fill our nightmares. He delights in the atmospheric, the character-driven, the psychological, and he is not afraid to bend the rules to achieve that.

If you listen closely, you'll hear the music and sea salt of his Scottish and Newfoundland heritage echoing in his words.

To follow Robert as he haunts fog-laden streets, visit him at his split personality places, on Facebook, Twitter, and Goodreads under the sign of Dale R. Long, or on his blog, drlong67.wordpress.com.

NEKOMATA

A.L. Tompkins

"THANK YOU, MR. RAMACHANDRAN!"

Abigail Seito scrambled out of the back of the minivan behind Satya. Satya's father waved to them from the driver's seat as the girls pulled out their overnight bags and dropped them onto the sidewalk before sliding the door shut again. Leaning in through the passenger's side window, Satya offered a grin.

"Thanks, Dad. I'll see you tomorrow."

With one last caution to behave for the Turners, Mr. Ramachandran waited for the girls to take their bags up to the house before he backed out of the driveway. They'd barely knocked when the door was tugged open, and they were dragged inside by a crowd of four other excited girls.

Satya and Abby waved once more as the minivan flashed its lights before driving off down the block, its silver paint reflecting the crimson glow of the setting sun.

The girls crowded into the living room, where a base camp of sorts had been set up. Sleeping bags had been arranged on the floor as well as pillows and bowls of chips. The other girls flopped down, resuming whatever conversation they'd been having before the latest arrival, making room for Abby and Satya to set up their own sleeping bags.

Abby only half-listened to the conversation flowing around her, feeling a little unsure. Glancing up from her backpack, she caught the grin Satya offered her, and managed a small one in return. She'd have never had the courage to accept Kelly's invitation if Satya hadn't come. All the other girls were near-strangers to her, though they seemed nice enough.

It had been hard to start at a new school and leave behind all her old friends, but she had to admit that moving to the suburbs meant that she had a much bigger room now. And there weren't so many people, or noisy streets, so Abby approved. Leaving the city had been a change, but Abby found that she liked the slower, quieter pace of Fairdale.

She'd never been very talkative or outgoing, and being the new kid in a class of other kids who had known each other since kindergarten had been an adjustment. Thank goodness for Satya. Satya, who had asked Abby about the book she was reading one recess and declared that they were friends afterwards, and actually meant it.

It had been just over a month since the start of the school year, and Abby had been shown around the town, introduced to so many people that she couldn't dream of remembering them all, not to mention being dragged home to the Ramachandran house for dinner more times than she could count.

With Satya, Abby no longer felt like the odd person out. She'd be grateful forever to the other girl, not that she'd ever be brave enough to say so.

"So," Satya said, tossing the thick braid of her hair back over her shoulder as she sat. "What's the plan? We have any good movies?"

"Yep!" Kelly picked up a remote, her ponytail bouncing with her excitement. "We can search Netflix for something we all want to watch."

Madison made a dismissive sound, picking idly at her nail polish. "There's nothing good on Netflix."

Emily dragged her laptop onto her knees, her sweater sliding off one skinny shoulder. "If there's something we want to see, I can download it."

"How many controllers do you have, Kelly?" Andrea asked, flexing her toes in brightly coloured socks. "We could play Xbox?"

Abby let herself get swept up in their eagerness, happy to be part of the group.

Until her backpack flexed against her knee, and shifted.

Emily pointed, her eyes wide behind the glasses she nervously pushed up her nose. "Did your bag just *move*?"

Abby felt the blush burn in her cheeks, and ducked her head forward to hide behind the curtain of her hair. She sighed and reached for the zipper of her bag, already knowing what she would find. It wasn't the first time he'd pulled this trick. He just didn't usually do it around other people.

Rei popped free once the zipper parted far enough for his head. The lanky white cat somehow managed to look elegant as he squeezed out of her purple canvas bag. He sat himself down on Abby's pillow, curling his long tail over his front paws and looking over the assembled girls with regal disdain. Abby hoped he hadn't tossed her clean socks out to make room for himself. The first time he'd stowed away in her school bag, he'd knocked out one of her textbooks to give himself more space.

"You brought a cat?" Andrea tugged on a strand of her curly hair. She sounded somewhere between fascinated and scandalized.

"No." Abby gave Rei an unimpressed look. "He brought himself. And he knows better."

Rei seemed indifferent to her scolding.

Madison squinted blue eyes, drawing back as if Rei might get hair on her clothing from across the room. "He's weird-looking. What kind of cat is that, anyway?"

Abby bristled, and pulled Rei into her lap. She might not be happy that he'd stowed away again, but Rei was a handsome cat. No one was allowed to make fun of him. She gave his ears a reassuring scratch, even if it was silly to think he'd have understood the comment.

When Satya leaned over to give him a pat, Rei relented enough to offer a small purr. She flashed a pleased smile, her teeth brilliantly white against the warm brown of her face. "He almost looks Siamese."

Emily frowned. "I thought they always had blue

eyes?"

Abby just shrugged, still playing with Rei's soft white ears. "I don't know. He was my grandmother's cat. I don't even know where she got him."

Rei had been her Grandmother's best friend, and when Baba lay on her deathbed in the hospital, Abby had promised to take care of him. Well, actually, she'd promised to love him. Baba had been very specific about that. She'd held Abby's hand, her dark eyes bright even though her fingers trembled. "He'll need you, Abigail, my Abby. He'll need you to love him."

Abby had swallowed her tears long enough to promise, and she meant to keep it.

She shook off the memory, working her fingers through short white fur.

Andrea offered her fingers for Rei to sniff. "How old is he?"

The question made Abby pause, because she honestly didn't know. Baba had had Rei for as long as Abby had been alive, and even before that, when her brother David was a baby. That made Rei at least sixteen.

She frowned, her arms tightening around Rei. *That must be old for a cat.* Even after three years, the loss of her Grandmother was a dull ache inside her chest. Abby didn't think she could lose Rei, too.

She was working herself up into a panic, when Rei lifted a soft paw to her chin, and turned those wide, gold eyes on her. She felt her worries fade away, as if soothed by a gentle hand. It just didn't seem important, and certainly nothing to get upset by.

Abby dipped her head to brush a soft kiss over that velvet paw, and Rei removed it with a good-natured chirp.

He let the other girls fawn over him, offering him pats and trying to tempt him with various bits of food. He sat back in Abby's lap and accepted it all as his due, like a king accepting accolades from his subjects.

Kelly offered a tentative hand, which had to be thoroughly examined before Rei unbent enough to allow her to pet him. A smile crept across her face. "I think he's cute. What's his name?"

"Rei." She gave it a soft roll, as her grandmother always had. The tom lifted his head to Abby, his eyes half-closed as the chime on his collar sounded gently.

"Is that Chinese?"

Abby fought not to frown, but she tilted her head forward again so the others couldn't see her expression. "It's Japanese."

Madison frowned. "Is that where you're from?"

Her hands stilled on Rei's soft coat as she shot a look at the other girl. "I'm from Toronto."

Madison rolled her eyes and shook her hair back from her face. "Yeah, whatever. I mean, is it where you're *from*?"

Abby drew back, suddenly uncomfortable. She clutched at Rei a little too tightly, and even his raspy purr couldn't help.

Satya sat forward, pinning Madison with a serious look. "You're being a tool."

Madison scowled, and opened her mouth like she was going to snap something back, but Emily leaned in before she could speak. She ran a hand down Rei's back, laughing when he arched into it. "What does his name mean?"

Grateful for the change in topic, Abby gave a small smile. "It means 'spirit'."

"Spirit? Like, a ghost?" Emily's brow wrinkled, but she continued to gently move her fingers down the cat's spine.

Abby nodded, moving her arm to scoop underneath Rei's back legs to lift him higher. "Yeah. Well, sort of. They mean different things, but the *kanji* can be used for either..." She trailed off, feeling awkward again when she realized the other girls were watching her with various expressions of confusion. Tilting her head forward again, she hid her blush against Rei's fur.

Satya grinned, stretching her legs out in front of her. "*Kanji* is a kind of writing. The character for Rei's name can mean either spirit, or ghost." She shrugged, and leaned back on her arms. "No big deal."

Abby offered up a grateful smile, while Rei kneaded her arm gently with his paws.

"Oh!" Kelly clapped her hands, rocking back on her heels. Her eyes were wide with excitement. "That's what we can do tonight!"

Jumping to her feet, she led the other girls to a closet that was jammed full of coats, boots, and boxes of forgotten junk. "My aunt gave me this present for my birthday, and I thought it was totally lame at the time. But it could be cool for us to mess around with tonight."

Scarves and mittens and tattered manuals for old electronics went flying as Kelly began tossing her way through the tightly-packed boxes. Rei stepped grudgingly out of the way as a pair of earmuffs came close to rolling into him. Once safely behind Abby's legs, the old cat sat and groomed one of his paws, as if in demonstration of how unimpressed he was with all of them.

"Ah!" Kelly tugged a glossy cardstock box free of the detritus, and offered it out for the other girls to inspect, her ponytail sliding forward over one shoulder.

Andrea looked the box over with some trepidation. "A Ouija board? Seriously?"

"Yeah, yeah, I know." Kelly tossed her hair back, and rolled her eyes. "That's what I thought when I opened it. I mean, it doesn't even take batteries. Plus it's like, forty years old or something. But it could be spooky fun, right?"

Satya laughed, and bent to rub Rei's ears. "Well, we already have one ghost here."

Emily shrugged, smiling shyly. "We can try. Worse comes to worst, and it's boring, I've got some scary movies on my laptop."

If the disdainful curl of her lip was anything to go by, Madison wasn't convinced. "You've got to be kidding. And what, your Mom's just going to let us light a bunch of candles and, like, hold a séance or whatever?"

Kelly shrugged, most of her enthusiasm leaking out of her voice. "Well, Mom's not here. She and Dad are gone for the weekend. It's just Dana, and she doesn't care what we do as long as we don't burn the place down or bug her too much."

Madison rolled her eyes, but Satya stepped forward to take Kelly's arm. "Come on, I bet it'll be fun and scary. And then we can watch a movie."

Bolstered by Satya's words, Kelly smiled and led the troop back toward the living room, with Madison sighing and dragging her feet as she brought up the rear. Abby settled back on her sleeping bag while Emily and Andrea dragged a low table closer, and Satya dimmed the lights.

Rei lay on Abby's pillow with his paws tucked under his body, and watched them all down the regal line of his nose. Kelly ducked out and returned with an armload of mismatched candles, and began setting them out around the room.

"I know the candles on the box are, like, black, but all I could find were these purple ones from Dana's room and these weird ones that smell like cinnamon that Mom usually burns at Christmas."

Emily frowned, and then pushed her glasses back up her nose. "You think it matters?"

"No, it doesn't matter! Because ghosts aren't real, stupid," Madison huffed.

Abby thought if Madison rolled her eyes any harder, she might strain something.

Andrea shot Madison a glare. "I don't think it would matter anyways. I mean, it's not like ghosts can smell, right?"

Emily chewed on her lip as she gave it some serious thought. "I don't know. In the movies, they don't usually cover that sort of thing, do they? Maybe I should look it up online?"

Kelly lit candles until their warm golden glow flickered all around the room. She bounced back over to the table, and began pulling the pieces out of the box and setting it up. "I'm sure it's fine. Help me figure out how it works."

"There's only two pieces, Kell." Andrea wound

a curl around her finger as she watched.

"Oh, yeah I guess. But there're instructions."

The soft light of the candles flickered in the dark, leaving the walls lost to shadow. The scent of cinnamon flooded the room, reminding Abby of *nama yatsuhashi*, a sweet her uncle had brought her from Kyoto. Rei gave a small sneeze, his tail flicking in agitation.

Kelly glanced over the folded instructions before tossing them back into the box. "Okay, it looks like we put the plastic thingy on the board and then touch it with our fingers and ask questions and like, any ghosts present will spell out the answers."

Emily blinked, and looked over the board. "But how will we know it isn't just one of us pushing the middle piece around?"

Andrea settled in at the table, curling her long legs under herself. "I guess we just have to promise each other not to. It won't work otherwise."

"God, you're all so lame. It's not going to work. There's no such thing as ghosts." Madison threw herself down on her sleeping bag, sulking.

Satya rolled her eyes, her voice clipped with irritation. "If you're just going to complain, don't play."

The look Madison shot Satya was mean. There was no other word for it. "Just shut up and get it over with, then."

Abby scooted forward, taking a place between Satya and Emily, happy to put her back to Madison's sulking, wishing that the girl hadn't come if she was just going to complain for the whole night.

There was a bunch of poking and giggling,

shoulders pressed in and arms stretched out so everyone could put the tips of their fingers on the planchette. Satya tossed her braid back, and Abby could feel the weighty slide of the thick tail against her shoulder.

"Okay," Kelly straightened her back, blowing her bangs out of her eyes. "This is serious." She had to pause when everyone burst out giggling. "Shh, okay. Everyone has to promise not to just push the thingy around. We have to let the ghosts move it."

"You're just going to be sitting around in a circle like a bunch of idiots when nothing happens, then." Madison grouched from her sleeping bag.

Rei's tail gave an irritated flick.

Abby frowned. "Hey, Kelly? Why did your aunt give you something to talk to ghosts with, anyways?"

"Oh my god." Kelly rolled her eyes. "Aunt Betty is so weird. She, like, lives on a farm with a landline and grows her own vegetables or whatever. She keeps offering to, like, clean my chakras or something, too. I can't even."

Satya laughed. "Wow. There's so many things wrong with that."

Andrea wiggled a little in place. "Okay, so what are we going to ask the ghosts? Oh! We should order pizza after this!"

Abby perked up. She loved pizza, but didn't get to eat it much. Her dad couldn't eat cheese, and pizza without it seemed kind of pointless.

The planchette under their fingers twitched, and lurched toward the corner of the board. *Yes.*

Everyone went still, before Kelly gave a shaky little laugh. "Okay, very funny. We can order pizza, it's no big deal."

Andrea stared. "That wasn't me!"

Satya glanced around. "Then who moved it?"

Emily gave a nervous giggle. "You're trying to tell me that ghosts want us to order pizza? Get real."

The planchette gave another lurch. *No.*

Kelly jerked her hands back, and then tried to hide the motion by snatching up the instructions again. "Um, it says we're supposed to ask questions for the ghosts to answer."

She gingerly replaced the barest tips of her fingers on the edge of the plastic, before clearing her throat. "Um...okay, so, like, are there any spirits present?"

The planchette lurched to the side, before returning to its previous position. *No.*

Satya frowned and shared a glance with Abby. "Wait, that doesn't make sense. If there's no spirits, then who's moving the piece?"

Madison made a disgusted sound, stomping over to stand beside the table. "Don't be stupid. One of you is shoving it around."

"If it were one of us, wouldn't we be trying to make everyone think we were a ghost? Not saying we weren't?" Emily pointed out quietly, not meeting Madison's glare.

Andrea started to giggle. "This is silly. It's kind of a dumb prank, too."

Abby frowned. For some reason, she didn't feel nervous, though she could tell the others all were, even if they denied it. Even Kelly who was demanding whoever was moving the game piece to fess up and quit trying to ruin things.

"If you're not a spirit, what are you?" Satya demanded.

The plastic twitched and slid underneath Abby's fingers, moving steadily around the board with lurches and arcs. *B-O-R-E-D.*

Kelly groaned. Emily and Andrea kept giggling, while Satya shot an amused glance at Abby before turning to Madison with one brow raised. "Wow, that's impressive. How did you get it to move without touching it?"

With a sneer, Madison dropped down next to Kelly, crossing her arms haughtily. "Very funny. Fine, ask another question. I'm going to watch and see who's moving it."

Emily rubbed her nose on her sleeve, trying to swallow her nervous laughter. "I'm not sure I want to play anymore."

Abby reached for Rei, scratching behind one velvety ear as he watched the board intently. His tail twitched lazily.

Kelly nodded. "You ask it a question, if you want."

"Fine, whatever." Madison rolled her eyes, as if everything were just too stupid for her to endure. "Will I become world famous?"

Everyone's eyes dropped down and fixed on the planchette as it began to dance around the board again. *H-E-A –*

"– ven forbid." Satya finished out loud, before dropping back with a loud whoop of laughter.

Madison was scarlet to her hairline, and sputtered a few times before she managed to speak. "That isn't funny! Who did that?"

Abby dropped her hands from the plastic wheel,

and fought not to laugh. Madison looked like her eyes might bug out of her skull. The girls were trying to hold back their giggles, some with more success than others, while the blonde girl raked them all with her furious gaze.

Only Satya laughed without shame, holding her stomach as she convulsed on Abby's sleeping bag. Rei stood when she jostled the pillow he lay on. The old cat stretched before lazily sauntering over to Abby and butting her arm with his forehead.

Madison jumped to her feet, still furious, and stood over Satya with an expression that made Abby uncomfortable. She crossed her arms over her chest again, pale eyes narrowed as she waited for Satya to calm down enough to hear her.

"You think that's funny? I know that was you, you bitch."

Kelly's eyes widened. Satya abruptly stopped laughing. "What did you call me?"

Abby stood hastily, leaving Rei sitting on the floor. The cat's ears perked forward in interest.

"You heard me. You think you're funny? Like you're ever going to be anything."

Satya's hands fisted for a second before she forcibly relaxed. "What's your problem, Madison? Yeah, I think it's funny. But I didn't write it."

"Then who did?" Madison shot a glare at the other girls, all of them frozen in shock. The ugly anger in that gaze made Abby feel a little sick to her stomach.

When no one admitted to anything, and the silence began to stretch, Madison turned back toward Satya. "No one else did it. It had to be you."

"Maybe a ghost did it."

"There's no such things as ghosts!"

Satya shrugged, though her eyes were still dark and angry. "Well, if no one wrote it, then I don't see any other explanations. So obviously, there are ghosts, and even they can see what a jerk you're being."

For a second, Abby thought there might be a real fight. Then Madison sank back on her heels, her lip twisting up into a sneer. "Prove it."

"What?" Satya looked at least as confused as Abby herself.

"I said prove it. You say a ghost moved that stupid thing around? Then *proooove* it."

Satya's brows drew down, her hands going to her hips. "How am I supposed to do that?"

Madison gave a triumphant smile, and Abby's stomach clenched. She knew Satya had played into Madison's hand, but didn't know how. Even when Madison spat out her answer, Abby still didn't understand. "Hearst House."

Satya blinked, and Andrea gasped. Abby turned in confusion to see Kelly and Emily go pale. *Why are they freaking out? What's the big deal with the Hearst House?*

Satya's posture wilted a little. "What about it?"

"If any place has proof that ghosts are real, it'll be there," Madison said. "So just go in and find some."

Andrea's eyes popped impossibly wide. "She can't go in there! It's all boarded up!"

Emily nodded so hard her glasses almost slipped off her nose. "Plus, it's been abandoned for, like, a hundred years."

"Fine. She doesn't have to go." Just as everyone

started to relax, Madison's lips twisted up into a nasty smirk. "She can just admit she's a liar, instead."

Abby watched Satya's face harden, saw the fury in her dark eyes, and spoke up before the other girl could open her mouth. "What's Hearst House?"

All five girls turned puzzled expressions her way. Rei lazily washed one ear. Emily reached for her phone, the screen giving her face a bluish cast as her thumbs flew over the screen.

"Oh, right." Kelly's giggle was a little too high-pitched. "I forgot you just moved here."

Andrea leaned forward, pushing back dark curly hair when it slid forward into her face. "Hearst House is this old, totally gross house up on Mill Street. No one lives there and it's falling down. It's really creepy."

Kelly's voice dropped to a whisper, as if afraid to be overheard. "Dana went there with some of her friends once, and she said there were all kinds of weird noises. She said they found a window they could get through, but no one wanted to go inside."

Emily looked up from her iPhone, the light casting strange shadows across her face. "The last people who bought it wanted to fix it up, but they only lived there for two weeks before moving out. That was twenty-two years ago, from what it says here."

Shivering, Andrea pulled her sleeping bag up around her shoulders. "My Mom said that a long time ago, the woman who lived there killed a bunch of kids. She got caught, but still. She's probably still there. That place is totally haunted."

"Aunt Betty says there's an unquiet spirit in the

house." Kelly giggled nervously, glancing over her shoulder. "She says that when she was in high school, one of her classmates went in on a dare and never came back out."

Satya rolled her eyes. "That's not true."

"Is so!" Kelly glared a bit, before hunching down again. "The police looked and everything. They never found him. Aunt Betty totally told me that."

Madison's smile was poisonously sweet. "See? It's perfect. You can find proof for sure. Unless you're scared."

Her chin tilted back, Satya stared down her nose at Madison. "I'm not afraid."

"Which means," Madison said, "you really don't believe in ghosts, and you're a liar, just like I said. Or, you're really stupid."

Abby swallowed hard. Ice had settled into her stomach, its chill fingers reaching out through her body. "Guys, come on. Why don't we just watch a movie or something?"

Kelly's smile was strained, but she pulled out a cellphone. "Yeah. We can still order pizza."

"No." Madison crossed her arms over her chest. "Either Satya gets some proof, or admits she's a liar."

Emily shook her head, her brown hair flaring with the movement. "I'm not going in there."

There was nothing friendly about Madison's smile. Her lips twisted up like a dog about to bite. "We'll wait outside. Just to make sure Satya actually goes in."

Satya's lip curled, peeling back from her teeth.

"I think Kelly's sister might notice us all

leaving." Andrea frowned, curling her hair around one finger. "Let's just forget it."

Kelly gave another nervous giggle, and glanced toward the kitchen. "Please. She's too busy texting her friends to notice we've left."

"Let's go, then." Madison rose to her feet, and grabbed her coat. "Satya can go in, and we'll wait outside."

As the others rose reluctantly to their feet, Abby found herself blurting out, "I'll go in with you."

She froze afterwards, her face feeling alternately hot and cold. The others stared at her like they'd never seen her before. There was a lump in her throat that was hard to swallow around. But somehow, with Rei purring in her arms, and the look of gratitude on Satya's face, she couldn't regret it.

IN ITS DAY, it might have been a pretty house, built with rosy red brick, with huge windows to let in the sunlight, and a couple of turrets that might have reminded Abby of princess towers. But now the wraparound porch was more ashy grey than white, the windows grimy or broken, and moss and ivy crawled over the brick. Parts of the roof sagged alarmingly, and the whole building seemed hunched, like a beaten dog waiting for the next kick.

Hearst House crouched on top of a hill in the older part of town, with a small forest at its back and the overgrown remains of a hedgerow surrounding it. The gardens that had lined the walkway were long-dead, and the gravel was so choked with weeds it was barely a lighter ribbon of lawn in the dark.

It wasn't hard to approach the back of the house unseen. The shadows were so thick and the shrubs so overgrown, they just had to keep their cellphones pocketed to avoid detection from anyone passing by on the road.

At the back of the house, one window gaped open, its glass long ago shattered. Someone had even removed the remaining jagged shards from the frame, making it almost too easy to slip inside.

Rei, who had refused to be left behind at Kelly's house, tensed himself to leap through the window. Abby caught him up in her arms just in time, and passed the indignant cat to Andrea.

"Can you hold him while we're inside? I don't want him getting hurt." It was the truth, but still, Abby hated to leave him behind. The night felt colder, the shadows more threatening, without Rei at her side.

Andrea nodded, carefully wrapping her arms under Rei's hind legs and around his middle. The tom didn't struggle or try to claw, but he fixed his huge golden eyes on Abby, the expression on his whiskered face almost reproachful.

Satya tugged down the bottom of her jacket. "Okay, we'll go in the house, find some stupid proof, and bring it back to you."

Madison rolled her eyes. "Wow, all this because you can't just admit you were moving a stupid toy? Whatever, your funeral."

Satya's back stiffened, and she turned to the dark hole of the window.

Abby swallowed and moved to follow. She glanced back when Rei shook his head hard enough to make the little silver chime on his collar jingle, and she gave him a tremulous smile.

"Be good. We'll be right back."

Rei's ears flattened, and his tail lashed back and forth violently, almost a blur.

With one last chin scratch, Abby took a deep breath, then shimmied through the dirty window after Satya, cellphone in hand.

If the ghosts don't kill us, Mom just might, Abby thought.

The room on the other side of the window was dingy and alien in the faint circle of light. It might have been a parlour or a study. A couch had collapsed on one side, upholstery rotted away. Most of the shelves on the wall had fallen apart, spilling brittle paper and cracked leather book spines to the sagging wooden floor. The wallpaper peeled down in spiraling curls, looking a bit like a cat had clawed at it.

Leaves and bits of trash had gathered in the corners, blown in through the broken window. It made a shushing sound, crunching underfoot as the girls slowly made their way toward the doorway that led to the rest of the house. The floor creaked and groaned underfoot, and Abby kept close to Satya's side, occasionally bumping the other girl with her arm or knee. Satya didn't complain.

"So," Abby finally found the courage to whisper. "What exactly is proof of ghosts?"

Satya gave a little huff of laughter, but her dark eyes were very wide. "I was kind of hoping you'd have an idea."

"Maybe pictures?" Abby said. "Or video?"

Or maybe us never coming out again, she thought, before immediately pushing it aside.

They shuffled across the floor together, the narrow beam of light darting around the room, cellphones gripped tightly. Dirt and grime coated everything, until Abby felt like she was looking through a sooty filter. Even the shadows seemed greasy, and Abby took pains to avoid the corners of the room.

When nothing resembling proof presented itself, and with both girls unwilling to sort through the trash and leaf rot on the floor, they made their way further into the house. The parlour room door was missing completely, one brass hinge half-twisted out of the wood of the frame.

They made their way toward the front of the house. There, a huge wooden staircase twisted along the wall and up to the second floor. The tiles in the hall were cracked and torn up in places, sliding under their feet. Satya took a step to the left, trying to see further up the stairs, then yelped as she threw herself backward when the floor sagged alarmingly under her weight.

When both girls had calmed their breathing and loosened their grip on each other, Satya cleared her throat.

"Maybe there's something upstairs? We should check out the bedrooms."

Abby sucked in a harsh breath, her eyes wide, and grabbed hold of Satya's arm. "Did you see that?"

She felt the other girl go tense under her hand,

statue-still. "See what?"

Abby, still staring across the foyer, raised a trembling hand to point. "Over there. There was a light or something."

There had also been the vaguest shape of a face, with big, dark eyes, but Abby wasn't willing to admit that, even to herself.

It caught her off guard when Satya wrenched her arm away, face and voice tight with anger. "That isn't funny, Abby!"

Abby's mouth dropped open, fear forgotten in the face of that fury. "I'm serious!"

"I thought you came to back me up, but if you're just here to try and make fun of me, or make me look stupid, you can just go." Turning her back, Satya marched toward the stairs. The thick braid of her hair swayed with each angry step. The motion reminded Abby of how Rei's tail lashed when he was angry.

"Satya, wait!" She put as much as she could into the whisper, not willing to raise her voice, but the other girl didn't turn.

Abby watched as Satya hugged the wall and carefully picked her way up the stairs. She shifted her feet, frightened and unsure whether she should follow or wait where she was. She wanted to leave, desperately, but didn't want to go without the other girl.

The light was back. Abby watched wide-eyed, not daring to breathe, as it wafted up from the floor in front of her. As insubstantial as fog, but glowing softly, it condensed into a cloud not much taller than she was.

Then it sharpened, and she found herself

looking into the misty outline of a boy's face.

He wasn't like Baba had taught her. This wasn't the *Yurei*, the lady ghost with her long, untamed dark hair. Nor was he like the other ghost tales Abby had learned; a quick glance down confirmed that while his body grew less distinct as it neared the floor, the misty outline of bare feet were clear enough.

They stared at each other for one long moment as Abby's heart pounded so hard in her chest she was surprised it didn't burst. The ghost boy's eyes were wide and dark, more hollows in his face than anything. He was young, she realized. Maybe even younger than she was.

Abby opened her mouth to call to Satya, but all that came out was a squeak of air. She felt frozen, as if the floor had grown over her feet to hold her in place. She swallowed, her mouth dust-dry, unable to do anything but stare.

The boy's chalky pale lips parted, his mouth opening as if to speak. No words emerged though, only an oozing black liquid that flowed like shadow down his chin, over his chest, and formed a growing oily puddle on the half-rotten floor.

Abby jerked back, her paralysis shattered. She didn't understand much, but she knew she didn't want that spreading pool of darkness to touch her.

She turned and bolted for the rear of the house, her back and fingers tingling with icy shock. Her breath pounded in her chest like the air had turned solid, and tears burned and blurred her vision.

But not so much that she didn't see the others.

There were more than a dozen now, clustered around the foyer. Half-visible mist children filled the room, with huge dark eyes that watched her, unblinking. Some were barely more than hovering balls of light a few inches from the ground, but somehow, she knew what they were. And she knew, in some cold dark place in her mind, that if she paused long enough and listened, she could know their names, and how they died.

Racing down the narrow hallway, she shook off that terrible knowledge, banishing it. All Abby wanted was to escape, to put a door between herself and the apparitions in the hall. Her footsteps sounded too large in her head, running shoes pounding out a terrible pulse of their own. She could barely hear over the roaring in her ears. Somehow, it made it worse that the ghosts were silent, only turning their heads to watch her flee.

The hallway stretched before her, impossibly long. Panic bubbled up, pressing her lungs flat until it burned to breathe around it. No matter how hard she ran, she never seemed to get any closer to the broken door frame that promised freedom. It felt like a nightmare, her limbs heavy as lead as she tucked her head down and willed her feet to go faster.

One foot came down a little too hard, and the soft wood gave way beneath her.

Terror closed her throat and froze her chest as she pitched forward into nothingness.

"I DON'T LIKE this. They've been gone too long." Kelly shivered, wrapping her arms around herself despite the warm weather.

Andrea nodded, her arms still clutching Rei. "Let's call them, tell them to come back. This place gives me the creeps."

Rei was absolutely silent, and other than an occasional twitch of his ears, he could have been a statue. Huge gold eyes were fixed on the dark window, his claws hooked into Andrea's sleeve.

"Whatever. No one made them go in."

Kelly turned on Madison, her voice a furious whisper. "*You* made them go in! If you hadn't been such a jerk, we wouldn't be here!"

Madison's eyes narrowed to dangerous slits. "Um, no. See, Satya was the one being a jerk. Pulling that crap with your stupid board, and then not having the guts to admit it to my face."

Shoving her glasses back up her nose, Emily shifted nervously. "What if they get hurt, though? Like, what if they get cut or something?"

"Oh my god, my Mom is going to kill me." Kelly bit her lip, skin prickling with goosebumps. "This is all your fault, Madison!"

Madison started to snap back, when a breath of warm air gusted out the window, redolent of the smell of dust and rot. The house groaned, old wood settling like some great beast disturbed from its slumber. Shadows rustled, skittering across the wooden porch around them in a rush of half-heard whispers.

The girls all froze, hearts pounding, breath catching in their throats. Fear prickled over their skin, and as one they began backing away.

Something on the other side of the window began to laugh, a quiet dry chuckle that made the hair on the back of their necks stand on end.

"What was that? What's happening?" Andrea's gaze darted, trying to follow the movement of the porch's shadows as they fluttered and shifted.

"Oh my God. Screw this." Madison turned and bolted down the street. She didn't look back.

Kelly scrambled to the road, hands clutched to her mouth, eyes wide in her pale face.

Emily hesitated, her limbs trembling. "What about Abby and Satya? We have to get them out!"

Andrea grabbed hold of the smaller girl with both hands, pulling her away from the house. "We'll go get help. Come on!"

Letting herself be dragged along, trying not to look too grateful, Emily noticed Andrea's empty arms and glanced around. "Wait, where's the cat?"

Andrea looked at her as if she was crazy. "What cat?"

When the girls turned to run, Emily's toe caught on a little leather collar lying discarded on the grass. The blow jostled it, making the tiny silver charm ring softly. Neither of them slowed down.

ABBY AWOKE TO darkness, with her face pressed against rough wood and her left side aching fiercely from shoulder to hip. She sucked in a few slow, shallow breaths, tasting mildew and dust on her tongue. The black was absolute, thick and heavy as it lay over her.

Shaking and trying not to cry, she rose unsteadily up on her hands, though her shoulder stung horribly. The wood squelched under her, the scent of rot rising, along with something older, something drier.

Shifting her hip, Abby felt something crunch underneath her. There was a snapping sound, thin and high, like when she'd stepped on a broken plate. She raised her one arm to wipe her face, smearing something warm over her cheek, while her other hand reached forward to feel what she was lying on.

The wooden floor of the basement had been soft and rotten, collapsing underneath her when she'd fallen from the floor above. Cold stone lay beneath it, sucking the heat out of her body where she half-sprawled across it. Her reaching hands found something else that rattled and cracked around her fingers. Smooth, thin sticks and little round bits of stone.

Abby fumbled for her phone, hands trembling almost too much to press the buttons. The screen had cracked in the fall, but it still lit up with its faint white glow.

She was in a room, surrounded by dirt and dust, and cold stone walls. There was only one heavy wooden door, and the hole in the ceiling she'd fallen through barely visible above her, just a lighter patch of shadows. Abby raised her arm to wipe at her running nose, and when she saw it come away wet with blood, she finally let flow the frightened tears that she'd been fighting back.

Hiccupping softly, she turned the faint light toward the ground to try and pull herself free from the broken planks of wood she'd fallen through.

The floor was covered in bones.

Between the rotten wood and the fieldstone was a layer of bone, yellowed and fragile with age. Tiny finger bones, curving ribs, broken bits of jaw cradling hollow teeth, and Abby could see a small skull, barely bigger than her fist, half-crushed from her falling on it.

Her fingers numb, she scrabbled backward blindly. Abby's mouth opened, but she couldn't force her voice past the icy grip of terror that closed her throat and stole her breath. The faint light from her phone made shadows dart and shift around her.

But no, the shadows were moving. Pooling and shifting, an inky blot that repelled the light. Abby froze again when she realized she wasn't alone. Fear pounded jagged ice down her nerves, holding her in place.

It wasn't anything like the glowing child spirits she'd seen upstairs. This shade was all glaring eyes and reaching fingers stretching along the ground, creeping toward her. It rose up, a tidal wave about to break over her and swallow her up.

When the first shadow finger wrapped over her ankle, Abby finally managed to suck in a shallow breath.

She opened her mouth and screamed.

A<small>NGER HAD CARRIED</small> her up the stairs and through the first doorway on her right. But even as Satya dragged the light of her cellphone over the dust-shrouded remains of a bedroom, guilt began to crowd the edges of her thoughts.

That wasn't fair, she thought to herself, ashamed. *Abby wouldn't try to scare me on purpose.*

Maybe she really had seen something. And even if she hadn't and was just jumping at shadows, she'd still volunteered to come along, despite how scared she was.

And I left her all alone.

Satya bit her lip, and hesitated. Maybe she should go back, get Abby, and apologize. They could come back upstairs together. Searching would go faster with two of them. They could get whatever proof Madison needed. As spooky as the old house was, the satisfaction of Madison having to admit she was wrong was worth the dirt and the gross smells.

Decision made, she turned to head back down the stairs, when the beam of her flashlight caught on something almost blindingly white in the dark.

A spool of old ribbon lay on the floor, partially hidden underneath an ancient wardrobe. The white satin was plain but delicate looking, completely untouched by the dust and dirt that covered the rest of the room. It gleamed slightly in the dark.

Uneasiness trickled down her spine to pool in her stomach. *Why would someone leave ribbon here? And why is something so dumb suddenly so very creepy?*

The scream almost made her jump out of her skin. High and terrified and far too real to be a ghost.

"Abby? Abby!"

Satya turned and bolted out of the bedroom, shoes sliding against the floor. She raced to the stairs, barely slowing as she thundered down them in a cloud of dust and groaning wood.

I never should have left Abby alone. What if she's

hurt? Satya would never forgive herself. She should have never taken this stupid dare, should never have let Madison goad her into something so dumb.

The last stair collapsed underneath her, sending her sprawling across the broken tiles of the front hall. Choking on dust and spitting up grit, she started to scramble back to her feet, when she looked up and met a pair of huge golden eyes.

Satya recoiled, before recognition set in. "Rei?"

The cat was different, sharper somehow. His features more angular, his legs longer. The golden rings of his irises gleamed like fire in the dark.

He turned without a sound and raced across the floor.

Satya blinked in surprise before rising to her feet and following. If anyone could find where Abby had gotten to, Rei would.

There was a door behind the upper staircase. Rei eeled through the narrow opening without looking back. Satya wrenched the door open to find a narrow wooden staircase descending into the basement. Holding her cellphone in one hand and the railing in the other, she followed the bobbing white shape of the cat into darkness.

Down there, the shadows felt *wrong* somehow. Cold and moist, they wrapped around her and clung to her skin. Satya fought the urge to hold her breath, as though the dark could slip inside her nose and down into her lungs if she wasn't careful. It felt like leeches against her skin, wriggling and writhing on her legs, trying to get a hold so they could feed.

Satya tried to ignore the feeling, but couldn't

stop herself from jumping the last couple of steps to the old fieldstone floor.

The basement was so crammed with junk it was hard for Satya to tell how big it was. Boxes and old furniture, sheet-covered bundles, and mouldering piles of who-knew-what made a dangerous labyrinth to navigate in the dark.

The cellphone's light made the shadows in the basement break apart and scuttle to the corners.

"Abby? Rei?" Satya shimmied between an old dressmaker's form and what looked like the remains of a sofa, the cushions rotted and two of its spindly wooden legs snapped off.

Pushing past some heaps of newspapers, Satya choked on the cloud of dust that rose up. She scrubbed her eyes clear, and opened them just in time to see a flicker of white fur disappear behind a steamer trunk. She hurried her way after Rei, trying not to trip or lose sight of the pale beacon of his fur, until finally he stopped before a collapsed bit of wall.

The fieldstone had long ago given way in this corner of the basement, spilling rock and soil into the room. Rei stood before the wall, his tail twitching in agitation, and for one unbelievable moment, Satya could have sworn the cat had *two* tails.

She shook her head, banishing the thought. "Rei, come on. We have to find Abby!" There was no sign of her in the basement. *What if the dumb cat's just chasing mice?*

Rei didn't so much as twitch an ear back to acknowledge her.

Satya had just taken a step forward to pick him

up and go looking for Abby somewhere else, when that elegant tail flicked once to the side. And one of the fallen bits of stone rolled out of the pile.

Satya froze at the movement, then started to laugh at herself. *The house is getting to me*, she thought. *As if a cat can move a chunk of rock by flicking its tail.*

But the tail flicked again, and yes, there were *definitely* two of them now. Twin white plumes that moved in graceful sweeping gestures, like a conductor's baton directing a symphony, and the chunks of masonry rolled away from the wall, taking the soil and debris with them. Finally the way was clear; an old wooden door set flush to the wall.

Rei's tails gave a hard flick to the side, and the door tore itself open with a sound of shrieking hinges, crashing against the stone.

The smell of earth and rot boiled up, but the cat didn't hesitate, only bounded forward into the room.

Satya stood, staring after him. And then she stepped forward, and followed him through the door.

ABBY CRAWLED BACKWARD, legs kicking out to push her further away from the thing that reached for her with strangling fingers. The wooden floor collapsed under her hands, and the sharp bones rattled as they dug into her palms as she moved. She couldn't tear her eyes away as the apparition drew closer, tattered shadows grasping.

NEKOMATA

A flash of white in the dark, and Rei was between her and the shade. Abby sucked in a shocked breath, mouth working silently.

He was no longer the small white cat that slept on her pillow at night. Somehow he'd tripled in size, standing taller than a German Shepherd. His tail – the tail he curled over his nose when he slept and tickled her chin with while he sat on her shoulder – had split in two, forking from the base of his body, and both halves lashed angrily, low to the ground.

The shadow tried to reach around Rei to get to Abby, and the cat struck, claws sinking deep into the darkness, accompanied by a low basso snarl that would have been more at home coming from a tiger than a tabby.

The shade retreated with an echoing hiss.

Rei reared back, teeth bared. It should have looked ridiculous, a cat standing on its hind legs. It wasn't. Firmly planted between Abby and the shadow, tails fanned out behind him and his front paws lifted— whether in defense or threat, Abby wasn't sure— he looked frightening. Alien.

Abby remembered the stories her grandmother used to tell her. They'd made her shiver, made her hide under the blankets at night, but she'd never believed them. Stories of the *Nekomata*, cats that grew so old that they became *Yokai*, supernatural creatures of frightening power. They were said to be malevolent and cunning, capable of doing great harm.

She remembered wrinkled hands smoothing over white fur as Baba held Rei in her lap, speaking quietly in Japanese as Abby had listened, entranced, by the stories.

Rei, who had been her grandmother's cat, and was now hers. He was *Nekomata*.

But he was still her Rei.

"Abby!"

The flashlight was blinding after so long in the dark. When her eyes cleared, Satya was beside her.

"Are you okay? What happened?" The other girl knelt next to her, hands hovering awkwardly. The light moved, illuminating Rei where he stood, and Satya's mouth fell open. "Is that...?"

Abby stared, a little dumbfounded. In the light of the cellphone, the shade was more defined. Only vaguely humanoid in shape, it reached hands tipped with absurdly long fingers toward them, hair moving in a halo around its head. Its eyes were open pits, a darker black than the night, determined and achingly hungry.

One shadow hand reached out toward Satya, but she didn't react. With a sense of cold dread, Abby thought, *Satya doesn't see what I see.*

She grabbed her friend's arm, trying to pull her out of reach of those grasping claws. The second her fingers closed on skin, Satya's face went almost grey, her dark eyes wide as she stared in horror.

Then Rei was there, claws raking the air. His teeth closed on a small bit of darkness and, shaking his head viciously, he tore.

The shade shrieked, a high discordant wail that pierced her ears. Abby clapped her hands to her head, trying to block out the sound as it went on and on.

Satya grabbed her arm and hauled her up with surprising strength. "Come on!" she cried, her eyes locked on the shade where it had retreated away from Rei's claws and fangs. "We need to get out of here!"

Abby let Satya drag her toward the door. Her legs felt as useless as rotten string. She kept craning her head around, trying to keep sight of Rei. She couldn't leave him behind. He was her cat. He'd saved her.

She didn't need to worry; Rei was backing up with them, keeping himself between the girls and the subdued shade. His twin tails moved, adjusting for balance, but his steps backward were oddly fluid and graceful. He waited in the door, ears flat to his skull and a warning growl bubbling up from his throat, until the girls made it through the confusing sprawl of debris and reached the stairs. Only then did he finally heed Abby's increasingly frantic calls, dropping back down to all four feet and bounding after them.

They hurried through the main floor of the house, treading carefully across the groaning floors. Abby kept seeing little wisps of light out of the corner of her eyes, but she ignored them, focused only on Satya and Rei and reaching the study window.

Satya had to help her over the ledge; the muscles on her left side were just one big ache. The rest of her shook, and no matter what she did she couldn't seem to stop it.

She didn't feel so bad when she realized Satya was shaking, too.

Once clear of the window, they didn't stop until they'd stumbled four blocks, finally collapsing on a bench close to a tiny park. Rei followed closely at their heels, and when they sat, he leaped up onto the bench to nestle between them.

He'd dwindled as they moved, until he was again just a small white cat, his single tail tucked demurely over his front paws.

Abby reached out a still trembling hand, stroking her fingers over silky ears and into the thicker fur at the nape of his neck. When the rumbling purr began, she finally was able to take a full breath. "Wait." She frowned. "Where's your collar, Rei?"

The old tom turned his head, showing her the leather collar gripped in his teeth. The silver chime rang softly with the movement. Abby carefully smoothed it back into place around his throat, and Rei's eyes slitted in pleasure, his purr growing louder.

Satya drew in a deep breath and let it out slowly. "What the heck was all that?"

"Ghosts, I think." Abby didn't stop stroking Rei's fur. The repetitive gesture was familiar and soothing for them both.

Satya didn't speak for three more breaths. Her brows drew down, dark eyes filled with concern. "Hey, are you okay? You must have fallen really hard."

Abby hurt all down one side of her body, and there was an itchy tightness on her face that told her blood was drying. But all she said was, "I'm fine."

"I'm sorry." When Abby gave her a confused look, Satya continued. "I should never have let Madison talk me into this. That was crazy."

Abby shook her head. "It's not your fault. I

wanted to come with you."

Satya didn't say anything, but Abby could tell the other girl didn't believe her.

"Do you want to go back to Kelly's?"

"So Madison can make fun of us for not getting any proof?" She hefted her phone. "I didn't even think to take a picture. You?"

"No. I was freaking or falling."

"Yeah," Satya said. "Lucky we had our own ghost there, huh?" She didn't meet Abby's eyes as she reached out to scratch between Rei's ears. "So, no Kelly?"

Abby shook her head, dark hair swinging. She didn't want to see the other girls. "No. I just want to go home. Can you call your dad? I think my phone is broken."

Satya nodded, pushing back the hair that had come loose from her braid. "Sure, okay. You can stay at my house, too, if you want."

Abby nodded, and kept running her fingers through Rei's fur until the shaking stopped.

After a few moments of silence, Satya's brows drew down. She turned an accusing look on Rei, pointing her finger dramatically.

"It was *you*! You were the one making the stupid Ouija board move!"

Abby opened her mouth to point out how silly that was, that Rei was more special than she'd known, but was still just a cat. Her voice died when Rei calmly raised his head, met Satya's eyes. And smiled.

◄✧►

The grass was cool under her feet, damp with early morning dew. It soaked into the cuffs of her pyjamas, the fabric cold and clammy against her skin. Moving without any conscious decision, her feet took her step by step up the gentle incline of the hill and toward the rotting planks and shadowed windows that made up Hearst House.

The moon turned the blades of grass to silver, and a low bank of fog curled around the porch, spilling down onto the lawn in searching tendrils. There were faces in the fog, drawn and pale, watching with huge dark eyes as Abby made her slow, hesitant march forward.

Mist brushed over her face, wrapping around her throat, cool and shivering, before yanking tight. Abby clawed at her neck, trying to suck in a desperate breath and straining backward with all her might. It pulled tighter, dragging her along like a reluctant dog on a leash.

When she placed her foot down on the first stair, the front door swung open, revealing nothing but inky darkness. Cold air rushed over her, thick with the smell of rot and mildew, as though the house had exhaled.

There was something waiting for her. Something old, and cruel, and *hungry*.

Abby woke with a start, shivering with fear and cold, tears tracing down her temples and into her hair.

Rei lay on her chest, his body solid and warm. He watched her out of narrow golden eyes, tail lashing in agitation.

For days she'd dreamed of the house, each night taking her closer and closer. For long moments,

Abby fought to breathe around the frantic hammering of her heart, her throat stinging where she'd clawed at it in her sleep. She felt like a baby, to be crying over a dream of all things, but she'd rather stay up all night than keep seeing the house when she closed her eyes. And she'd rather never sleep again than find out what happened when she finally reached the door.

Abby had to swallow twice before she could force her voice past the lump of remembered terror. Staring at Rei, she said, "It won't ever let us go, will it?"

A.L. TOMPKINS IS a writer from Ontario, Canada. She holds an Honours B.Sc. in Biology, and is usually found working with animals, or in conservation.

A.L. lives with her dog, and a senile old cat that rules the house with an iron paw.

When not writing, A.L. is usually reading anything she can get her hands on, or gaming.

PART THREE:
MONSTERS

Hell is empty and all the devils are here.

Shakespeare
The Tempest

FIGHT OR FLIGHT

Tobin Elliott

"**A**RE YOU SCARED?" he asked as he looked at me sidelong, a grin firmly fixed in place. "Am I scaring you?"

There was, of course, only one acceptable answer.

BY THE TIME he climbed back in the car, smiling and cursing, with me still hiding behind the big bench seat, he was splashed with blood.

He remained behind the wheel, not moving, for a long minute. He didn't start the car. He made no movements. No squeaking of the leather bench seat. Motionless. I remained motionless as well, taking shallow, silent sips of air.

I thought I knew him, but now I wasn't so sure.

This person sitting a few feet away from me, covered in blood…who was he?

Ten minutes ago, I would have sworn he would never hurt me. Scare me? Yes. Hurt me? Never.

Now I had no idea what he was capable of.

He was my father.

EARLIER THAT DAY, Dad had taken me to the Ex—The Canadian National Exhibition—in Toronto. The annual signal to so many children that summer was drawing to a close, and this was their last chance to have a full day of adrenaline-soaked, sugar-blasted, gut-bloating fun.

For me, the day held so much promise. Dad, unlike Mom, would be okay with the more exciting rides. The Tilt-a-Whirl. The Mighty Flyer roller coaster. And on this day, he didn't disappoint. Any ride he could get me on, we took.

We also went on quite a few that I shouldn't have been able to get on. In these cases, the guy working the ride, usually a stringy-haired teenager with a cigarette dangling from the corner of his mouth, would hold up a stick, dirty brown from years of greasy teen palms, beside me. I would stand as straight as I could, trying to subtly lift my heels to increase my height to meet that piece of black electrician's tape marking off minimum height for the ride. I often failed to reach the required stature, but only by degrees of an inch.

In each case, before the teen—Dad called them "carnies"—could turn to Dad to deny me the ride, my father would be holding out some money, usually a two-dollar bill. "Come on," he'd say every time, but with his mouth stretched to a grin tight enough that it altered the sounds until it came out *cahm ahn*.

Not once were we denied a ride, though it must have cost Dad a small fortune that day. But for both of us, it was worth it. It was all about the ride. Any opportunity to flush adrenaline through our veins, he seemed willing to take. Any opportunity to feel the warm summer air stream past our faces. Any chance to feel like we were flying.

The day had held so much promise. A promise of fun, of screams of fear and screams of laughter, of food that tasted like summer, of a day spent companionably with my father.

Until the afternoon, it delivered on that promise.

FLIGHT. THE THING my father lived for. His only dream, his one passion.

Throughout most of his marriage to my mother, my father was somewhere else in the world. The Arctic. Africa. Spain. Greenland. Brazil. Everywhere but home.

Back when the world was dividing along the lines of peace and war, when teens were growing their hair, loving freely, tuning in, turning on, and dropping out, his job was to be the onboard mechanic for a plane, usually a Douglas DC-3, a terrifyingly loud propeller-driven beast. His company, J. V. Aviation—a name I loved just because of the rhyme—would be hired to fly the plane over different locations, scouting for areas to mine certain minerals. As long as the plane itself was working, my Dad had a lot of time to himself.

The locations were exotic, but flying meant freedom. He was free to drink, to fight, to womanize. No commitments other than getting on that plane on time. He had a wife at home, but that niggling detail never slowed his wanderlust.

Then, things began to change. When my mother became pregnant, he promised he would stay home and be a father. The wanderlust would be repressed. He may have even believed himself as he spoke that promise.

Three days after my birth, he packed for another flight. "What about your promise?" my mother asked. "What about the baby?"

He picked up his battered suitcase, opened the door and, without a backward glance, walked through it.

Just like that, he was in flight again.

BY EARLY AFTERNOON, as we walked the Midway, he made his signature move.

He'd run his palm down from nose to chin. As his mouth emerged, his teeth were bared in a grimace.

I hated that look, because I knew it would come again soon.

It meant he had a thirst.

EVENTUALLY, DUE IN large part to his drinking, he

did stay home. He couldn't be counted on to ensure a plane was in working order when he couldn't ensure *he* was in working order himself, so he was let go. He was a man who could fix anything, so he took odd mechanical jobs. Anything from lawnmowers to large trucks. But they all paled beside his glory days.

Trapped at home with his wife and kid, his wings clipped, he started to unravel. There was no escape, no way back to the sky.

Instead, he could only fly on wings of alcohol.

HE TOLD ME to wait, then went to a nearby booth on the Midway. We were still easily in view of each other, but I couldn't hear what he said as he talked to the long-haired, tattooed carny.

It seemed to take some back and forth, but eventually some money crossed hands, and the carny slid something across to my father.

He nodded to the guy and came back to me.

We walked away from the Midway, Dad ignoring my questions about where we were going. Eventually, we found a place that resembled a waiting room or an administrative office. There was no one in the room. Empty chairs lined two of the walls. It reminded me of a doctor's office. I'm guessing the building still stands, and in the intervening years I've gone looking for it, but never found it again. Some innocuous little office with a front area. I've always wondered why it was open back then, considering no one was there, and the only answer I ever came up with was: those were different days back then.

Dad sunk to his haunches so he was eye-to-eye with me. "Okay bud, I gotta do something." Again with the scrubbing hand, the grimace. "And I need you to stay here, okay?"

"I can't go with you?"

"No, bud," he said. "You can't. It's not a place for kids."

Suddenly I was worried.

"You're not scared, are ya?" he said. There was a grin on his face, but when I looked in his eyes, I realized they held no humour. His eyes were cold, judging.

I *was* scared, but even at that age, I knew I probably shouldn't admit it. I did not want to be judged as weak. It had been a good day up to now, and I didn't want to ruin it by being a sissy.

My silence seemed to be the right response, as his eyes softened, though just a fraction.

"I won't be long," he said. "Besides, I got you something." His hand—the one that didn't scrub his face—came around from behind his back. In it, he held a beautiful little toy car. The Batmobile. The one Batman and Robin tooled around in every week on the TV show.

He showed me the rockets that could launch from the pipes. He showed me the little blade—disappointingly dull, but still—that popped out of the front bumper. It was the coolest toy I had ever seen.

"You think, if I give this to you, you can play quietly here for a few minutes while I'm gone?"

I stared at the car, at how the shiny black paint caught the afternoon sunlight and gleamed. How the red pinstriping just seemed to accentuate the fins.

"Yeah," I said, happy that I'd shut my mouth earlier.

Dad stood, ruffled my hair and said, "Of course you can. Thanks, bud."

He handed me the car, told me once again that he wouldn't be long. Then, he walked back through the door and turned right. I watched him through the large, floor-to-ceiling windows that lined the one wall of the office.

I caught a glimpse of his hand coming back up to stroke his mouth as he walked out of view.

Into flight.

SOON, HE'D BECOME paranoid. I learned all of this later, only knowing at the time that Dad was acting a bit weird. Later, it was easier to understand what muddied thoughts slithered through his brain: *Of course my wife is cheating on me. She's sleeping around with any goddamn guy that'll give her a smile. Hell, she's a good-looking dame, and that's the price a guy's gotta pay, right?*

When she caught him tapping their telephones so he could listen in from the line in his garage, she took me, and we left. It happened only three days after the car incident. As Mom explained to me when I was older, "The crazy was escalating." There was only so much fight in her.

She chose flight this time.

I WAITED IN that room, playing with the Batmobile, solving crimes for Commissioner Gordon and beating the Joker, the Riddler, and the Penguin, stopping them from taking over Gotham.

But there was only so much I could do with one toy. And there was nothing else to do in the room. There was only one door other than the exit, and it was locked. Six chairs lined the room, three along one window, three more along the window on the next wall. And a desk sat at the other end.

I kept watching the big clock that hung on one wall, and soon, I decided to make a game of it.

When the big hand is on the 9, he'll be back.

But he wasn't.

When the big hand is on the 12.

On the 3.

I tried each one of them three times.

Later, I changed the game to, *When the big hand is on the 12, I'll go look for him.* The numbers continued to change in that game too.

Somewhere in the middle of these games, a different kind of desperation set in. I had to pee. And once the realization was on me, it escalated quickly from mild discomfort to agony.

I don't know how long I sat in the chair, wobbling my knees side to side in a desperate attempt to ease the feeling, staring out that window. I wanted desperately to go find a washroom, but the fear that Dad would show up while I was gone was too great. Greater than my own suffering.

I circled the little room again, hoping to miraculously find a door that led to a washroom, even though I'd thoroughly scanned the room several times in the past few hours.

Once I'd gotten up to check the room, I couldn't sit down again. It wasn't a pressure any longer, it was a throbbing ache, cramping arcs of torment through my guts. Walking around the room seemed to help, if only a little.

Then it didn't anymore. If I didn't do something about it, and do it *now*, I would piss my pants.

My Dad had no patience for anyone who wet themselves.

I trotted to the desk and looked quickly out the windows. I was invisible in here. No one looked in, no one saw me. I pulled the chair out from the desk, the legs juddering on the carpet, then I ducked down into the space under the desk. I almost peed myself just with the act of bending down.

On my knees, I undid the button on my pants, and pulled down the fly. My fingers seemed dumb somehow, stupid and fumbling. My eyes watered as I hooked my thumbs and pushed down both pants and underwear until my dick popped out, stiff with the need to pee. I let go.

At first, it was simply relief. The simple act of letting my bladder go, yet those initial tears now flowed down my face, my body unclenched itself and I shuddered hard enough that I thought I might fall.

Instead, I watched, almost laughed at the wobbling stream of piss that seemed to come endlessly from my body.

Next, the sound, the pattering of piss on carpet, brought me down from the heights of ecstasy. The stream of urine hit the carpet with a hard, pattering *tactactac* noise, so unlike the splashing in a toilet, that it reminded me I was going where I shouldn't be going. *What am I doing? This is wrong!* But I couldn't stop it.

Finally, about the time the arc of liquid was showing some sign of lessening, the harsh odour of my own waste absorbing into the carpet made me want to puke. The smell made me feel guilty, even as my body felt better.

When I finished, I scrabbled backward on my knees until I was out from under the desk. I still kept my head low, to be sure no one saw me as I pulled up my pants and refastened them. Only when I was done did I cautiously peek over the top of the desk.

No one looked in. No one had seen me.

Then a horrible thought occurred. *What if Dad came by and looked in and didn't see me and thought I was gone? What if that happened?*

The sheer terror in that thought brought more tears. I told myself he would have opened the door. He would have stuck his head in. I would have heard it.

But I didn't believe it.

He would have thought I was scared.

THE THING MY mother and I referred to as "the car incident" happened just before we moved out.

Mom was out and Dad was watching me. He'd spent much of the day pacing the house like a caged animal. The pacing was broken only by frequent trips into his bedroom, usually right after the familiar palm to mouth motion and the accompanying grimace.

In the early afternoon, he came out of the bedroom and stated he had to go somewhere.

He grabbed his jacket, wallet, and keys. As he pulled on his shoes, he seemed a little surprised to see me standing there, my own coat and shoes on. "Right," he said. We left.

All these years later, I can't remember where we went, or why we went. Only a few seconds, maybe a minute of that trip remain imbedded in my mind.

We drove down a busy road. I know this because I always challenged myself to name all the cars. This one was a Mustang. That one was a Corvair. That other one a Corvette. Bonus points if I could name the year.

Without warning, my father said, "You ready?"

He didn't give me a chance to respond.

Our car seemed to dig in and throw itself forward. Dad had slammed his foot down on the gas, and suddenly, we rocketed down the road. His hand twitched as he steered, weaving between the slower cars, with only his wrist on the top of the steering wheel, his eyes squinted down, that smile, that horrible smile, twisting his lips.

I stared first at him, then out at the road, and I found I couldn't tear my eyes away. We passed the cars as though they were parked on the road, and we were the only thing in motion. They're taken for granted these days, but back then, I couldn't have told you if our car even had seatbelts. If it did, I do know they were never used. I kept one hand tightly on the light blue vinyl of the bench seat, and the other clutching the armrest. It was the only thing that kept me from sliding as we snaked through the cars.

Then, ahead, I saw the traffic lights. We'd be on them in seconds.

They were yellow.

A memory flashed through my brain then. My mother clutching my hand as we stood by an intersection, her other hand pointing up to the traffic lights, explaining when to walk and when not to. Explaining and then having me repeat it back. Explaining again, repeating it back.

"I don't ever want you to forget," she'd said. "You can't forget. It's important." Her eyes were on me as she said, "Those cars are big and you're small. You have to see them because they can't see you. And you have to know the lights, because if you don't, if you forget, you could get yourself killed. You hear me?" This last punctuated by a shake of my hand in hers.

I'd heard her.

And now we were going to go through the lights when they were the wrong colour. What if there was some other kid out there, waiting for the lights to change? What if he didn't know he had to see us, because we couldn't see him? We were going to get ourselves killed. The two of us and maybe someone else.

"Dad?" I said.

He didn't respond, he just kept flying down the road. There was a slower car in front of us. Dad jerked our car to the left, and then there was another car coming right at us. At the last second, Dad blew by the first car and jerked us back into our lane as the second car shot by us, horn screaming.

"Dad!"

He turned his head slightly, his eyes flicking between me and the road. "What?"

"Can you slow down?"

"Why?" I watched as the grin pulled his lips thin and bared his teeth. I stared at the man I had known my entire life. But who was he? Was this my father? Because it felt like I sat beside a stranger. Black hair, shot through with iron grey, his nose, slightly off-centre, the humourless twist of his mouth. Then his slitted, handsome eyes—eyes both familiar and alien—stopped their flicking and focused solely on me. He said, "Are you scared?" That grin. "Am I scaring you?"

I broke the gaze between us, terrified of what was rushing at us. Another light was coming up fast.

There was no right answer here. If I told him a lie, he'd keep driving like this. If I told the truth…

"Yes," I said, my voice trembling. "You're scaring me, Dad." The words were a betrayal. I couldn't look at him.

He muttered something under his breath, then, very deliberately, placed both hands on the wheel, and stomped on the brake. Our car slid, the tires skidding, trying and failing to grab the pavement, until we stopped a few feet short of the red light. I turned my head to my father as the stink of burned rubber hit me.

"Better now?" he said. The musicality of his voice told me he didn't give a shit, that I'd embarrassed him.

That I hadn't been strong enough.

That I should have chosen fight instead of flight.

We sat at the intersection, horns honking around us, until the lights had turned green and red and green again four times.

My mother and I moved out three days later.

AS THE SUN dipped low, it shone directly into the office. There were blinds I could pull down, but I didn't want to, in case Dad couldn't see me, or I couldn't see him.

The room warmed like an oven, slowly cooking me. The funk of my pee bit at my nostrils, so I chose the chair farthest from the desk, positioned so I could see out all of the windows.

He has to come soon, I thought. *He couldn't have forgotten me.*

It must be another test, like the car. To see if I'm scared. I'll show him. I won't be scared and if he asks, I'll be cool and tell him no. Act bored.

But I was scared.

The last gambit I had was to make deals. If he wouldn't come back by specific times, I would bring him back through force of will. *If I hold my breath for a full minute,* I bargained, *he'll come back.*

I felt my face go red, and I pounded the chair, willing my lungs to hold on, but they couldn't, and I started breathing again at about the forty second mark.

When that didn't work, I moved to something easier. *If I squeeze the Batmobile so hard that my hands hurt for two minutes…*

FIGHT OR FLIGHT

I gripped the toy tight and clenched my fingers around it, watching my knuckles go white, feeling sharp pains where metal dug into my hands. Still, I squeezed, squeezed harder, the car shaking in my fists as I watched the clock.

I was left with painful indentations in my palms and fingers, but little else.

If I keep my eyes closed for as long as possible, the next noise I hear will be Dad opening the door.

This one scared me, because it meant taking my eyes off the windows. *What if he didn't see me?* Still, nothing would prove I wasn't scared more than making myself blind, allowing the world to pass by as I sat, unknowing, in that stupid chair.

I checked the clock, then slowly, deliberately, I closed my eyes.

I may have fallen asleep. I sat there a long time. When I next looked at the clock, the numbers didn't make sense. The hands seemed to be nowhere near where they were before. And it was darker outside now, the sky pinkening.

Finally, I became terrified that he might have come and, thinking I was asleep, gone again. With that thought, my eyes snapped open. I looked out at all the people, all the parents with their kids, walking by. I scanned desperately for him.

Then my father walked by the window.

"Dad!"

I scooped up my Batmobile and ran for the door, chasing after him.

THEY PACKED OUR belongings into two separate

stacks in the living room. Our pile seemed huge beside the small, pitiful lump of stuff my Dad had separated out.

Mom and I moved into a house that had been made into three apartments. My father moved in with his sister, a large, black-haired woman who scared the hell out of me.

Every time I saw my father after that, he didn't seem that interested in me. We'd go to a movie, he'd buy me a model car or airplane to build, and then we'd go back to his sister's place. He'd get a drink of something, I never knew what it was, but I was always captivated by the gold liquid and the two ice cubes. He'd drink a few of these, then fall asleep on the couch with the television on, and I'd build my model, keeping quiet to avoid drawing the attention of my scary aunt.

She'd feed me, then Mom would pick me up when it got dark.

I didn't really enjoy those visits.

I knew I'd failed him in some way. Admitting my fear.

That's why I'd been so excited for the Ex.

My father wasn't a tall man, and I was just a kid, so it would have been easy to lose him in the crowd. I pumped my legs and called to him, doing everything I could to keep up.

It wasn't as hard as it looked. My father walked like I did after he would spin me around and around. I'd try and walk afterward, but the whole world seemed to be sliding past me, and I'd have to throw out my arms just to keep my balance. It looked like someone had done the same thing to Dad. He kept angling off to his left a bit, then he'd catch himself, or grab sloppily at sign or booth or person, then angle back to his destination.

At one point, in the parking lot, Dad stumbled a bit, and leaned against a lamppost. I took this as my chance. Dad never locked the doors. He always said if someone wanted to steal his hunk of junk, then they were more than welcome to its problems. I ran past his blind spot around to the passenger side of his car, opened the rear door and climbed in, pulling the door shut behind me, wincing at the clunk.

If pressed, I could not have explained why I felt the need for stealth, exactly why I had to sneak into my father's car. Maybe it was in the way he walked past the waiting room without acknowledging me. Maybe it was the way he stumbled grimly to the car. And maybe it was just something unexplainable, yet palpably there. I simply knew it would be better to get into the car and remain unseen until we got home.

It took a long couple of minutes, but he eventually made it to the car as well. I stayed low, crouching in the footwell behind the front seat. I heard him stumble into the driver's seat, muttering curses. I heard the car start up, then felt the movement as we backed up. Dad's arm, dark with hair, came up and gripped the top of the seat as he turned to look.

We were on our way home.

◄✧►

I SETTLED MYSELF as best I could on the floor. It was tough with that big hump in the middle where the driveshaft ran. Dad didn't make it any easier when he took corners really fast or abruptly changed lanes.

He kept up a steady stream of muttering. I couldn't make most of it out, but I knew a lot of it was swearing.

The car movements became increasingly erratic, like we were in bumper cars at the Ex instead of a real car. Dad's speech got louder, but he also laughed a couple of times, though it wasn't the easy wheezing laugh I was used to. This was a lower, somehow nastier thing. I didn't like it. It didn't sound like anything was really funny, and I knew he'd have that grin on his face, the one he had on when he asked me if I was scared.

Then there was the sound of metal on metal, followed by the short bark of laughter, and I felt the car first slow, then stop. Dad shut the engine off and got out of the car.

I took the chance and raised my head just enough to see over the seat. My father and another man, younger, taller, and better dressed, seemed to be arguing. Dad's face, though lit starkly by the headlights, was red. His eyes were narrowed down and his hands were in constant motion, but mostly he kept jabbing a finger in the taller man's face.

After the third or fourth time, the taller man slapped my father's hand away. I said, "Aw, you shouldn't ought'a—" then my father punched him in the face.

The man rocked back, shocked, and my father

hit him again. Blood spurted from the man's nose, and that seemed to enrage my Dad. He punched the man in the stomach, his arm a battering ram. The man's eyes bulged and his mouth formed an *O* that would have been comical in other circumstances as he hunched forward, hands wrapped protectively around his midsection, his face spraying blood. My father, taking his time, placed one hand almost reverently on the back of the other man's head. Then, just as deliberately, he brought a knee up into the man's downturned face, his own expression somewhere between a snarl and a grin.

At that point, the man dropped out of sight below the front hood of the car, but I watched as my father's back raised and lowered as his arm rose and fell, rose and fell, rose and fell. Each time his fist came up, it was darker, spraying strings of blood that caught the rays of the setting sun.

BY THE TIME he climbed back in the car, smiling and cursing, with me still hiding behind the big bench seat, he was splashed with blood.

He remained there, behind the wheel, for a long minute. He didn't start the car, he made no movements. No squeaking of the leather bench seat. Motionless. So I remained motionless as well, taking small, shallow sips of silent air.

He started the car, and I risked a look out the side window as we pulled away.

I couldn't even see the man's face. Just a too-large smear of dark across the pavement.

When we got home, it took me a long time to actually get up the nerve to leave the car. By the time I entered my aunt's house, my father was passed out on his bed.

I'd been forgotten.

THERE ARE A lot of holes in my memory of that day, but that's to be expected. I was five.

Twenty years on, it kept coming back to me, and my mind worried at it like picking at a scab. Not so much reconstructing it as reverse engineering it from the knowledge of the kind of man my father was. And the man I was becoming.

While trying to make sense of that day, and wondering exactly how many people he'd done that to, I wrote him a long letter asking him about it. Asking for some explanation. *Any* explanation.

Telling him what it had done to me.

Before I could send it, he passed away. His final flight.

I put the envelope in his cheap casket when I kissed him goodbye for the last time.

IT ALL CAME together for me when I was thirty-five.

My son, a small reflection of myself at that age, sat in the passenger seat of my car as I drove him to a soccer practice across town. He sat, fidgety, humming along to some song on the radio by a band I'd never heard of. And as I looked at him, a deep well of understanding opened up for me. I had to turn away to hide the shameful, ridiculous tears that threatened to spill down my face.

When I had control, I gripped the wheel with both hands. Then I pressed my foot hard on the pedal, mashing it to the floor.

The car jumped forward, engine howling, as I pushed the car through the traffic, sliding between too-slow vehicles, blaring horns, and upraised middle fingers. Ahead of me, there was a light just turning from green to yellow.

I flicked a glance at my boy and saw his eyes, wide and staring. He saw the light too.

I ran the light.

"Dad?" my son said, his voice quavering, high-pitched, almost girlish.

"What?" I said, and turned to him, grinning. "You scared?"

MY WIFE TOOK my boy and moved away the next day.

She stared at me with a look of utter disappointment. The separation had been coming for a while now, the look on her face becoming more and more commonplace over the past weeks.

At one point, with their bags packed and standing by the door, my son's face red from crying, she took my hand in both of hers. I stared at the gold band on my fourth finger as she asked me why I was doing this to them. Why I was acting this way.

I didn't look at her as I said, "I don't know."

She held my hand a little longer, her breath

coming in short, hitching gasps. I know what she wanted. She wanted me to look at her, to tell her it was going to be okay. She wanted me to take her in my arms. She wanted me to explain *why* I was acting this way.

I knew why, of course. But I couldn't tell her.

I HAD COME to realize something my father obviously recognized a long time ago.

I realized that a family made me weak.

If I cared about my wife, if I cared about my son, then I would always have a worry in the back of my mind. What if something happened to them? What if I let them down?

To worry about anyone other than myself was to be weak. If I loved them, then I worried about them. If I worried about them, I was scared.

I couldn't be scared.

If it was just me, I could choose to fight or choose flight. Anyone else complicated the equation.

If you had nothing to lose, you had nothing to fear.

My Dad realized this. He knew it when he left me when I was first born. He knew it when he scared me in the car. He knew what he was doing. He knew he was pushing me away.

He knew it when he abandoned me at the CNE. Maybe not consciously, but he knew it. He knew cutting me out would make him strong. Make me strong. He chose flight.

After all those years, I finally understood my

father. I finally got his message. I knew why he did what he did. All of what he did.

I wasn't scared anymore.

NOW, FORTY YEARS past the day I discovered who my father really was, forty years since the Ex, with my wife gone, my kid refusing to talk to me, and my job long abandoned, I have little to do with my time.

So I drive.

I drive the highways. And I watch for a certain type of person, a certain look.

It's not a cursory look, the kind that someone gives me in passing. Someone whose eyes slide by without ever really registering me, like all those people who walked by me that day at the CNE. They're not worth my time. They're sheep.

No. I want the look that sticks. The eyes that actually see me, the look of disdain betrays the passing of their judgement.

It didn't take long this time. It never does.

AT THE LIGHTS. She glanced over, first at my car, taking in the scrapes and dents, then she raised her eyes, resting them for the briefest moment on my own. A beautiful woman.

Until the beauty scampered away from her face. Her mouth made a small *moue* of distaste at what she saw. Her face clouded, and she didn't so much look away from me as reject me from her world.

That's all I needed to *know* her. Her values. Her beliefs. Her life.

She went through her days knowing she was better than the rest, that others looked at her with lust, with jealousy, with need, and she took her small joys in rejecting them. She lived her good life, but only on the condition that nothing went bad. Life could only be good under her strict conditions.

Without those conditions, she was nothing. A quivering mass of jelly, shrinking from the ugliness in the world.

Her, then.

She pulled away from the lights the moment they turned green. I followed behind, waiting for my moment. I had practiced my patience until it was as calm and as still as the noose, as quiet as the blade of the guillotine.

I was as patient as the unfired bullet.

She turned to a quieter road. There were houses, but behind them were more sheep. More who wouldn't intervene, because it would change their conditions. My hands tightened on the steering wheel in anticipation.

I pulled out as though to pass her. I judged it correctly and clipped her front fender, pulling back in. I heard the satisfying crump of plastic and metal pushed beyond their limits. I saw the woman spit a tight expletive, look around quickly, then pull to the side of the road. I did the same.

I waited a half-second until she was out of the car. I exited mine to the staccato attack of her anger. "What the fuck are you—"

I said nothing. I crossed the short distance quickly, my fist coming up into her warm smooth face, trying my best to push my knuckles through her skin into her skull, loving the way her eyes widened, the huff of breath. Loving the feel of contact with her.

And with that first hit, as my knuckles drove into her soft, pitiful flesh, I felt myself harden. I felt the rush and tingle in my scalp, in my balls, in the flutter of my breath.

And I knew what I would feel next.

As bone impacted on skin-cushioned bone, I felt my father.

As her warm blood kissed my hand, I felt love.

As her cries caressed my ears, I heard my father's message.

And as she fell away from me, I felt like I was flying.

"Are you scared?" I said, not keeping the grin from my face, not wanting to. "Am I scaring you?"

There was, of course, only one acceptable answer.

TOBIN ELLIOTT HAS written for most of his life. After some unfortunate incidents with walls and permanent markers, he switched to safer things like pens and paper, and later, typewriters and then computers. Though science fiction was his first love, horror has always had a powerful hold on him, even back before he wore big boy pants. He likes to have the shit scared out of him, and he likes scaring the shit out of others. Somehow, it always comes down to shit with Tobin.

Tobin has written (but not yet published) several novels in his Aphotic World series. He's had three horror novellas published, as well as a couple of stories in anthologies. He's a member of the Writers' Community of Durham Region (WCDR), and an annual participant in the Muskoka Novel Marathon, a 72-hour writing marathon to raise money for adult literacy programs.

When he's not doing all that stuff, he's likely complaining about how everyone drops the last T in his last name, he's avoiding power tools and breakable things, or he's trying (and likely failing) to make his amazing wife of 25 years laugh, or doing what he can to embarrass his son or daughter, or just hanging with the two cats and one dog. Or, you know, talking about shit. 'Cuz it always comes down to shit with Tobin.

If you're interested in more ramblings by Tobin, you can check him out on Facebook, Twitter, Goodreads, (all searchable through "Tobin Elliott") and at his website, tobinelliott.com.

MULE

Pat Flewwelling

FOR NOW, THE bruise was pale on his bony face, except for a small ragged red mark, as if the skin had ruptured from so much swelling. Not that the boarding attendant was looking down at him to notice anything amiss. Tomorrow, the bruise would turn all sorts of colours, but it would be blamed on bed rails and seizures. The bruising between his legs would be harder to explain away. Not that he could tell anyone what happened.

Oh, Joshua could make his feelings known. He could express shock, outrage, and pain, and what he lacked in volume, he made up for in pitch. He had what the specialists called a behavioural problem, because yelling and thrashing is considered uncivilized, even if one's assigned personal service worker is busy stuffing foreign objects, like cocaine-filled condoms, into one's body cavities. It was his behavioural problem that had earned him the bruise on his face.

Of course, even if Joshua could get out an intelligible word or two, the people who should care wouldn't know, because Joshua was leaving the country. As far as Customs knew, Alan – his PSW – was taking Joshua to a family funeral in Portland, Oregon. Well, at least Alan got the state right.

Alan had bought two tickets to Portland, but only one of them was round-trip.

This was their sixth funerary voyage now – remarkable for a forty-year-old ward of the state – but no one behind a desk seemed to notice how much of Joshua's family was dying off. Orphaned when he was eleven, Joshua had long since been an assisted-living tourist, never staying in one place longer than nine months, the perennial victim of budgetary cutbacks and his own behavioural foibles. So no one ever kept track of how many supposed relatives had died before. This was the fifth time Joshua and Alan had ended up in the same institution together, probably because Alan had some behavioural problems of his own, and no one wanted to keep him on any given staff for long. And because Joshua and Alan were a matched pair of bastards, a holiday out of country for them meant a holiday for everyone else.

But, even if there was an investigation underway, Joshua wouldn't return to see justice done.

And for all those days in between... I'll see you die first, you prick! I'll see you torn to shreds.

Joshua's tensely twisted arm writhed like an

atrophied snake, slaloming toward a punchable face somewhere above and behind him. He yelled again – more like a deep, manly moo than a real yell.

"He hates to fly," Alan said to the boarding attendant, and he sighed his most saintly sigh.

She smiled her most saintly smile, and said, "You can go ahead and get him seated." She handed back the boarding pass and passports. She reached for Joshua's hand, reeking of public reassurance and personal unease. Joshua recoiled and mooed again, straining to claw Alan's face, desperate to explain that this trip was illegal and one-way, and that there were foreign objects falling out of his colon. "Does he need anything else?" she asked.

I'm down here, bitch. Alive, aware, and in first-person. Yes, I need something else. How about a lawyer? Or a shotgun? Or hell, just a little eye contact!

"No, no," Alan answered quickly. "And uh…" He leaned over Joshua, so they could keep the conversation just between single man and pretty woman. "He'll settle down soon. It takes about twenty minutes for his meds to kick in. He'll be fine." Joshua could hear the wink in Alan's voice.

"We'll have to put his chair in cargo, of course."

Customs always did a thorough search of his chair. Pat-down, flashlights, sniffer dogs, all that. They never found anything, because, although Alan was an idiot, he wasn't that stupid. Customs also performed a cursory search of Joshua's body with a metal detector, but Joshua was confident the condoms weren't filled with metal filings. As unofficial policy, Customs didn't perform many cavity searches on squirming, shouting, six-foot-tall men with continence problems.

"Of course," Alan said, blooming with magnanimity. "You do what you've got to do. It's all good. I can help him into his seat and out again." Alan's hand smelled of latex, lubricant, and baby-food shit. He patted Joshua on the shoulder. "I won't let him out of my sight."

Of course you won't. My anus is worth half a million dollars.

Joshua began to lose some of the acuity in his sense of touch. His wriggling arm fell stiff against his lap, making his whole body tilt forward and strain against the straps that held him in his chair.

"There you go," Alan said, now squeezing Joshua's shoulder.

As they rolled down the boarding corridor, Alan's hand slid down Joshua's shoulder to his chest.

Die in a fire.

"Just relax," Alan said, "and it'll be over before you know it."

IT WAS OVER before he knew it. The flight, at least. The ride out of town was a long and literal shit-show, not because they couldn't find someone with wheelchair accessible transport, but because Joshua had an ill-timed poo-nami, with brown slime funnelling up his crack to the small of his back, and down into his pant legs, leaking even into the material under the cushion of his chair. Joshua laughed and flung his rigidly bent arms in delight.

He had released a glorious, messy shit upon his enemies, and it was good. It took forty-five minutes at the side of the road to get everything cleaned up, Joshua included. Joshua didn't even mind showing off his taint to the drivers pealing their horns in disgust as they drove by.

Only by luck had the condoms come out intact. He counted his blessings on both hands. Joshua had never tried a cocaine enema before, but he knew that was not how he wanted to shuffle off this mortal coil.

What had made it so odd was that Alan hadn't fed Joshua in almost two days, to prevent exactly this from happening. But Joshua's metabolism had been slowing down for weeks – a sign of things to come, no doubt, and one of the many reasons why Alan may have bought only that one return ticket. Maybe Joshua's autonomous colon had planned its own revenge.

After that, they drove with the windows open, hoping that maybe some mountainous forest air might help clear out the stink. Three hours later, everything still stunk. They arrived after dark, and Alan and the driver left him in the van while they both went in to shower and change.

Joshua couldn't see much through the windshield except for a poorly-lit house – a three-storey pretension transplanted from a field of McMansions, with a clearing used as a parking lot. There were four cars and a truck out front, each crouching low to the ground, gleaming with wealth and horsepower. He couldn't see the trees, since there were no side windows in the van, but he knew he was far from civilization. They'd driven on a dirt track for the last forty-five minutes of the trip, and now, over the accelerating thump of music coming from the house, Joshua could hear ancient redwoods whispering and creaking in the wind. He heard no animals. No birds. Not even a lonesome owl.

This wasn't the place they usually came to. It didn't feel right at all. Maybe he'd watched too many movies, but even in the dark, it seemed like a place this remote should have wildlife and other noises. Maybe the lights scared away the animals. Maybe it was the music. Whatever it was, something just felt *off* about the place. Anticipatory.

Well hell, I am about to be murdered. It's no wonder I'm on edge.

The air turned cool and dewy, but refreshingly so.

An hour later, he thought about how anticlimactic "dying due to exposure" would look on the death certificate. After all he'd suffered, he at least wanted his final showdown. He wanted to hear the villainous monologue, and to stare death in the barrel. This was…sad. This was how seniors with Alzheimer's bit it, when their families couldn't afford health care anymore. Stick 'em outside, pretend like they'd wandered off in the night and got lost. Organize search parties and cry on TV. That was all right for old folks. That was social commentary. But this…

I mean, come on, you're narcos! You've got to have a gun somewhere. Don't be lazy.

Two more hours later, Joshua woke from a doze, stiff with the cold. Someone had opened the side door of the van. He tensed his arms and chest, ready for a fight.

This was not Alan. Instead, judging by the van's interior lights, this was a woman with braids. She was swearing up a storm, and twice, she spat tobacco. Joshua took an instant liking to her.

"How the hell does this thing work?" she asked a half-dozen times. After several attempts to pull the ramp out, Joshua yelled, "*ngaaaa*," and she said, "I'm working on it! God. Give me a second." Softer, Joshua said, "*ngaaa*" and thrust his whole arm in the general direction of the side door's frame, where the ramp control buttons were. She followed his line of sight, rolled her eyes, and jumped out of the ramp's path as it unfolded. "Why the hell did they leave you out here this whole damned time? God. Idiots." Once the ramp was down, she came in crouching. It took her some time to realize that she could push the wheelchair without tipping it forward if she released the brakes first. "Bad enough they brought you out here in the first place. Cowards – if they'd wanted you dead, they should have done it fast and humanely."

Joshua grunted his agreement.

"Hey...can you understand me?" she asked.

Joshua groaned four or five syllables in a skillful attempt at reply. His crooked arms waved uselessly while she drove his chair over the pebbly clearing. The front wheels stuck in loose sand.

"Mags," she said. "That's my name." She grunted as she pushed his chair out of the dirt. "I suppose you've got a name and you're going to keep it to yourself."

"Nga."

"Can I give you a name? Sons of bitches won't

tell me the one you've already got. How's *Ricardo* sound to you?"

He choked out a surprised laugh.

"Englebert. I'll call you Englebert, after Englebert Humperdinck. How's that?"

He bellowed a happy, monosyllabic hooray and waved his arms some more. He bent his elbow and stretched rheumatic fingers over his shoulder. She shook his hand as best as she could.

She sighed. "I shouldn't have named you. You don't name cows. You shouldn't name mules. Makes it harder when the day comes, y'know?"

His stomach sank. *So you're the tough they've sent to kill me? Well…I can't complain about the company. At least between us, it's just business, right?*

"Stay here," she said, leaving his wheelchair behind. "I'll get a ramp set up at the back door. "

She had parked his chair at the side of the house. Security lights flooded the wide lawn that surrounded the property, but the glow stopped where the trees began. If not for the cold, Joshua would have enjoyed himself. He'd never smelled so much fresh cedar, nor had the scent of fallen leaves been so pungent. The air was crisp, so he thought the stars might be brighter and sharper, too. But no luck. The flood lamps were too bright, and the forest canopy too closely knotted.

He heard something in the trees, furtive and fast.

Mags came around the corner from the back of the house, hugging herself and casting a wary eye on the forest, where Joshua was looking. She stopped short.

Did you see that too? he wondered. *Red eyes*

reflecting back the light.

"Shit," she breathed. "Damn. I shouldn't have left you out here even for a second. I thought they only prowled by day."

"Waa," Joshua warbled.

"Cougars, I mean. I'd heard about them in the area, but we haven't actually seen any for the last ten years."

Joshua's mouth worked as he tried to say, "Oh," but his voice, lips, and tongue were all out of sync.

"Bastards," she said. "Look at you. Sons of bitches. I promise you, Englebert, they'll get *theirs* in the end!" She laughed abruptly. "So to speak."

Joshua managed a bitter laugh.

She leaned closer to Joshua's ears as she put her shoulders into her work, heaving Joshua up the untrustworthy plank she'd thrown down on the stairs. "I'll let you in on a little secret."

Joshua was all ears.

"I have friends who are coming," Mags whispered. "Good friends. You'll be all right. Just trust me and follow my lead."

Joshua's heart swelled. It wasn't so much about living or dying. He'd given up caring one way or the other. But revenge, that was a different matter! If he could stick around long enough to see Alan get his own cavities probed, then by God, he'd hang onto life by tooth and nail.

By the time Mags got him into the kitchen, she was glistening with sweat. She kept only one light on – the one in the range hood – so it was still hard to see her. The kitchen was immense, with multiple faceless refrigerators fit for a chef, and knives and pans dangling from wrought iron fixtures hanging from the tiled ceiling. Everything was spotless, and open, and made of glass, marble, stainless steel, or blackened iron.

"Yeah, sweet digs, eh?" Mags asked. "And they say crime doesn't pay." She was older than he'd expected. Her voice was young, but she had a Depression-era farmer look about her, right down to the grey streaks in her braids. "Well, maybe crime doesn't pay, but the benefits can't be beat. Don't go anywhere. I'm going to check the van for any luggage or whatever. Sure as hell Asshat Alan didn't bring anything in with him. Hey – did you shit on him?"

Joshua grinned, arched his back and spread his chest. If he'd had one, he'd have wagged his tail.

"Sweet. Good job, bro." She patted him on the shoulder, and left.

Somewhere else in the house, one song ended and a new track began, louder than ever. Joshua could hear men and women laughing. He was sure he heard Alan screaming something about streaking across the quad, and that got them howling with laughter.

But under the manic joy, there was a desperate strain in Alan's voice, like he was riding shotgun in a street race, and the car had just hit a wet patch.

Someone changed the playlist. Now, instead of irritating hip hop, it was becoming simpler, louder, more primal.

Alan laughed too fast and too seriously. "No man, I'm good. I-I-I can't hold it together – no – " His laugh sounded spasmodic. A woman was talking, her voice ribboning words together in time with the music. Alan was panting. "Oh God," Alan said. "Oh yeah. Oh God yeah. Yes."

A dark-haired man walked into the kitchen from the hall, flicking on an overhead light, and sipping straight from a bottle. When he tipped the bottle down, he jumped and stared at Joshua, who sat in his chair in the middle of the kitchen, trying hard to look innocent. The man was sweating, and his light brown eyes were bright, wide, and wet.

Elsewhere, Alan groaned ecstatically and began to chant, "Yes, yes, yes," and it was clearly making both Joshua and the dark-haired man physically uncomfortable.

Mags walked in through the back door, talking around the wad of tobacco in the pouch of her cheek. "I found a bag with medicine in it. There's a box of needles here, says you're supposed to have a shot once every four hours? I'm guessing it's – "

She stopped in her tracks. She looked like she was about to swallow her chaw.

The dark-haired man peeled back his lips. The grimace made the bridge of his nose seem a lot wider. "I gave you the night off."

"I'm sorry, Mr. Stuyvesant. I was on my way out," Mags stammered. She sounded a hell of a lot more timid than when she had been swearing and spitting tobacco.

"I told you to leave, Margaret."

"A-and I did leave, but on my way out, I heard somebody in the van, and I thought – "

"You weren't supposed to come back."

"I…I thought you might…need him," she answered. As if in afterthought, Mags stepped on the pedal of a steel garbage pail and spat her coffee-brown chew into it. "Thought it'd be better than leaving him outside." She jarred when her foot slipped, and the lid of the garbage pail clanged shut. "You know, in case of…in case somebody…"

"In case of *what*?" Stuyvesant snarled.

In the other room, Alan blurted, "What? Wha…what the hell?" Louder, higher, he screamed, "What the hell! What the hell!" Someone turned up the thumping jungle drums, but it wasn't enough to drown out the startled gargling noise that followed.

Well, this sure wasn't the way I expected things to go.

Then Joshua began to wonder about that return ticket, and whose name was actually on it. All this time, he'd assumed he was the one making the one-way trip…but maybe Alan knew too much and kept too little secret. A PSW doesn't make that much money, after all. Maybe he had a crouching black sports car of his own back home.

But damn it, I'm missing the best part!

When heavy things began to tumble in the other room, Mags gripped Joshua's shoulder.

The dark-haired man was coming closer, and he smelled of something other than beer. He smelled of leather, ammonia, crotch sweat, and wet dog. He wore eyeliner.

Wait…how'd I miss that before? Guy-liner? And why is it getting thicker?

"You…" Stuyvesant growled. "Weren't. Supposed. To come back." He slammed the beer bottle on a counter, making Mags jump and Joshua flail. Mags stepped between her boss and her charge. She held one of the needles in her hand. It was a preloaded needle, likely Joshua's nightly dose of Cogentin, which was supposed to relax his arms and stop him from making all his involuntary ugly faces. What it did was make his heart race, as if it was a shot of adrenaline.

Stuyvesant undid the top button of his collar. His throat was hairy. Joshua's eyes widened and bulged. The hair was coarse, straight, grey and white, and it was growing. Stuyvesant stomped forward, curving his arms, flexing his dirty hands. He grinned, showing off teeth that lengthened and sharpened. Mags gasped and blindly thrust the needle at him like a dagger.

My God…this is really happening! I'm awake, I'm not dreaming, I'm watching this happen. His heart pounded. *Shit, this is exactly what I wished would happen! I'd wanted to see Alan shredded! Claws would do the trick. God, if I'd known this would happen, I would have wished it three years ago!*

"There are consequences," Stuyvesant said, chewing up the syllables and spitting out hate and desire. His shirt tore open across the chest and over the biceps, with more grey and white hair bursting through the ragged spots. Mags was breathing hard, and her hands shook.

"*Ngo!*" Joshua shouted, though he meant to say 'go'. His life was short anyhow, and this was a far more interesting way to die. "Mah. Ngo!" Not only was she in grave danger, but she was blocking the view. He pushed at her, trying to move her to the side, out of his way. She didn't even seem to feel his touch.

"There are grave – " Stuyvesant slurped bubbling drool – "consequences for disobeying your employer…" The last word was lost in a long, mumbled growl. His mouth had extended into a muzzle. Small, yellow eyes started from his lengthening skull.

Mags screamed and stabbed the air with the needle, missing Stuyvesant by a mile. "Stay away from him!"

The werewolf laughed its inhuman laugh. "It's not him I want."

Joshua understood: Mags had already seen too much. Mags could talk. Mags could fight back.

Then the werewolf turned his knowing, derisive eyes down on the extra witness in the room. Joshua could see all and tell no one.

No, take me! he thought at the beast, but emotion tangled the already knotted neural pathways and no voice came out.

Mags bolted for the kitchen door.

She didn't get far.

The werewolf had tried to leap over Joshua and his chair, but – for all his lack of muscular control – Joshua's reflexes were good. His arms went up, tangling the werewolf's legs. All three of them tumbled to the floor, with Joshua still strapped into his overturned wheelchair. Joshua slapped at the werewolf, trying to die, and maybe buy Mags some time. She'd said her friends were on the way. Surely one of *them* had a gun.

The werewolf recovered first. He grabbed Mags by the throat and, with his free hand, smacked Joshua away, making him skid on his side, in his chair, all the way across the tile floor until the wheels banged against a wall. Joshua was dazed and lacked the muscle control required to crane his neck and witness what was happening to Mags. All he could see was his skeletal lap, the underside of a table, the open kitchen door, and a wood-panelled hallway beyond.

But he could hear just fine, and in graphic detail: a muffled scream pinched into silence, a hand convulsively slapping the marble countertop, joints cracking, and pots banging together and ringing. Then something wet and hollow fell to the floor, like an overripe coconut. Mags' head bowled under the table toward Joshua, jumping each time her nose contacted the floor. Loose, ragged, bloody skin hung where her throat had been. Her head rolled to a stop an arm's length away, with one braid draped across her open eyes.

In the other room, more lycanthropic voices growled sick laughter. From the hall came the sound of wet laundry slapping on the floor, over and over. Joshua saw a bloody hand hook into the grout between tiles as Alan reached around the door frame. He dragged himself off the carpeted hallway floor onto the white tiles, pausing every now and then to fish-mouth for air, or to cup the torn ruin of his throat. He stretched out his hand toward Joshua. He collapsed. He roused to swim across the floor in languid, halting strokes. He looked up briefly, but that stretched his neck so that air whistled out of his exposed and lacerated trachea. Alan kept his head down after that. His hands slipped in the spreading slick of his blood, and he banged his face on the kitchen floor.

Something hot and wet fell on Joshua's face. It slithered down the side of his nose to splat beside his left eye. He couldn't focus on it. It was too close. But given the lip-smacking and grunting noises coming from the kitchen table, he figured he'd been hit with leftovers.

Alan roused again, gargling for more air. Two more strokes across the floor, and he had his bloodstained hand wrapped around Joshua's ankle. He pulled with extraordinary strength, and Joshua slid, wheelchair and all, toward the man he'd wished dead. Alan passed out and let go.

Joshua wasn't having fun anymore.

Sniffing loudly, a pair of growling werewolves appeared in the doorway, stooped so low their nails scraped the tiles. One of the werewolves caught Alan by a leg and pulled him out of the kitchen, his bloody face squeaking across the tiles. They dragged him down the hall and out of sight. Werewolves squabbled, teeth clacking.

Stuyvesant came around to Joshua's side of the table carrying Mags' broken torso in his paws. Her leg swung limply from her broken hip, still sheathed in her ruined jeans. Stuyvesant let her body tumble to the floor right by Joshua's face. The werewolf was out of breath. He grunted and began pushing his meal closer to where Joshua lay. When he was satisfied, Stuyvesant hunched over her body and bit strips out of her thigh, denim and all. He kept his yellow eyes on Joshua the whole time. He ripped and swallowed, nuzzled and ripped again. When Joshua didn't react, Stuyvesant separated her leg from her hip with a sickening pop, and he laid it against Joshua's body, as if Joshua was an altar, or a plate. Her leg was still warm, and it bled through Joshua's clothes. A growling chuckle resonated deep in the monster's huge chest. Outraged, Joshua tried to knee

Stuyvesant in the ribs. Stuyvesant snapped red teeth in Joshua's face.

Something was sticking out of the fur in Stuyvesant's right shoulder. Joshua wriggled until he could free one arm and raise it high enough to thread his fingers through the fur. The werewolf snarled, but he didn't jerk away. He was too busy grabbing both ends of Mags' ruined thigh and biting down on the bone, cracking it open. Joshua reached, and reached, and finally, he had hold of the barrel of the needle swinging from Stuyvesant's matted, sweaty fur. His spasmodic fingers couldn't curl around the barrel, so, with all his fury, he smacked the plunger with the palm of his hand.

Stuyvesant snorted and slashed Joshua's scrawny arm away, a second too late. The needle waved like a lance in a bull's hide.

Joshua's arm stung. Blood dripped from three gashes across his wrist.

Also not how I thought I'd die.

Stuyvesant tried to pluck the needle from his shoulder, but either his arm was too short, his back too broad, or his chest too big. Frustrated, he roared in Joshua's face.

Joshua smelled coppery breath and saw the tongue arch behind the small, uniform bottom front teeth. The breath hitched. Stuyvesant lurched upright, then to the left, then curling over his pricked shoulder. His right arm went limp. Stuyvesant panted and whined. His bulging eyes were bloodshot. He pawed weakly at his chest and gasped for air. He yelped and crushed the fur under his claws, as if trying to keep his heart from leaping out between his ribs. His nose and ears dripped red. Vessels burst in his eyes, and he gasped again. He coughed once. Blood sprayed from his lips and spattered on Joshua's face.

The werewolf's neck lolled. His shoulders sank, his spine gave out, and the werewolf withered sideways onto the floor, barely breathing, tongue unrolling to unleash a tide of fleshy vomit.

Cogentin, Joshua thought. *Makes my heart race too. Was there too much in the needle?* Then he wondered if cocaine and lycanthropic adrenaline had already super-charged Stuyvesant's heart, and the Cogentin was the nail in the werewolf's coffin.

Holy shit, Joshua thought. *I just killed a werewolf. A guy like me, knocked over in my wheelchair, armed with nothing but a needle I can barely hold. And I just killed a werewolf with my bare hands.*

The Alan Feast continued in the other room for hours. The sound of the gorging orgy turned Joshua's stomach and grated on his nerves. He covered his ears with his hands, smearing four different blood types across his face. He waited for them to come in to finish him off, but every time they passed in the hall, they kept on going. Joshua would make a bony dessert at best, but they didn't seem at all interested. One even pissed in the bathroom and flushed a toilet.

An hour later, Joshua closed his fists and tried to block out the noise of two werewolves rutting and banging each other against the kitchen wall. When they finished, one of them came scavenging, and Joshua tensed, closed his eyes, and awaited the inevitable. He heard lupine nostrils snuffling about, but the werewolf turned up his nose at the easy meal-on-wheels. Instead, it picked up Mags' head, sniffed it, dropped it again, and left. The head came to rest facing Joshua, dead eyes unfocused.

I could kill you all, Joshua thought. He opened his hand.

His hand opened flat and straight. His arm moved slowly and smoothly, unkinking after decades of contortions.

Something was warming in his blood.

What the hell?

His heart boomed. His veins felt bloated, and every extremity tingled and burned.

No…really? Really?! Already?

He was alive. He was a killer, a hunter, alive, *alive*. He'd made his first kill before he'd even been turned, and he was *alive*. Strong. Powerful. Dominant.

Mags seemed to be staring at him. Her open mouth drew closed into a grim line, as dead flesh seized in rigor. *Take it and use it*, her expression seemed to say.

He had little strength and practically no control in his legs yet, but he had enough dexterity to pop the seat belt and release himself from the chair that had kept him prisoner for nearly twenty-nine years. He crawled across the floor, not really sure where he was going. There was a ringing in his ears, and he could see his own pulse in the corners of his vision. *Will it hurt?* he wondered. *Will I change back as a whole and normal man?*

His hand slipped on a piece of intestine.

She was the first person to talk to me. She was the first person to give a damn. She was the first woman to treat me like a person, and you ate her!

He found the limp backpack Alan used to stash

all of Joshua's meds, and inside was the spilled-open box of needles. He reached into the pack, and when he pulled out the box, he found the back of his hand was dotted with new fur.

Boy, that didn't take long, did it?

He had one needle in his hand when he heard a window shatter, followed by two more windows, all on the ground floor. The window in the kitchen's back door blew in, and a canister rolled in spewing, yellow smoke. Joshua covered his mouth and nose with his forearm. Behind him, in the main foyer, the heavy door shot open.

"Police! Get down on the floor! On the floor! On the – "

Joshua tilted one ear back as it grew and filled with the syncopated sound of human and lycanthropic heartbeats. A man was gagging on bad smells and disbelief.

"Oh my God," someone cried, while someone else shouted, "There! There!"

It was impossible to tell how many guns shot how many bullets, but they weren't doing much harm. Grown men shrieked and died. More guns went off – shotguns, by the sound of them. Joshua crawled back across the kitchen, skating on all fours through smeared blood. More shots. Bodies fell. He'd come to the rescue. He'd save Mags' friends – the sheriff's office, or the DEA, maybe. Drugs, they knew. Werewolves, they didn't. But *he* knew. He alone knew how to kill werewolves. He now had hands agile enough to deliver the fatal dose, too. He could do it. He *would* do it. He crawled to the kitchen door frame, with a loaded needle in one hand.

One shotgun opened fire, and a werewolf's head disappeared, bursting like a furry balloon loaded with chunks of white gyprock, grey goose liver, and raspberry jam.

There didn't seem such a pressing need for Cogentin anymore.

Someone kicked open the kitchen door, aiming a rifle at Joshua's face. Behind him, three sets of boots landed hard on the flagstone hallway floor. "Is he one of them?" asked a hysterical voice. "Is he one of them? Kill it!"

Joshua sat back on his heels, raised his hands and dropped the needle.

I wonder, he thought. He put one foot flat on the floor.

"Stay down! Stay down!"

"Kill it!"

Shaking and slipping on the blood, Joshua got to his feet and stood all six feet tall. He looked death in the barrel and thought, *This was the best day ever.*

IT IS RUMOURED that Pat Flewwelling hatched from a rooster's egg during a lunar eclipse on the night of the Spring Equinox. On her seventh birthday, following a run-in with an ill-tempered *strigoi*, she was cursed with the ability to see into frightening parallel dimensions, leaving her often unable to discern one world from the other. For weeks at a time, she retreats into her lair, hidden in the tunnels beneath an abandoned factory in Oshawa, Ontario, and can only be enticed from her enchanted den by an offering of steaks and craft beer. After many years observing several realms at once, she began to write down what she saw in the realities just to the left of our own, and has created such reports as *Helix: Blight of Exiles*, and *Helix: Plague of Ghouls*. Her stare is unnerving, because she's not just staring through you…she's watching the monster standing at your back. She has learned one pearl of wisdom that is true in all dimensions: you shouldn't believe everything you read.

VICTIM OF LOVE

Samantha Banik

"A word, a glance, a touch are sufficient to fire the magazine of passion in the heart, and to desolate forever an existence."
Sabine Baring-Gould

Village of Cachtice
December, 1610

"TIBOR, PLEASE, DO not let them take her. Not our Anna," the girl's mother whispered, her tears glistening in the torch light.

"We've spoken of this. There is no other choice. It comes for her this night."

"Please, no…my baby…"

"Do not fret, Mama," Anna said. "I will go. I would go and see you and Papa unharmed."

Anna stepped forward to embrace her mother, the sound of her own heart beating heavily in her ears.

"You are brave, my child." Her father's voice gave her courage. He held out his hand to her. "Come, let us show them how brave you are."

She accepted it and followed willingly out into the night toward an uncertain future, her mother's cries of desperation behind her.

The thrum of hoof beats were heard long before the great, ebony carriage charged forth, drawn by six massive, black beasts. With eyes rolling and nostrils flared they advanced, the blood red froth at their snarling mouths running in rivulets down their powerful necks. The shouts of the drivers rose above the rattle of the chains and the thunderous hooves.

Anna trembled at the sight, the carriage lurching to a stop before her. The animals pawed the earth and snorted great plumes of foggy breath in the chill of the night. Anna's gaze darted to the looming figure that assisted a much shorter man from his seat atop the carriage.

Once on the ground, the small man made his way to her and her father, extending his hand as he approached them. "Are you ready for your new life, my dear?"

Anna hesitated at the kindness in his voice, for it did not match his eyes. Her father squeezed her hand, holding her in place. A cold sliver of fear pierced her heart.

"Come along. My name is Janos. I believe the

Countess will be very excited to meet you." The man paused for a moment to look up at her father. "My compliments, good sir," he said. "You've raised a pretty one. My Lady tends to favour the red-haired ones."

Her father's grip loosened as the man's cold, clammy hand tightened around her wrist. The connection was lost completely as she was pulled toward the carriage.

She had heard the rumours of those who had chosen to run and hide. Entire families destroyed by sudden plague and other mysterious afflictions. She had seen many of her friends taken on a promise of a fine education and the teaching of etiquette fit for a young woman. She had seen them go, yet none had returned.

These days, there were no such assurances. Only fear of a much greater evil forced the hands of the families that stayed, stripped of their young, their daughters, and their blood. Tales of sorcery and torture spread throughout the lands, and the people, driven by superstition, conformed. More children could be had. Much better to appease than die a horrid death. Better that than face the twisted, hellish mind of a maniac. Give her what she wanted, and time would heal gaping hearts.

"THE COMPLAINTS HAVE been many these six years. Many, many more these two months. The people will not hold back much longer, Thurzo. Anger and grief have taken over the fear. They would see their daughters back where they belong."

Gyorgy Thurzo stood before his king, who was adamant a party be sent to Cachtice to investigate the fate of numerous young women.

"Majesty, you know as well as I that I am in no position to make such a move. The family is inflexible. She is to be left alone. Besides, do you know what kind of attention this would bring?"

"Just a few men, Thurzo. You may find nothing, and that is my hope, but there is enough proof to warrant questioning. The people fear for their children. Surely you, her charge, must know her ways?"

"I have been removed from her these long years, sire. What I do remember is that she is an ill-tempered, narcissistic woman who runs her household with an iron fist. We know many who fit that mold, sire. Besides, she will not see me."

King Matthias shook his head and turned to look out the window, exhaling a long-held breath. "Her children?"

"They, like myself, no longer have contact with her."

"Then, as your king, I can only demand that you go. It is an order."

"They will not like it. I will have her uncles before me with questions. I have no need for that kind of audience."

"Then there is no justice."

"It is not a matter of justice, sire. It is a matter of keeping my head upon my shoulders in the literal sense, not to mention yours, and those of the court."

"Do you have any idea the numbers we are talking about here? Twelve these two weeks, hundreds these past years. I cannot stand by any longer."

Thurzo sighed as King Matthias turned back to him with pleading eyes, the humanity in them overwhelming.

"Very well, sire. I go only because it is your command."

"Thank you. You are a good man, Thurzo. Whatever you find, please promise you will do nothing. Do not provoke. And then, return and tell me what you have seen."

"You look lovely, my Lady."

"Oh, Katarina, your constant compliments bore me. This gown bores me. Bring me the red one," the Countess Elizabeth Bathory replied, watching the girl as she crossed to the bureau.

A sleek, black cat leapt onto the vanity, its tail pointed to the ceiling as it brushed its body against Elizabeth's arm in search of attention.

"Hello, my darling," Elizabeth crooned as she stroked it, a gentle staccato of delight rumbling from its throat.

"The carriage has come," Katarina said as she plucked the red gown from its place on the rack. "Janos said you would be delighted."

She hung the garment with care on the cloak hook beside the vanity and looked on with ardent longing at her mistress' reflection in the mirror, one of several in the room. The walls were lined with the bright glimmer of the looking glasses in various sizes, all in gilded frames. The light of many candles reflecting back cast long shadows beyond everything they touched.

"Do you hear that, my darling?" Elizabeth lifted the cat's head, rubbing the feline under its chin, the drone of its satisfaction continuing. "You will feast this night. Go, tell your brothers and sisters."

The black cat mewled, jumped from the dresser, and slinked across the room. Elizabeth waved her hand and the door opened enough for the animal to escape. She waved again and the door closed after it with a soft clunk.

Elizabeth pressed her long, elegant fingers to her cheekbones, pulling the skin back just enough to remove the faint lines of age. "Yes…delighted."

Katarina lifted the heavy coil of ebony hair from her mistress' back and draped it over the Countess' shoulder. "You are so good to us," she said as her slender fingers picked away the buttons that ran down the length of the emerald gown her lady wore.

Elizabeth turned, interrupting the girl's work, and cupped Katarina's jaw, brushing a thumb over her soft lips. "I am good to you because you deserve it, my love."

A sharp knock came at the door and the women turned as it opened, Elizabeth's eyes narrowing in annoyance.

"My Lady, we are ready for you."

"Thank you, Janos," Elizabeth said as Katarina continued to undress her mistress.

Elizabeth looked over the small man in her doorway, whose head was far too big for his body. He walked as if each step pained him. She had asked him once if it did, and he had laughed and said, "Not any more than it would you." A good friend, Janos, strong despite his inadequacies and fierce with a quick wit, one that matched her own. A kindred spirit, perhaps.

"I have a gift for you," he said. "A beautiful morsel. I saved her just for you."

"Excellent. We'll be along. Any troubles this night?"

"Not a single whisper."

"Then they are learning," Elizabeth said, stepping out of the garment that lay at her feet.

Janos' eyes roamed over her body, and she leered at him, running a hand down her side, enjoying the way he wanted her. He boldly met her gaze for a moment before he took his leave.

"My robe, Katarina."

THE ROOM WAS uncomfortably warm, as she always demanded. It hadn't always been so precise, but as the years went by and her arcane knowledge increased, the more elaborate the ablution became. Bathing was an institution; everything had to be immaculate. The temperature, the mood, and the lighting all played their parts, as well as the people who attended the ritual.

The fire in the massive hearth burned hot. The bath, sunken into the floor before the great pyre, was full almost to the brim. The flickering light of the many candles that littered the room reflected off the surface of the liquid that filled it. Janos stood near, a young girl by his side, her head held high, though her pale, trembling chin gave away her inner panic.

"My gift for you, my Lady. I thought perhaps you would enjoy her company."

Elizabeth took in the girl's naked beauty, with her long, red hair brushed into a glossy sheen and draped over one shoulder, soft tendrils framing her face. The light illuminated her dark eyes and danced on her pretty skin, shadows falling over the contours of her body.

Elizabeth smiled as her gaze fell to the awaiting tub and held up her hand for Katarina to take, supporting her as she walked to the edge of the bath. As time went on, bathing became more frequent, once weekly these days.

"What is your name, child?" Elizabeth spoke to the red-headed girl without looking at her, her gaze on the flames that licked the top of the stone hearth.

The girl hesitated, and Janos prodded her in the arm. "Answer your mistress," he growled.

"Anna…my name is Anna." The girl sobbed and dropped her head to hide her face.

"Never avert your eyes…"

"Janos, enough now," Elizabeth said in a soothing tone. "Come, Anna. Come with me."

Anna was quivering so she could hardly walk the few steps. Elizabeth felt her terror. It ebbed and flowed around her like an invisible tide, pulling and pushing as thoughts of her family's safety collided with the urge to flee from the room and escape.

"There now," Elizabeth said, touching a finger to the girl's chin, lifting her face to search her eyes. "You are a brave one, Anna. I can sense it. And a desperate beauty. Stunning."

Elizabeth moved the hand at Anna's chin to grasp the spill of smooth, copper hair, letting it fall through her fingers. Anna held her gaze, and Elizabeth felt some of the tension leave the girl's body.

"You fear me?"

The girl nodded, her eyes wide.

A harsh, female voice came from behind the two. "My Lady, a gentleman's here to see you."

Dorotya. Elizabeth hissed and turned to give a sharp retort to the fair-haired woman standing in the doorway, but held her tongue when she saw the familiar silhouette beside her trembling attendant.

"My Lord," Elizabeth said, a knowing smile creeping across her lips. She looked over her company, the irritation of being interrupted instantly forgotten. "What brings you to Cachtice?"

"My Lady. I have business in Vienna. I could not pass by without seeing you, though I fear I am disrupting your toilet. Shall I occupy myself while you finish?"

The voice that spoke the words was faint, yet commanded the attention of the entire room, every eye following the gentleman who approached their mistress, as if floating through time.

Even in the warming light of the fire, the man was ghastly pale, his skin as smooth as alabaster, his age a mystery. When he spoke, his blood-red lips seemed not to move. He reached a hand out to Elizabeth, the fingers almost too long for the graceful appendage, the nails, sharpened to points, no less than daggers. She took his hand and watched as he brushed cool lips over her knuckles.

"Nonsense, my Lord. I would invite you to join me. Please." Elizabeth gestured to the edge of the bath.

He eyed the liquid, the corner of his mouth twitching as he did so. "You are too kind, my Lady. An invitation that I should never decline."

"You are always welcome. Tell me, how are my uncles? Do they serve Transylvania well?" Elizabeth removed her robe, and Katarina took it from her outstretched hand.

"Quite well, my Lady," he replied, his appreciative eyes wandering over the hollows and curves of her body.

"Mmmm…I shall come to visit soon." She dipped a toe into the dark, shimmering liquid and sighed. "Still warm."

Elizabeth stiffened at the feeling of icy hands on her hips then immediately relaxed against his Lordship's body, snaking a hand up to rest on his cheek. "It would be a joy to have you," he whispered into her hair, his fingers trailing over her skin.

She closed her eyes as a sigh fell from her lips. "I have missed you."

He surveyed the scene before them, taking in every detail with interest. "But you do go through such an arduous process in your ablutions."

"Ritual pleases the soul, my Lord. You should try it sometime," she said, turning in his arms to drape hers around his neck. He bent to kiss her, but she pushed him away.

Elizabeth stepped into the bath and sank down, the black fluid welling up over the sides, sizzling on the scorching hot stones as it rolled closer to the hearth. The smell of sweet, coppery metal filled the room.

"Yes," he said, dismissing the idea. "Such a waste," he murmured, though his voice carried throughout the chamber. "So many to shed so much, simply to bathe?" His eyes darkened and filled with lust. "Shall I teach you to drink from the source so that you may have your fill, insanely delirious in the knowledge that the blood seeps through your veins, youth claiming you from the inside out? You shall be forever eternal, my Lady."

"I like to learn new things. I would enjoy that very much, I think. You are perfect in every way, my Lord."

"Oh, come now, there are those who think me depraved."

"Not I. Quite the opposite. I adore you and your beautiful mind." She lifted a leg from the bath to point her toes at him, the thick fluid caressing her skin as it ran down her leg. She smiled at the desire in his eyes as she slipped her leg back into the tub. "We do a great service, you and I. Those that think otherwise, they are blind to these gifts we bring upon them. They do not appreciate how we love them and shower them with affection, give them everything they need before they give us what we need. It is a perfect situation."

"It is true, my Lady. Alas, it is the way of society. Fear. The masses fear too much. They are afraid to embrace such pleasures."

"Yes. I suppose you are right."

"Of course I am right. Imagine for a moment if they did not."

"Yes. I think that I should like it better the way it is, the fear."

"I do not doubt that you do." His Lordship smiled, the gesture cutting his face in two.

"Katarina, fetch his Lordship a crystal goblet. Take your fill, my Lord. And then you may show me this new way."

"It would please me more to show you first. Besides, I prefer it from the source. I am sure the bath is warm, but can it compare to the heat at the back of the throat? The burn as it becomes a part of you? No, my Lady, I think your experience pales in comparison."

The power of his words tugged at Elizabeth's core, and the heat of wanting touched the apples of her cheeks. "Very well," she breathed, turning her head to the girl, who had returned to her place beside Janos. "Anna. Come." She lifted her hand from the bath, beads of red rolling down her arm dripping back into the liquid in which she sat.

The girl shook with fear, her eyes wide, darting from Elizabeth to his Lordship. "Blood? Is that…blood?"

"Go to your mistress!" Janos bellowed when she did not move.

Anna whimpered and took a step, her legs heavy with fright.

His Lordship held out his hand to her, and she cringed as she slipped her hand into his.

"Such beautiful skin," he purred, pulling her into his arms, brushing her hair away to expose her neck. He ran a cool finger down the creamy slope causing the girl to quiver. "Here," he said, stopping just below Anna's jaw, his eyes catching Elizabeth's gaze. "Where you can feel the beating of her heart," he said, entwining his fingers into her hair, drawing her head to the side.

"Please…" Anna moaned. "Please, my Lord."

"Hush, child," he said, the calmness in his voice soothing the terror away. She stilled and arched against him, her hand moving up to grasp his waist, her will now his. He pressed a thumbnail into her flesh, and she mewled, bowing into him. He let out a low growl, his eyes rolling back into his head as he clamped his mouth over the well of blood, cutting off the stream that had begun to flow freely down the girl's back. His hands gripped her, holding her steady as he drank, Elizabeth looking on with a lurid smile etched on her face.

She rose from the bath, the dark, red blood spilling onto the floor and running in rivulets down the length of her body. Janos hurried to lay down fresh, white linens, Katarina assisting Elizabeth from the tub. She walked toward his Lordship, bloody footprints seeping into the material as she went, the droplets falling from her hair leaving a crimson trail in her wake.

She reached the two, his Lordship releasing his mouth from the girl, his head falling back to expose two sharp fangs and eyes that were as black as pitch, the pupils dilated in his pleasure. Elizabeth turned the girl from him, her own mouth finding the vein, and she drank, feeling the girl weaken in her arms.

"My Lady, you are a natural," his Lordship said, placing a hand on Elizabeth's head, stroking her hair.

She let go of the girl and smiled with bloody

teeth, removing a spot of blood from her lip with a fingertip, popping her finger in her mouth. "Janos, take her to the great hall. Give my darlings their fill. They feast well this night," Elizabeth said as Anna's body slid to the floor at her feet. She knelt down and placed a hand on the girl's forehead. "You have done well, my child. I had such wonderful plans for you. The fire would have cleansed your soul and the stitching would have made your mouth look even prettier, but it would be rude to ignore my guest. You understand, do you not, my child? Still, you are blessed, and you are loved. Say it, my Anna, say it. You are blessed and your Lady loves you."

"I am blessed. My Lady loves me…"

"Good girl," Elizabeth said and rose, her gaze resting on his Lordship's. "Do you stay with me long, my Lord?"

"I have but a few hours, my Lady."

Elizabeth held out her hand to him. "Then let us retire, while the blood still warms you."

"My Lady! The men from the villages, they come!" Janos cried from the doorway of Elizabeth's chambers, startling the two women within.

"Open the gates," Elizabeth said with little interest, tucking a stray hair back into the braided chignon she wore.

"But, my Lady…" Katarina turned from the table where she had been organizing her Ladyship's implements with care.

"Let them come, and they will see." Elizabeth

turned to Janos as he entered into the room, his lips tight and eyes wary. "They will see how gracious I am. They will see how I help my children. How I give them pleasure, and how they love me."

"But they will kill you," Katarina said.

"Kill me? Why ever would they do that, my child?" Elizabeth walked to Katarina and placed her hand upon the pale, smooth cheek that was tinged with fear. "Do not fret. I am protected. Nothing shall happen to me, though it pleases me that you worry. You will be rewarded."

"But…they do not understand…"

"Hush now," Elizabeth said, placing her thumb over the girl's lips. "Come, let us show them. Let us show them, you and I, my Katarina."

A shiver ran down the young girl's spine as her mistress looped an arm about her tiny waist and led her away.

THE CHILL IN the room did nothing to calm the heat that had risen in Katarina's flesh, yet she shivered still. The rope bindings cutting into the skin of her wrists that were tied above her head to iron rings protruding crudely from a thick slab of wood. Her ankles were hobbled and secured to the dense wooden beam that ran parallel to the one above. She stared at the ceiling, not daring to make eye contact with anyone in the room. She had known this day would come, and she relished it. Her mistress loved her, and now she would know just how deeply.

Fingertips traced over her, causing tiny bumps

to rise up on her skin, and she closed her eyes.

"Look at you, so beautiful. I have longed to taste you. I will take my time with you, sweet one."

"Yes, my Lady," Katarina whispered.

"Sir, the gate stands open, as does the door within. What would you have us do?"

"Open?" A cold chill ran up Thurzo's spine.

"Yes, sir. There are no guards. Do you think it a trap?"

"It may be, though it makes little sense. We go in silence, at dusk. Keep watch and keep hidden. They have all come?"

"We are eleven strong, sir."

"Let us hope that is enough."

Thurzo stood at the entrance of Cachtice Castle and listened. The only sounds he heard were the nervous jitters of his men that hovered around him, each one as curious as the next about what might lie within. He pushed against the heavy, oaken door, opening it further, the dense odour of death greeting him. He placed a hand to his nose, swallowed back bile-filled saliva, and cleared his throat, holding his other hand in the air to cease the murmurs and hushed exclamations that spilled from the group.

He pressed forward, the ancient, rusted hinges giving way with much resistance, their protest echoing throughout the dark, stone hallways.

Thurzo squinted, his eyes slowly adjusting to the lack of light, and he proceeded through into the great hall. A barren emptiness met him; tall, grey pillars, all intricately designed, circled the room. Bare walls, cold, damp rock, and a looming silence made him think for a moment that they were alone and, perhaps, too late.

He motioned for his men to fan out and search the area, the putrid stench of rotting flesh growing stronger as they moved further from the door. He could hear the coughs and gags of his men resonant in the dimness, his own stomach nearly giving way as he shuffled forward.

"Sir! Here, here. I've found something. Someone."

Thurzo headed toward the commotion, four of his men standing over a dark silhouette sprawled on the floor. "Bring me light! A torch!"

"And here!" Another voice called from the other side of the room.

Thurzo came to stand with the group of four as a man, illuminated in a circle of torchlight, made his way to them. Thurzo's heart immediately slid into his throat at the sight before him.

The corpse of a woman lay at his feet, the sharp, acrid scent of roasted flesh and brimstone insulting his senses. The lower half of her body was reduced to little more than blackened bones as if she had been dipped into the flames of a very hot fire. Her legs stuck out at awkward angles from the rest of her like a disfigured skeleton. The flesh that remained upon them hung like crackling by threads of scorched sinew. Thurzo sank to his knees, stifling a sob.

The robe she wore was melted and stuck to the remains of her torso where her arms lay motionless, her hands folded together at peace. The fingers had blackened and curled around themselves and the fragments of twine at her wrists had melted into the skin where they were bound.

Thurzo's eyes took in the horror before him, his stomach churning with each new sight. Her hair was singed almost to her scalp, scorched patches of skull peeking out through the matted locks. Her mouth had been sewn shut, the crude stitches drawn tight enough that the thread had cut through the skin in some spots, the white of her teeth visible through the holes. He placed a gentle hand to her forehead and closed his eyes. She had been someone's daughter.

He opened his eyes again, looking into the dark holes where her eyes had been and shivered as they gaped back at him. He clenched his jaw to stop it from quivering and swallowed hard, trying to stay the remnants of the supper lying heavy in his gut.

The man holding the torch gagged, turning away to expel the contents of his stomach. The body, now engulfed again in shadow, brought Thurzo back into himself enough to regain his composure.

"The other body, where is it?" he spoke gruffly to the man on his right.

Finding his voice, though shaken as he was, the man replied, "Behind the pillar, just there, sir." The man pointed ahead, where a second group of men hovered beyond the realm of light.

"Come with the torch, if you've finished." He spoke to the torch-bearer who followed him at once.

"She's still breathing, sir, but it is doubtful she will live much longer."

Thurzo knelt beside the second naked body, ragged gasps escaping the dry, cracked lips of a young woman of similar character to the first. Her mouth was moving but no sound left her lips. He leaned in and turned his head, straining to make out the sounds.

"I am loved…I am blessed…my Lady loves me…I am loved…I am…"

A cold chill ran over Thurzo's skin, and he pulled away from her to look down into her face.

"Anna?" The torch-bearer's voice cracked. "No, Anna, no, no!"

"You know this girl, Tibor?" Thurzo looked up into the horrified face of the man next to him, then relieved him of the flame he held.

The grieving man dropped to his knees clasping the poor girl's head between shaking hands. "Anna, my love, what have they done to you?"

She had been pierced numerous times through her torso, the bigger holes still seeping blood. The smaller ones had dried into flaky, rust-coloured splotches. There was a wound at her neck with two smaller holes on either side of it. The girl swallowed, the desiccation in her throat audible. Thurzo started as her hand came to rest on his knee, limp and pale.

"What has happened to you, dear girl?" he asked, placing a hand over hers.

"I am blessed." The words grated against his soul as she forced them through her lips, the whisper of impending death covering the syllables as she spoke them.

Her hand slid from his as she passed, leaving him with the looming feeling of powerlessness. He clenched his jaw and rose, the moans and sobs of the young torch-bearer feeding his anger.

"Sir?"

"Yes?" Thurzo hissed through his teeth and spun on the man who had spoken.

The man, eyes wide with fear, pointed with a shaky hand over Thurzo's shoulder. Thurzo whirled and stopped short, unsure of what he was seeing. Black, soundless splodges moved toward them in the dim light, snaking their way along the corridor like sleek serpents with twitching tails. The man beside Thurzo crossed himself and cursed under his breath as several pairs of eyes glimmered in the light of the torch as they moved closer to the group.

"Cats…" A breathy voice came from one of the men behind Thurzo. "They eat the souls of anyone who has ill will toward their mistress…we must leave this place!"

Thurzo's heart raced. "We stay," he said, gripping the hilt of the sword at his side. The words of his king echoed in his ears. *'Do not provoke.'* "Go, that way!" He pointed in the opposite direction of the black mob edging closer, their hisses and growls raising the hairs down the back of Thurzo's neck. "Go now!"

Thurzo hauled Tibor from his knees, and the group of men ran toward the other side of the great hall, the looming spill of dark, angry bodies following them like a storm cloud about to burst. The men stopped as one before the opening of another corridor, pitch black and ominous. The smell was much worse here. The heaviness of rotting corpses crawled deep into Thurzo's sinuses.

Thurzo looked back, eager to press on, but the feline mob behind them had withdrawn its pursuit, its attention turned to the bodies of the fallen girls. The glaring had split into two, each now covering the corpses, howling and heckling as they consumed their feast.

A sob came from Thurzo's right. He turned to see the haunted eyes of Tibor, the ache of his loss touching Thurzo's heart. Thurzo laid a hand on the man's shoulder, though it would offer little consolation.

"What is that?" a man whispered.

"What is what?" Thurzo asked, returning his gaze to the sight behind them. He was not sure he wanted to know any more.

"Listen…"

Thurzo stood stock-still, his hearing alert. A faint thrum, with voices? Singing? No, chanting. A rolling beat seeped through the hallways, keeping time with Thurzo's heart. The group followed the sound until they came to stop outside a room with heavy double doors, the vibrations of the music from within giving the men a sense of what they might find when they entered.

"The Devil's music," one of the men whispered.

Thurzo lifted a hand to silence his men as he pulled on the handle, the sudden intrusion of the rhythm and voices spilling out into the hallway. His group stood frozen behind him as his eyes ran around the room.

It was dark, lit only by a few candles at intervals

around the circular room. Along the walls were several hooded figures, men or women, Thurzo could not tell. The beat came from their heavy boots as they stamped down on the stone floor, the hymn itself from their mouths.

On the other side of the room, a figure could be seen, standing in the middle of a darkened space, a shadowed wall behind it. There was no ceiling, only the night sky above, the moon's rays peeking out from behind a single cloud.

THE VOICES ROSE up in the darkness, wrapping around Elizabeth, her own melodic drone joining them in harmony, and she felt her body still and bend to it. The drum of boots continued, softly at first, then rising up, echoing off the dense stone walls, the crescendo taking over the beat of her heart.

She closed her eyes, the blood coursing through her veins like wildfire, and as she opened them again, set on Katarina, she became aware of the unsettled reaction from the men that had just entered the room. She smiled as she lifted her hand, a circle of large candles lighting themselves one by one around the perimeter of the platform. The intake of several breaths sounded off behind her as the light touched the wooden rack to which Katarina was bound.

"Sorceress!" a man's voice echoed.

Ignoring the outburst, Elizabeth stepped forward to the edge of the altar, the song escaping her lips like a hymn. As one, the commanding blend of voices of all of her children joined her own falsetto, fueling the power growing inside of her. She raised her hand to her Katarina, the girl's eyes closing as the rise and fall of her mistress' voice consumed her, the deep tone of the song awakening her soul.

A quick, subtle movement of fingers, and the girl's bindings unlatched. As she stepped forward, the sash of her robes fell away, the long, white, flowing material billowing out around her like a seraph's mantle. The pins in her hair scattered to the floor, the long tendrils flowing down her back in waves of silky, blonde curls.

Elizabeth sighed at the sight, her fingers tingling with need to touch the fair skin, to taste the sweet life that ran through heated veins. Her mouth watered and her eyes widened as the overwhelming pang of love welled up in her chest, a single tear escaping her lashes. She let it roll quietly down her cheek.

Katarina's eyes opened to hers, the once pale green orbs now afire, glowing in the candlelight a bright orange, flicking crimson and blue as they burned, matching her mistress'. The girl raised her hands to the sky, the long sleeves of her gown like wings as she stepped forward, her hair lifting and swirling out behind her, caught in a draft that wasn't there.

The chanting became stronger, louder, the voices matching Elizabeth's anthem as she sang to her Katarina, guiding the girl toward her, fluid and silent. She created Katarina's every step; played her body like an instrument, her eyes flashing and sparking as she grew closer. Katarina sank to her knees before her mistress, who brought a hand to rest on her soft, flaxen hair. She fell forward to bow at her Lady's feet, then rose to her knees again clasping Elizabeth about the waist.

Elizabeth stopped chanting, yet the voices carried on the haunting melody. She held out her arms to the girl and watched as tiny hands clasped hers, then lifted Katarina to her feet. Katarina's skin was warm and flushed. Elizabeth could feel it through her own robes, and she smiled into the beautiful face before her. So much love.

Their fiery eyes locked on one another and as their lips came together, the outer edge of the circle in which they stood ignited in an explosion of flames, engulfing them in a ring of fire. Their audience gasped collectively as the great pillars of flame grew, reaching for the star-filled sky above them. Light flashed around the two as they touched, their fingers entwining.

THURZO LET OUT a stifled breath, his frown deepening. His skin was crawling with fear as he observed the two women. How was he to defeat such a woman? One who could control flame and fire and the people around her?

"Sir…what would you have us do?" his man whispered. Two figures stepped in front of them. One was a woman, who held a small, wide-eyed girl with curled blonde hair, a thumb wedged between her lips for comfort. Beside her was a very short man, almost the size of the young boy he clutched in his arms.

Thurzo eyed the two small children, the fine, metal blades of daggers digging into the delicate skin of their necks. The woman leered, challenging him to make a move, the imp beside her smiled with heinous intent, wishing a reason to let the knife filet the tender young thing in his embrace.

Beyond them, a wall of women appeared, clad in red robes, armed with spears. They were flanked by two men in crude metal armour, heavy spheres of iron encased in sharp spikes dangling from chains at their sides, waiting to spill the blood and break the bones of his men.

Thurzo shook his head in defeat. There was no way to stop it. Not without losing more lives. They were outnumbered. He could only look on and let his mind consider a plan of escape. He would return with more men, reinforcements, and a better strategy. He had all the proof he could handle.

A scream pierced the air. Thurzo's attention darted back to the two women. It had been Elizabeth. She shrieked again, her arms raised to the heavens with her head thrown back, her long, ebony hair escaping its bindings. In a whirlwind of black and gold, Katarina's flowing tresses joined Elizabeth's in dance.

Elizabeth caught the girl's gaze once more, caressing her shoulders, slipping her thumbs under the edges of Katarina's robe. She guided the silky fabric down her arms, letting it pool to the floor, her skin pale and shimmering in the firelight.

Elizabeth ran a delicate hand over the young woman's torso and up to cup her breast, her eyes searching the girl's. Katarina smiled back, moving her hair to the side to bare her throat. Elizabeth's hand moved up to caress the milky plane.

"I am yours, my Lady. Take of me what you will."

Thurzo shook his head. He had heard the words, yet it should have been impossible over the drone of the song and the distance between him and the altar. Still, he had heard them.

"No," he breathed, stepping forward. His men tensed behind him, ready to move.

"I remind you, sir, of what you shall accomplish in taking action," the small man growled, the boy in his arm whimpering as the steely edge nicked through skin. A bead of blood oozed from the cut, and Thurzo raised a hand to stay his men. "Please." The imp gestured to the stage.

Thurzo turned in time to see Elizabeth sink a sharpened thumbnail into Katarina's jugular vein. Her body trembled as dark, red blood welled up and trickled down over her collar bone.

The girl tilted her head back as if in ecstasy as Elizabeth's tongue caught the bead before her mouth settled over the wound. She drank for what seemed like an eternity, drawing back only when the girl's hand clutched at Elizabeth's shoulder.

Elizabeth drew her away, Katarina's skin gone pale from blood loss, but the dark glimmer of unconditional love was still there in the depths of her eyes as she regarded her mistress. Elizabeth turned to the congregation and raised her hands, her gaze settling on Thurzo. Her mouth curled into a slow smile as recognition glinted in her eyes.

Thurzo blinked and rubbed his eyes, sure that the woman standing before them was years younger than the one which he had first laid eyes on, upon entering the room. Though he could not be sure that she had not always looked that way. His mind was obscured, tainted with all that he had witnessed so far this night.

Elizabeth beckoned a young boy standing in the shadows to her right. The child stepped forward, a large silver platter in his hands. He lifted it to his mistress and bowed as Elizabeth picked up the object that lay upon it, then resumed his place to the side. Elizabeth pointed her arms to the sky once more, in her hands a large dagger, the sharp blade luminous in the light of the fire. The voices became louder, escalating into a thunderous roar, and Thurzo winced, his eyes keen on the woman holding the knife.

Elizabeth turned back to Katarina, their eyes meeting, the latter nodding in acceptance. Elizabeth walked to the circle of candles, the girl following closely behind.

"My child." Elizabeth gestured, and the girl leaned forward, her neck exposed to the flames beneath her.

"Enough!" Thurzo's voice rang out, bringing the congregation to immediate silence, the dagger in Elizabeth's hand pressed against the girl's throat.

The armed group that surrounded Thurzo and his men tightened their circle. Thurzo turned his attention to the man and woman holding the children. He held up a hand to stop their blades. "Please," he said, his voice breathy and pleading. "Please do not harm them. They are innocents."

Janos smiled, the wickedness of his soul showing through, and Thurzo regretted immediately his outburst. Thurzo's eyes fell to the small boy whose wet, blue eyes were fixed on him, not much older than his own son, asleep in his bed at home. The muscles of Janos' forearm tightened as he gripped the dagger, set to swipe it across the boy's throat.

"Please…" Thurzo begged.

"Janos." The room turned to Elizabeth. "Release the children."

Janos glared at her, his loyalty wavering only a moment before he dropped his hand away, letting go his captive. He gave a nod to the woman holding the small girl, and with some reluctance, she freed her quarry as well. The two ran into Thurzo's open arms and clutched his waist, burying their faces into his sides.

"Stand down, my children," Elizabeth said, moving away from Katarina. "Let the man speak his words."

The room pulled back as one, weapons relaxing.

"Countess Bathory. Elizabeth." Thurzo's voice echoed in the silent room.

"It's lovely to see you, Gyorgy," she replied, dabbing at Katarina's blood still wet on her lips. She threw him an unreadable smile, one that made him wary. Though it seemed she had surrendered, her voice still carried a quiet confidence. "It has been far too long."

Thurzo stepped forward, removing the children from his person, handing them over to the man on his left. He glanced about the room, noticing that the hooded figures that lined the wall were chained there, unable to move more than their feet. His mind recalculated his odds. Not so outnumbered.

"My Lady, you are under arrest for the

abduction, torture, and murder of hundreds of souls."

The congregation gasped, voices filled with dissention and disbelief rang out.

Thurzo turned to the man on his right, now holding the small, blonde girl in his arms. "Go. Tell King Matthias what we have witnessed. Bring the notaries."

"Yes, sir."

"Under arrest?" Elizabeth said, a sweet, musical laughter escaping her bloodied lips. "Whatever for?"

Thurzo turned to her. "I have told you. For what you have done, you can only hope that your uncles will speak on your behalf. You are to remain here, shut away in your quarters until such time as a trial can be arranged. Your staff will be detained and questioned, and your prisoners set free." Thurzo spoke calmly, gesturing to his men to seize the armed as he walked to the altar. "May God forgive you," he said, crossing himself, his thoughts on the many souls lost at the hands of the woman before him. As he approached her, he knew in his heart that she would not pay for her sins. She was protected beneath the veil of royalty, and he loathed himself for being party to it. But sadly, it was the way of things.

"As you wish, my dear Gyorgy. As you wish," Elizabeth purred, making her way to stand before him. "But you must tell me, for I do not understand my crime." She tilted her head, the whisper of a smile on her delicate mouth.

She was beautiful. Even more so in the dim light, her skin smooth and porcelain, lips plump and inviting. He felt himself drawn to her, caught in her dark gaze, and he closed his eyes as her hands cupped his face. He suddenly felt drunk.

"Tell me, Gyorgy, what have I done that is so terrible?" Her voice wove itself around him, creating waves of longing that washed over his entire body. "There are no prisoners here. These are my children. I love all of my children. I treat them as if they were my own. I give them gifts, just as they give me their gift. I honour them." Thurzo's breaths had gone shallow, and his body moved to press against hers, placing his hands on her hips. "Yes," she whispered in his ear, her hands roaming freely. "My dearest husband Ferenc picked you for me. Why have you not come to see me, lover?"

"I have tried, my Lady. I have attempted many times to honour your husband's request and look after you, but you turned me away."

"Sir?" A voice from behind broke the spell, and Thurzo stepped hastily away from the Countess.

"Forgive me," Thurzo said, more to his man than to Elizabeth. He shook his head to clear the fog that had clouded his judgement, wary of the powers she was rumoured to wield. "Take her to her chambers," he barked, angry with himself for letting her get to him in that way, the thought of his sweet wife escalating his temper. "She is to be isolated. No one speaks to her. Four of your best guards at her door at all times. No one gets by. Am I understood?"

"Yes, sir."

Thurzo stood with clenched jaw as she was escorted away, her face contorting into rage. "What have I done? Tell me, how is love *wrong*?" She fought against the hands that held her, the guards dragging her down the hall as she shrieked at them to release her.

A ball of heat grew in his chest as his disdain for the murderess took over his senses. So much death, so much terror. "Hold."

The guards stopped, while Thurzo continued forward. The Countess' eyes wandered over him with lust and smugness. He reached out and grabbed the hand of the girl that would have bled out over the fire, had he not stopped the ceremony. He stalked toward Elizabeth, the girl whimpering and stumbling behind him.

"Do you love her?" he asked through his teeth, stopping before Elizabeth. The girl squirmed to be free of his grip. He savagely pulled the girl forward, Elizabeth's eyes cool and calculating as she held Thurzo's gaze, a silent smile twitching at the corner of her mouth. "Do you love her?" he bellowed, his voice bouncing off of the stone walls.

Elizabeth winced and looked over the face of the girl, her features softening as she did so. "I do, my Katarina," she said.

"You love her, yet you would slit her throat and spill her blood? Kill her for your enjoyment, for your vile, disjointed pleasure?"

"No, you do not understand, I honour her..."

Thurzo turned to Katarina. "Do you feel honoured? Do you love this woman as she does you?"

"Yes, she is my Lady…"

Thurzo raised his hand and slapped Katarina swiftly across the face. She cried out, lifting a hand to her cheek, a red welt already visible on her pale skin. She cowered in his arms, but he saw her eyes clear, her hands clutching at his shirt, searching for shelter. The heavy veil of Elizabeth's spell had finally lifted from her mind.

"No," she whispered. "No," she said again with fear as she turned in Thurzo's arms to look at Elizabeth.

Elizabeth's eyes widened. "Katarina?"

Katarina stepped back behind Thurzo. "Please, take me away from this place. I will tell you everything, please…"

"Take her away," Thurzo said, waving away the guards and their prisoner.

"Katarina!"

"Come," Thurzo said, putting an arm around the shivering girl. "It is over now."

"Katarina!"

August, 1614

"Majesty, Sir, word has come from Cachtice Castle in regard to the Countess…" King Matthias' guard entered the room without invitation.

Gyorgy Thurzo eyed King Matthias. Neither surprise nor remorse was to be found in the gaze they shared, only reserved acknowledgement.

Thurzo turned to the guard. "Her body is to be moved to the family crypt – "

"That's the thing, sir. Her body is gone."

"Gone?"

"There is no body, sir. Andreas saw her fall to

the floor, but when the guards entered her chambers, they found it empty. No sign of her or a struggle, like she was never there at all."

"God help us…"

"My Lady, your life has just begun."

"Thank you, my Lord. Where shall we go?"

"Why, anywhere you would like, I should think."

"I have a longing to go to Hungary first. I've an old friend I wish to…drop in on." Elizabeth smiled, keen to see Thurzo's face once more. She laughed wildly as the power of his Lordship's blood raced through her veins.

"Then we shall go to Hungary, my Lady."

"And then you shall teach me this new life, my Lord. And we will feed."

Samantha Banik's passion for writing began early in her life, the spark ignited by the works of Austen and Brontë. Being a technical writer for Mazda Canada with many years of experience in the automotive industry, Samantha loves nothing more than to let loose and explore her more creative side by dabbling in the Historical Romance and Historical Horror genres. Samantha craves the nostalgic feelings that stir when delving into the bloody pasts of the notable women who have graced the centuries before us. Whether it is love or death, for Samantha, both come with a great amount of emotion when words flow onto the page.

Samantha has had several articles published in the *Orono Weekly Times*, the town in which she grew up, and is currently working on two novels that fall into the Historical Romance genre. Samantha enjoys spending time with her beautiful four-year-old daughter whose youth and passion for life is truly inspirational.

PIECES

Tobin Elliott & Robert E. Walton

"The whole is greater than the sum of its parts."
Aristotle

IN THE BEGINNING, there was the darkness, formless and empty, and though he struggled against it, fought it, still it came. Then there was light. Again. Light and life. And Aldini thought it was good. But lately, he found the darkness a comfort, a balm, and had come to enjoy how it helped him blank his mind.

The curtains allowed a sliver of light to split the darkness, the only stimulus he allowed. It was a focus, an anchor, and it kept the darkness at arm's length. It kept his mind from travelling too far back or too far away.

In the darkest corner of his room, beyond the blade of light, he detected movement. Was it a rustle of cloth, the grate of bone on bone, a glint of an eye? Did Death lurk there? Waiting as she had for…what? Years? Or was it decades, perhaps centuries? The numbers made his head hurt. He lowered his gaze to his lap, to his trembling, mismatched hands. Abominations, yes, but better than making eye contact with Death.

Forgetting the thing in the corner, for he knew it would go away in time, he focused his fragile attention on that trembling limb. His hand.

In his slow, imprecise mind, he considered this. *His* hand? He raised it to the light and examined the hand as he turned it over and back through the curtain of dust motes. The old saying goes, to know something innately is to know it like the back of one's hand. But he didn't know the hand he held out. A part of his brain told him it was familiar, but he couldn't place the memory.

The palm was lined, but not deeply. It wasn't creased with years of toil. The fingers flexed smoothly, with no pain, its joints untouched by the swell of arthritis. He rolled it over to examine its back. He used a finger of the opposite hand—this one a bit larger, brutish—to trace the line of a tattoo that started between the knuckles and wound back in a curling design to his wrist. A tattoo that should crawl up his arm like some slow-moving lizard, yet the smooth tracery ended cleanly and abruptly just past his wrist. His finger paused at that abrupt end. Though it was difficult to determine colours, he could see the fine blond hairs of his hand change to thick, dark, wiry curls on his forearm. *Whose was this?*

He dropped the hand back into his lap before

he could follow that path of thought.

There came a soft knock at his door, followed by an equally soft, feminine voice. *"Excusez-moi,* Monsieur Aldini, would you like to come for lunch?"

The intrusion dragged him from his inner world, back into that damned Belgian nursing home.

"Un attimo, per favore."

In the crack of light, he pulled an old ratty housecoat over his broad shoulders and straightened it as best he could. It barely hung to the tops of his thighs, far too small for his massive frame. He slid his feet into his slippers, the original colour a mystery, now covered with silver duct tape. A temporary sole had been taped onto one slipper, the right, to raise it almost two inches. No matter how much they built up the base, he always felt off-balance, and he cursed himself for the carelessness that it represented. He tossed a once-splendid silk scarf around his neck, arranging it just so, and opened the door. Even with his dark glasses in place, the light from the hallway exploded in his head like a million flashbulbs.

"Bonjour, Monsieur Aldini, did you sleep well?"

An impossibly young, excessively friendly orderly stood in the hallway smiling at him. A small triangular cap with a red cross and a blue stripe held her straight, dark hair back. Her casual pink, short-sleeved tunic and matching pants made her look like one of the many dolls in his room. The large, male orderly standing next to her patiently held the handles of an oversized wheelchair, his matching blue uniform taut across bulging muscles. The orderly resembled one of the blue-tighted heroes from the colourful comic books popular with some of the other patrons of the home. He was a mule in human form and Aldini wondered what secrets were buried inside him.

He responded to the orderly's question with an absent-minded nod, even though he hadn't slept at all. It had been so long since he last slept, he couldn't remember what it was like except that it was too close to death.

The death he had avoided for so long.

She flicked on the light switch. "Oh, you always keep dis room so dark, like eet is the grave? Dis is not good for you, m'sieu. Not, uh, healthy?" Aldini smiled at that last word. *Ell-tee.* She leaned deeper into the room, now that the light was on. He'd only have to shut it off later.

"I see you 'ave made another dolly. But, Monsieur Aldini, one arm, *il est trop grand*! Too…too big!" She stepped in his room and snatched the doll from the table. "It is you, *non*?"

Aldini stared at the doll. He hadn't noticed the difference in the arms before. His eyes flicked from her French manicured hands, to his own, and then to the male orderly's hands. Calloused, likely from the interminable repetitions to forge his body into its current shape, but the hands...*magnifico*! No, he was not a comic book character; he was a fine Roman statue.

They are both fine specimens, Aldini thought.

They stood, waiting for him and he realized he'd drifted slightly, and had taken too long to do the expected, to get in the chair. He lowered his mismatched eyes and shuffled toward the proffered wheelchair.

The chair, all shining aluminum and leather, groaned as he eased his weight into it. Even sitting, he was almost eye-to-eye with the orderly. The female placed the doll back in his room, pulled the door closed and turned to him, smiling. "*Prêt?*" she said.

"Yes," he said. "I am ready." The male orderly wheeled him to the lunchroom to dine with the rest of the old folks.

He knew their names…once.

ALDINI STARED DOWN at his supposedly gourmet lunch. It sat on the table flanked by a glass of watered-down apple juice and a pudding cup. He frowned at the plastic container. Butterscotch, never a favourite.

He shifted his attention to the main course. A plate of mashed potatoes, likely from a box; some unrecognizable, shapeless, green vegetable with the consistency of toothpaste served only to add some much-needed colour to the plate, garnished with a couple of spears of pickles of dubious quality. Finishing off this bounty, two small, pale chicken legs, or drumlets, as the staff would call them. Nothing like what his mother would make.

His mother.

He hadn't thought of her in over a hundred years. He shook his head, hoping the movement would shake the memories of her from his overtaxed mind.

Aldini stared down at his food. The drumlets,

placed with their fat ends touching and their narrow ends splayed out, no doubt someone's idea of fine presentation, looked obscene to him.

Memory sparked in his head like a lightning flash. The sights, sounds, and smells of the cafeteria faded.

Aldini crouched behind the couch in his uncle's den, his fingers pushing small divots into the fabric. He would suffer a beating if he was caught.

His Uncle Luigi and two other men—a professor and a doctor?—stood, huddled together, looking down at something on his uncle's desk. On it was a polished silver tray and on the tray sat two chicken drumlets…

No, not chicken.

Something else. Something… Aldini's mind ground slowly toward the answer. *They were… They were…*

Frog's legs. The memory sharpened again.

His uncle turned to a black machine. Wires snaked from this humming device and connected to the frog's legs. He turned a dial. The hum, already strange and making Aldini's teeth grind together, now cycled up, vibrating in his ears, filling the room. His grip tightened, his knuckles whitened ridges on the back of the couch. The hairs on his arms stood on end.

"More," the doctor said. His uncle turned the knob and the hum pitched higher still. The buzzing made Aldini want to bolt from the room. Then he saw a wondrous thing and forgot about running.

The frog's legs twitched.

And twitched again.

They twitched and twitched until it looked like they were dancing.

Aldini, still a boy, didn't comprehend what he was witnessing, but he felt a prickling in his scalp. His excitement filled the air like the buzz of the electricity.

"Monsieur Aldini, are you all right? You 'ave not eaten a bite."

Aldini blinked away the fragments of the memory. How he wished he could change things, stop time and remain in a life-moment of his own choosing. But time was his enemy. Time was death.

He nodded at the orderly, "I am. I am… alive."

He watched a raised eyebrow, and pursed lips replace the smile as she stared back at him.

"Pardon me, what I mean is, I am, as you say, okay." He raised the thicker hand, made a circle with his thumb and forefinger.

She smiled again. "Your daughter is 'ere to see you."

Daughter?

Aldini's attention shifted to the wall of frosted glass panes set in whitewashed wood paneling at the opposite end of the room. A pair of similarly adorned French doors separated the dining room where he sat from the reception area.

The doors swung inward and a tall woman entered the room. She nodded her thanks to the orderlies holding the doors for her.

Daughter?

All eyes turned her way as she approached Aldini. She moved with a grace that belied her height. He studied her as she crossed the room. Long black hair flowed over her short fur jacket, a leopard print scarf around her neck. Black leather pants ended in calf-high boots. She eased into the chair next to Aldini.

"Father." She spoke it with false reverence, and the word grated his senses. "Do you remember Francesca today?"

She dropped her oversized purse on the table and peered over her turquoise cat's-eye sunglasses at him.

Arrestingly blue eyes. He remembered those eyes. Specifically chosen because of a carousel he rode on as a child, before…

Screams filled his head as the dining room faded. Those blue eyes remained. They stared up at him. All around him, the undulating wails of the wounded and dying filled the air. Flames flickered. He pulled away the wreckage that pinned the blue eyes down. He threw the plane seats aside, no match for his brute strength, and scooped the broken body into his arms.

He ducked his head and melted into the night with his prize.

"Father?"

"Chesca, please, I am right here."

The blue eyes vanished. Once again, hidden by a veneer of dark plastic lenses as she slid her sunglasses back in place. "You were, and yet you were not." She reached into the large bag, now between her boots. "I brought you some more doll parts. The customer is very specific. Be extra careful."

"Indeed." Aldini brought his hand up to take the package, but stopped when his sleeve slipped back. The truncated tattoo and jagged scar stared back at him, ugly by comparison with her smooth hands and pristinely lacquered nails at the end of beautiful, expressive fingers.

He scooped the package into his lap and pulled his sleeves back down, wondering where his gloves were.

Francesca scanned the room before returning her attention to Aldini. "I think it is time to see the therapist again. You need to work on...your joints. If you sit all day, they will seize up."

Aldini shook his head, suddenly animated. "No. It hurts too much. I don't want to go. Please, leave me be."

Francesca slammed her hand on the table. The frog's legs...no, not frog's legs, chicken legs...drumlets, flew through the air. The plate shattered into bits held together only by the green mystery vegetable paste. The Formica table top cracked.

The room fell silent save for the tinkling of plate pieces.

"Father, be more careful." Francesca waved off the approaching orderlies and offered them her most charming, apologetic smile. "I will clean it up."

"You are quite sure?" one asked. "It's no bother."

She smiled, showing perfect teeth, and pulled her glasses from her face, unleashing those eyes again. "Thank you, but no." She had already slipped the broken crockery into Aldini's cloth napkin. "Talk of physiotherapy sometimes upsets him."

The orderly nodded in sympathy. "None of them really like it."

"And yet it helps so much," she said as she levelled those eyes on her father again. Aldini fought tears. He couldn't keep up with the conversation. Couldn't explain to them that she was not who she said she was. Couldn't form the words.

I was brilliant once.

"…Quite the shame too," Francesca was saying. "He is as gentle as they come, really."

She turned her attention back to Aldini. "I will return tomorrow at five in the evening."

He watched her stand, smooth nonexistent wrinkles from her pants, and walk away, either unaware, or more likely uncaring of the admiring stares by many of the staff and even some of the patrons.

When the frosted glass of the closing door obscured her, after the harsh clack of her heels had faded, he looked down at the ruins of his lunch. The drumlets lay on the table in the exact position they were on his plate earlier; splayed. He could have sworn he saw one move.

Aldini slipped the pudding cup into his robe pocket. He closed his eyes and did his best to shut out the world and those wretched legs as he waited for the orderly to take him back to his room.

PIECES

THE BIG ORDERLY came in to rouse him from the darkness. Aldini sighed regretfully, now more a willing companion to the dark than the light. Was there a song? A poem? A sonnet? Something from his past that seemed to fit? Something about darkness as an old friend?

As the orderly helped pull his wretched, failing frame from the bed, the thought was lost. Then again, so was the name of the orderly, a man who had told Aldini his name at almost every meeting. Ingwe? Ingram? Lost. All lost.

The orderly used those magnificent, well-muscled hands to wash and dress Aldini.

"You seem sad today," he said. "Are you not excited to be spending some time with your daughter? She'll be here any minute."

He was once a brilliant man.

"M'sieu?"

"I created her, you know," Aldini said. "My Chesca."

The orderly — *Inigo?* — smiled indulgently at him. "Of course you did. It goes without saying, does it not?"

"What goes without saying?" He'd forgotten more than most men would know in a lifetime, but he couldn't forget the sound of his daughter's voice.

No matter what throat the sound came from.

"Madame Aldini," the orderly said, and there was something in the sound of his voice that chafed Aldini. *The fool is entranced by her,* he thought. *Of course he is. It was how we made her to be.*

Francesca entered then, gliding into the room, smoothly settling herself on the bed, placing her small clutch beside her as she moved a concerned hand to Aldini's back. She turned the full gaze of those eyes on Ichabod, the orderly. "Please, call me Francesca. 'Madame Aldini' makes me feel…" She unleashed the full wattage of her smile on the man. "…so old."

"I assure you, Francesca," and the way the orderly emphasized her name made Aldini's gorge rise, "you are far from old. Barely hitting your prime. A flower just coming to bloom."

Aldini didn't think it possible, but he watched as his daughter brightened her smile for the orderly. Was the man simply blind to her manipulations? Or was it Aldini's two hundred years of experience that made it so obvious to him?

"And," the orderly continued, "as we will be spending the next few days together, you may call me Ingvar."

Ingvar! Of course!

The orderly pulled a small bag from the closet and gathered Aldini's toiletries, all the while talking and flirting shamelessly with Francesa. Aldini was disgusted. His own daughter, offering her wares like a common harlot.

Like the ones I played with over a hundred years ago.

He hadn't replaced a limb in years and had needed to get back into the process of cutting again. Five ladies of the evening had been enough to get him back in practice.

And now Francesca offered herself in much the same way. The language was less vulgar, but the intention was not.

And Ing… – *damn my mind all to hell, I've forgotten again* – the orderly, equally as brazen, with the woman's father sitting right beside her. *They've forgotten me, as well.*

Then the realization hit him. Something — *Ibrahim?* — had said.

"…we will be spending the next few days together…"

We?

"Excuse me…er, Ignacio," he said, ignoring the smiles from both his daughter and the orderly. "You mentioned something about spending a few days together?"

"Yes," Francesca said. "It took an exorbitant amount of money, but I've arranged for both Ingvar and Victoria…" At Aldini's quizzical expression, she laughed, put a hand on his massive shoulder and said, "That very sweet little nurse. The one with the charming accent?" Aldini nodded. Yes, he knew the one. "Anyway, I've arranged for both of them to come along."

She turned back to the lecherous orderly. "The two of you have such a calming effect on my father that I, quite sadly, lack." Of course, the simpering idiot filled the air with platitudes to Francesca, all of which she happily accepted.

When the orderly finally finished — taking far longer than he normally would — he reluctantly left the room, stating he would retrieve his own travel bag, and alert Victoria that they were ready to go. Francesca smiled her approval.

As the orderly left the room, the smile fell from Francesca's face. She turned to Aldini. "I know what you're thinking, Father. And yes, I will likely bed him once or twice. But I'm more concerned with you," she said. She gathered his mismatched hands in her own, pushed his sleeve up to expose the break in the tattoo, then further, to reveal most of the limb. "This arm/hand combination is sloppy. And the arm needs replacing."

Aldini looked down at his hands.

"I'm securing your replacement parts," she said.

"I'M AFRAID YOU needed replacement parts," Carver said.

The voice floated through the haze of pain. Aldini grasped at it. A lifeline that tied him to this world and kept him from being swept into the blackness that sucked at him.

Images from the previous day bounced off him like flotsam in a whirlpool.

A pale body, fresh from the gallows, strapped to a table at the centre of a lecture hall filled with physicians, scientists, and common gawkers.

As with all the crowds before them, they gasped in shock as the body on the table convulsed under Aldini's manipulations. Aldini turned the dial on his machine up another notch. He could feel his teeth ache and the hairs on his arms stand up as the hum of electricity filled the room.

He touched the metal rod to the neck of the corpse. Its teeth chattered like it was trying to talk, its eyelids fluttered.

He heard, with some satisfaction, a collective inhalation from the audience and a short scream as women and men alike fainted.

The sharp smell of ozone filled the air. Now,

emboldened by the audience's reaction, he would deliver the *coup de grâce*. Yes, it was time to try something new, something he had read about in a three-volume pulp novel, a lurid tale published anonymously, but rumoured to have been written by the wife of the poet, Percy Shelley. Aldini had spoken of it with his new friend, Carver, a well-connected and revered doctor. All of this, from the jumping frog's legs to this poor soul's chattering teeth, had been inspired by Carver, and then the sparks of imagination and electricity, as together they pushed the boundaries further and further.

Modern Prometheus, indeed.

Aldini had never worked with an intact corpse before, and even as he performed for the audience, he felt a deeper thrill in his own bones.

He touched the rod to the top of the body's head, right on the portion of brain he had exposed early in the lecture. The body arched its back off the table. A low moan issued from its pale lips then grew in volume to a piercing scream. People fled the room. Aldini stood frozen to the spot in both horror and fascination. The body continued to scream. Then its arms moved. Like lightning, they flailed. The corpse—*can it still be considered a corpse?* Aldini's overwrought mind wondered—opened its eyes for the first time, and Aldini realized it saw him.

The corpse sees me. Dear Lord in Heaven!

The eyes searched his frantically, and, finding no help there, jerked about the room, settling on Aldini's machine.

And still the scream came from its horrible, broken lungs.

The corpse very deliberately made a fist and punched the machine.

Blue light filled the space. Aldini's own screams joined those of the corpse as the smell of burning flesh and hair engulfed him.

First, there was darkness. Then Carver's voice came to him, pushing it aside.

When he opened his eyes, Carver smiled down at him, "We did it! You live, you live!"

Did what?

Aldini tried to raise his hand but it wouldn't move. He tried again.

Carver's smile faded. "No, no, lie still. You'll rupture the sutures. This will take some getting used to, my friend. Your limbs will be foreign to you, and you will have to learn to do a number of basic functions all over again. But, your theories were correct." Carver danced around the table. "Do you realize what we have accomplished here?"

Aldini still didn't understand.

"My God, man," Carver said. "You were *dead*. And now you live again." He leaned forward, close to Aldini's eyes. He raised his hand, shot it away from him, fingers splayed. "You were *over there…* And now…" He brought the hand back, squeezing it to a fist. "You are *here*."

"We're here."

The van stopped at a large bay door at the far

side of a warehouse-sized building. Aside from the immensity of the structure, it was otherwise completely forgettable, nestled among several other vacant and similarly nondescript buildings. No logo or sign proclaimed its business. Only a set of numbers to indicate its address on the quiet, mostly deserted street.

"The economics of our times, I'm afraid," Francesca said.

"You rent dis place?" Victoria said.

"Yes. Some of my company's research is done here, away from the distraction of my main location." She leaned toward Ingvar. "Keeps those prying eyes away." Ingvar smiled back at her, much too broadly for the comment.

Victoria ignored this. "And your business is…?"

"Medical. Technology." She waved a hand, dismissing it.

"This is where we will be staying?" Ingvar asked.

"Yes," Francesca said. "I have all the necessary equipment and supplies. It's easier to bring everyone here, including Father. Far from the madding crowd."

The two orderlies turned back to the building, neither showing much enthusiasm. "Ah, I see you are underwhelmed. I assure you, you will have all the comforts of home." She pressed a button on her smartphone, entered a swipe code, and the bay door first trembled, then rose to reveal the inside of the structure.

Francesca drove the vehicle inside, then touched another button, and the door trundled down behind them.

"*Mon Dieu*," Victoria said as she took in the vast space. Like a modernized set from an old movie, it looked less warehouse or hospital and more gothic mansion.

"Indeed," Francesca said.

The three exited the vehicle, and Victoria gathered the travel bags while Ingvar pulled the wheelchair from the back and got Aldini settled.

ALDINI SAT IN the darkness surrounded by medical equipment. Each implement glinted in the faint glow of Francesca's computer monitor. Tools that were both intimately familiar and yet stubbornly foreign. He ran his fingers over them, one at a time, as though touch would spark memory.

He'd had to leave his sleeping quarters, so close to his daughter's. He had been lying sprawled on his bed, his mismatched limbs trembling from unfamiliar use, when the noises started from the next room over. Not loud at first, but distracting.

Then, they became loud. His daughter. And that orderly. The large male. Rutting like animals and not caring who knew. It wasn't proper. It wasn't respectful.

It was unseemly.

He'd finally had to haul his overlarge frame to unsteady feet and lumber out of the front area where he and Francesca stayed in opulent comfort, out to the darkened floor of the warehouse, subdivided into various areas of research.

Above him, toward the back, a second level seemed to hang from the ceiling. The area where the orderlies—including the one that currently sweated against his daughter's naked body—stayed. What, in his day, would have been known as the servants' quarters. Those hierarchies no longer existed. There were times he wished they still did.

Damn her! She showed so much contempt for the gift he had given her. *Life*.

He cast his eyes around the warehouse, picking out details to distract him from the maelstrom in his head. Then he saw it.

His bag. Casually tossed under a desk, beside a slim briefcase of Francesca's. Someone must have thought it was hers. Why wouldn't they?

It was full of doll parts.

He bent, caught the corner of the bag between thumb and finger, and slid it closer to him. He reached inside and removed a delicate doll head. The weight of the porcelain felt pleasingly substantial in his hands.

There were other parts in there. Arms and legs and torsos.

But it was the heads he liked the best.

This was a new one, brought to him by his daughter. The eyes were blue, and the hair, long and dark, fell in waves over his hands.

It reminded him of Francesca. Not the animal in the other room, but the one he had made.

The better version.

Aldini took the porcelain limbs out of the bag one at a time, turning each over in his thick hands before placing them in precise order on the metal tray in front of him. As he moved to place the last arm, to complete the small body, the tremors got him. Like something had short-circuited in his body, his hands began to shake, small tremors at first but quickly escalating to violent convulsions. His eyes rolled back in his head. His tongue beat at the back of his clenched and grinding teeth.

He initially thought the crunching sound was him biting hard enough to crack his molars, but the sound came from farther away. Down by his hand. A crunch, then delicate tinkling.

"*Ch, ch, ch.*" The sounds spat out of his mouth and dribbled down his chin. He forced a deep breath in through his nose and willed the attack away. In control again, but too late for the fragile porcelain arm that had been in his hand. It lay in pieces on the floor.

He tentatively drew out another limb and placed it on the tray. He examined his work. The doll examined him back, blue eyes staring. Accusing.

The left arm was too big. But that wasn't right, it had been too small. The doll on the table wasn't a doll anymore. As the screams from the other room changed, a small, rational part of his mind realized this for what it was—falling back into yet another memory. The screams took on a more frantic pitch, "*Mio bambino*! My baby! Where is my baby?"

Aldini bundled the still form in old towels and tucked it in the laundry cart next to an identical bundle while the doctor and the nurse comforted the mother.

Perfect specimens? No, not in a physical sense, but they were perfect to him. He would show Carver. He would make life from this miscarriage. One of the laundry cart's castors chattered its agreement as Aldini wheeled it out of the room.

The vision faded, and the dark lab returned.

Somewhat calmed, he sat in the dark, running his hands over cold porcelain, much as that beast ran his hands over the woman he called daughter, and waited until the distant sounds fell away.

Until silence came, he could sift through the jumbled memories squeezed into his overburdened mind.

IT HAD BEEN years since Carver had brought him back to life. Initially, they had worked together, Aldini soaking up Carver's ideas and techniques like a hungry sponge. Then, they worked to perfect it. At times, it was necessary for Carver to find Aldini better hands; better eyes so he could perform the exacting work of reanimating the dead.

When Aldini proposed a new experiment, Carver stared at the patchwork man, disgusted.

"A child?"

"A baby," Aldini said. "Preferably a stillborn, albeit a recent one."

"You're mad."

Aldini chose to consider himself ambitious.

With neither willing to back down, there was a swift and final falling out. Carver cut himself off from Aldini, refusing to admit him if he appeared on Carver's doorstep, refusing to reply to his written entreaties.

The surgeon, though brilliant, was stubborn.

Carver would go on to much greater heights,

becoming the president of the Royal College of Surgeons and a doctor to royalty. He also wrote the most ridiculous, lurid tales of horror, spinning stories of body snatching and the reanimation of corpses. Aldini took these as very clear messages of how Carver now felt about Aldini and their work together.

Of course, with his standing in high society, he could never admit his role, nor out Aldini without hurting himself.

This suited Aldini just fine. It allowed him to continue his work.

And continue it he did.

In the weeks following Carver's departure, Aldini set up his laboratory to receive its next patient. And Aldini took to watching the pregnant women in his area.

Frustratingly, most of the women delivered healthy, robust babies.

Thankfully, in the span of two weeks, there were two that did not. His prayers had been answered.

Aldini took both.

Two perfect specimens.

Aldini looked up from the two porcelain dolls on the tray.

He watched in darkness as the orderly, wearing only a bathrobe and a grin, exited the front area and crossed the warehouse floor to ascend the stairs. He listened as the man climbed to his quarters, his feet making soft noises on the cold metal risers. He heard the *click-clack* of the heavy door as it closed behind him. For a few blessed minutes, all was still again, and Aldini was in the quiet darkness he knew so well.

He stroked the doll's hair.

Minutes later, the door to the front area opened once more, and Francesca, wearing a silk robe that clung to her, concealing very little, entered the warehouse. She stopped, and Aldini watched as she scanned the massive room.

"Here," he said. She located the voice and strode to him, bare feet whispering on the immaculate floor.

As she approached, he took the utmost care as he set the doll's head down on the desk and said, "Are you whole now?"

"Father, why are you here? I looked in your room, then got worried when I didn't see you there."

"Are. You. Whole?" He banged his fist down on the table making the surgical instruments clatter. The doll's head jumped, as if in surprise. The sounds echoed shockingly in the warehouse.

"Keep your voice down. They'll hear you."

"They? You mean..." He didn't finish the thought. "You didn't seem to worry about anyone hearing you for the last hour or so," he said.

She smiled and tightened the belt on her robe.

Aldini shook his head. "You never were satisfied. You complained about the scars. You always wanted more. To be better than those around you. You never understood that it was never about the vessel. It has always been about the spark contained within."

"But father, surely even you can see that the

spark is so much brighter when the vessel is perfection." Francesca sat in the chair in front of her computer screen. "I brought you here to show you that we no longer need to resort to the barbaric methods of old."

She spun the screen around. Aldini flinched in its glow and raised a hand to shield his eyes.

"I've been doing my own research. I…" She paused. "I know you're having capacity issues with memory. Should I wait until you receive the—"

"Get on with it, woman," he said.

She gave him a curt nod. He saw by the line of her mouth, the bend of her eyebrows that he had upset her. No one talked to the all-powerful Francesca Aldini this way.

Except her creator, he thought.

She turned back to the computer, maneuvering the mouse. "I have finally completed a full-scale, detailed mapping of the human brain. The separating of higher and lower functions."

I, he thought. *She says 'I did it.'* He knew better. His mismatched eyes swept around the facility and, seeing the equipment, the technology, he knew far more than just she had worked on this. But his Francesca would always take full credit. The puppet had cut her strings.

She hadn't noticed, or simply chose to ignore, the drifting of his attention and continued to talk. "In essence, it is possible to remove the higher functions like creativity, thought process and emotions, from the lower functions. The basic machinations of movement, the maintenance of heartbeat and breathing."

She stopped, turned to him, fixing him in her

gaze. He heard the passion in her voice, saw it in her gestures.

"Pain and touch are all part of the higher functions. Pleasure as well," her eyes flicked for a moment to the orderly's chambers. "It took me a while to figure that one out, but once I did, it all fell into place." She clicked the mouse. An image of the human brain appeared. She clicked again, and it was overlaid with a spider web-like map. One more click and the brain broke into sections, then each of the sections slid away from each other. The webs stretched, and more filled in, until the exploded view filled the screen.

"Do you understand what I'm saying, Father?"

Aldini caught the general idea, but his thoughts scattered like a deck of cards in the wind. Holding a complex thought felt like trying to hold pudding in a clenched fist. So much of it escaped his grasp. He nodded, but didn't truly see.

Francesca noticed this as well. He saw the disappointed look on her face. "You will, Father. When we give you a treatment, you will." She put a comforting hand on his knee. "All you need to know right now is that there will be no more need to harvest body parts as they fail. No more scars, just…perfection. You and I are both alive only because we walk on the bones of the long dead."

"It is easy to make someone dead. There is no science in that."

"But there *is* science in Death."

"No! You will not speak her name aloud." Aldini took a shuddering breath trying to calm his nerves. "No, the human body is frail and weak. The true science is in the reigniting of life. Making that life eternal is where the magic lies." He rubbed his face with his mismatched hand. "A magic that has eluded me in all my travels."

"But I hold the key to unlocking that magic."

"Then why do you need me?" The answers she might give terrified him.

"Father," she said, "my studies are all virtual, all theoretical. But you? You have practical experience. No one knows more about the human body's nervous system than you do." She smiled and tapped at his temple. "It's all in there, trapped. You forget, Father, I can run electricity through you, the stuff of your life, and it will revitalize you."

"No." Aldini wept. "It burns."

"The lightning exacts its price, Father. It gives life, but it takes payment in pain. Soon though, soon there will be no more pain."

And though her words said one thing, he understood what she meant. *Soon, I will let you die your final death and, after more than two hundred years, there will be no more pain for you.*

And with this realization, he understood that, regardless of the life he had given her, her heart would always remain a cold, dead thing. He'd read somewhere that evil was born into this world through a baptism of fire. But, he knew that sometimes it was simply put there, created out of the cast-offs, just as he had done all those years ago.

She smiled at him again, a slow sensual smile that may have worked on him before when he was...before Carver. But now, it just sickened him. "Besides, I have two perfect specimens. One for you, and one for me."

"What do you mean, 'two perfect specimens'?"

"As I said. The pretty little French girl is for me. I'll download my brain's — well, I guess it would be my software — into her, and we'll do the same for you with Ingvar."

"Download?"

"Father, you know this. I know you do. Download. Put in to. Your mind — not your brain, but your mind, all that you are — will go into Ingvar's brain."

"You wish to…download me into this man." A statement, not a question.

"Yes. That is correct." She smiled her million-watt smile to show him how pleased she was that the old man got it.

"You wish to download me, your own father, into the body of the man you just had intercourse with?"

Francesca laughed. "Intercourse? Father, really? We were not engaging in conversation. We were fucking."

"Don't be so crude, daughter. It is beneath you."

"No, it's not. This isn't the repressed nineteenth century you remember as a child. Women do that now. We fu—"

"Enough." She was trying to shock him now. They both knew she was succeeding. He'd had quite enough. He sighed, trying to get a grip on his anger. "In essence, when this is all said and done, daughter, you will look at the man that you let between your legs, and he will now be your father. That is correct, yes?"

Francesca stared at him for a moment, a nail

absently clacking on the hard surface of the table. Once again, Aldini considered that she was not used to anyone speaking to her like this. People prostrated themselves to the rich and powerful woman. They did as they were told.

Still, he, of all people, had earned the right to act as her equal.

She opened her perfect mouth, then closed it again. She stood, tightening her robe, her mouth a trim, tight line. "I do not have to explain myself to you, Father. If I want to choose a lover, I will choose whomever I want. After all, it is only a 'vessel' is it not?"

"And apparently choose him to be your father at a later date." Aldini offered her a humourless smile.

"If you believe my choice is unacceptable, you are free to make your own." She padded away from him, toward the door to the front chambers. "I know you have *exacting* standards, Father," she tossed over her shoulder.

"Indeed I do, Chesca." He reached for the doll head. Turning it in his hands, he considered it as he said, "You should be thankful for my exacting standards."

She stopped. He saw her head lower. "And why is that, *Father*?" she said finally.

"Because, had I standards as loose as your morals, *daughter*, your legs and hips and breasts and mouth and eyes and hair wouldn't have been good enough to entice that man into the vagina that I *also* chose for you."

She stood, not moving, only her hands clenching and unclenching, for a long minute. Then, without another word, she stalked toward the door, and slammed it shut behind her.

The pieces of the doll's head fell from his hands, nothing but broken shards of crockery now.

Ruined.

Aldini sat in the dark, listening to the dying echoes.

"Put this in your mouth." She smiled. "I don't want to have to replace your tongue like last time."

Aldini, strapped to the table, obediently opened his mouth, and she slid the mouth guard in.

The old, familiar table was now in a small, insulated and soundproofed room off to one side of the warehouse. Thick cables ran to it like veins and arteries to a heart. "The power running through here won't blow out the electronics, and whatever noise you make inside can't be heard outside."

Aldini tended to make a lot of noise during the procedure.

He strained his head against the strap holding it down. He wanted to watch her, to make sure she did it right and didn't add any of her "new ways". Instead, he resigned himself to listening as she clacked instructions into her computer. In the past, he would have heard the coils warming up as the electricity gathered at their core, the click of the dial as she ramped up the voltage. He would have had time to brace himself.

None of that happened though. Not a word of warning or even the courtesy of a countdown from his daughter. The voltage hit him like God Himself, and the thundering power kicked Aldini upwards against the straps holding him down.

It burns.

The frog's legs kicked at the table. *Frog's legs? No.* His own legs twitched and bucked, muscles threatening to tear from bone. The violence of the movement loosened the straps around his ankles enough to allow his heels to bang a staccato on the table. A metallic taste filled his mouth. The mouthpiece ground between his teeth. His tongue battered against the guard as it fought for release. His eyes rolled back in his head. A freight train thundered through his brain, each window a still scene from his past, a memory. The train moved at such speed all the images blurred together until they became one moving picture. A high-pitched keening filled his ears. The sound started deep in his chest and built until it escaped his lips as fast as the train in his head sped past his mind's eye.

It burns!

Then, without warning, the burning fell away.

Somewhere, far off in the distance, his body still juddered against the table, his lips still pulled back in a rictus. But he was separate from that now. He'd entered the eye of this electric tornado.

This is new, he thought with an unaccustomed calm.

He wondered briefly why this had happened, then chose not to question the gift. Instead, he took stock, separate from his broken, patchwork body, but still intimate with it.

And, as he examined himself, he knew then that, like an old battery, this would be his last charge. This vessel could take no more. He had never really been alive. All the parts never truly lived, they were simply re-animated. He was a doll mimicking life, nothing more.

All those years he tried radical alternatives, anything to reinject these cells with life. He traveled everywhere, talked with anyone who might have held the sliver of a solution. When those failed, he sought far more outlandish theories, even studying with a madwoman, going so far as to bathe in the blood of children. When that proved fruitless, he approached her uncle about his vampyric secret to immortality, but the gaunt, white man refused him. "Your flesh has already tasted death. I can do nothing for you, nor would I wish to. You are an abomination."

I am an abomination, he thought. *A mere simulacrum of life.*

But as the electricity filled him, as his mind responded, he became aware of something else. Behind the train that was his life, his mind, another train moved. One he had never noticed before. And yet, as it made itself known, he could only think, *My God, how have I never seen this until now?*

As it came into focus, his creation's voice intruded. She stood at his side. He could feel her there, feel her panic. "Father, what are you doing? I can't shut the machine down. I'll have to pull the plug!"

The scream worked its way up from deep in his chest, tearing through his throat as his jaw unclenched, and the guard was spit from his mouth. "*Nooooo!*"

Aldini ripped his arm free of the constraints and backhanded her across the room.

In his mind, the second train stopped. Instantly, Aldini knew it. He had known it all along, just as all humans—all those of living flesh—knew it, but genetics had kept buried. It was the door, the access point to all the unused parts of the brain.

A quote came to him then, from a book he had long ago forsaken. *In my Father's house are many mansions.* Though his body still bucked and rocked with the voltage, in his mind, in the calm of the storm, he smiled. *Ten per cent indeed.*

He heard her stirring. Felt her move to the wall. Pull the large lever. As suddenly as it had appeared, and only seconds since it had started, the electricity was gone. It didn't matter. Aldini had what he needed. He knew what he needed to do.

"ARE YOU NOT tired, father?" Francesca rubbed at her red-rimmed eyes. "We've been at this for hours."

Aldini did his best to be subtle as he put a bit more bend in his posture, a touch more droop in his eyes. "Perhaps a little, Chesca, but this is important."

Since he'd come off the table, wobbly at first, the world spinning, he'd quickly recovered. Far quicker than he let on to his daughter. His brain reeled with new thoughts, with incredible insights. He realized now that he—and every other human—saw the world through a constricted tunnel.

Now, he saw it all.

And it was glorious.

Still, he'd then had to suffer through Francesca checking him over to see if he was okay. His heart rate had actually slowed, and he'd had to concentrate with all his newfound power to pass the ECG and EEG, and any minor anomalies were explained by the sheer amount of electricity that had been pushed through his body. Manipulating the results was not a difficult thing for him now.

Then he'd convinced her, with a lot of low-level pleading that was, quite frankly, beneath him, to show him more about her brain mapping system. Fifteen hours later, he'd finally exhausted her.

Better yet. He now knew not only what he needed to do, he knew how to accomplish it.

Faking a yawn, Aldini stretched. "You are right. This tired old brain cannot hold information like it used to." He gave her a sad grin. "Perhaps you'll be able to fix that."

"Perhaps," she said, propping her chin on a fist. Her look should have been unreadable, but Aldini saw right through her. Saw her intent. "You realize the problem, don't you, Father?"

"Problem?"

"You've lived in this…" She gestured a hand up and down to indicate his body. "…This interchangeable shell for two centuries." She sighed, dropped her tired hand back to her lap. "You were never meant to live."

He didn't trust himself to speak.

"You were an *experiment*. A way to test a hypothesis. Nothing more."

"Yet, I live."

"If you call this living, I guess you do."

"And you live, daughter."

"But we live in reanimated flesh. Spoiled meat." Her eyes drooped in a slow blink. "I want more, Father. I want to live. Really live. No matter the cost."

"Even if it means stealing someone else's body?"

"You have done so for two hundred years."

"I took only those whose life had already fled the vessel. You would take the living."

"I would."

Aldini faked another yawn. "Let's consider this again in the morning. I grow weary."

Francesca looked relieved. "Yes, tomorrow."

They both walked back to their chambers. At his door, she leaned up and kissed him. "Good night, father. Sleep well. Tomorrow, your world will change."

"Good night, Chesca," he said. Then he walked into his room and stood, listening as his daughter prepared for bed. It took no time at all for her to fall into an exhausted sleep, though, for Aldini, his mind whirling, it seemed like hours.

And through his waiting, one thought circled his mind.

Who is the greater abomination?

When he was sure she was fully asleep, he went back to the lab.

FOR THE LAST time, there was darkness.

Then, through the formless void, there came a finger of light. Francesca peered out through strange, blurry eyes.

She was in her father's nursing home room, or was it her room? She was confused. There was something wrong with her, and she could not place her finger on it.

Her finger? His finger? She was lost. What was she doing in this room? Her body didn't respond. Not the way it should. Not the way it used to respond. Smooth, supple movements were now heavy, clunky. Awkward.

She raised a hand to look at it more closely, but there was a knock at the door. She looked up as the door opened, and the petite nurse, *what was her name?* came in with a tray of food.

"Daughter?" The nurse gave a small smile, as though they shared a secret. "Are you in there?"

"Victoria?" The word felt foreign and lumpy to both her ear and her mouth. Then, the realization dawned on her. "Father?"

"In a sense," the nurse said. "You are now both father and daughter. The most incestuous pairing ever."

"What did you do to me?"

"That vessel is old, now, Chesca. It's dying its final death." The pretty nurse's brows furrowed. "I extracted the essence of my mind, the knowledge, the experience, and left the rest behind." She tapped the side of Francesca's head. "It's still in there. All the memories of my dreams. The insipid conversations. The food I ate. Almost every memory of my long-dead mother." The nurse smiled. "I left all that behind. With you."

Francesca's tongue felt thick in her mouth, but the strange feeling didn't stop there. Her whole body felt foreign. She raised her hand to touch her lips, and a man's hand came into view. Her mouth worked, but she formed no words.

"You still don't understand. You're confused. Of course you are," the nurse said. "I gave you three gifts, daughter. The first is the kindness you would have spared me; I let you live." She reached out, and Francesca felt the cool hand on her brow.

"The second gift was to leave you with part of me. Granted, daughter, it is the worst of my memories, but as this body fails, I hope you find some small comfort in sharing your final moments with a part of me."

"Why?" Francesca croaked, but the part of her mind left over from him, already knew.

"Because, daughter," the nurse said. Her father's intonation, a female voice. "You were only an experiment," Aldini continued. "Another method, another path of research to see if I could increase my own longevity. You were wrong. It wasn't me, it was *you* that was never supposed to survive. When I made you, it was merely to prove a point, that I could create life, not to bring life from a broken womb."

The nurse moved to the door and flicked on the overhead light. Francesca squinted at its glow.

"It hurts, doesn't it?" The nurse—*her father!*—said as she adjusted her hat in the mirror over the dresser. In the reflection, Francesca saw the nurse – her father – smile at her discomfort. At her struggling to cover her eyes – his eyes! - with a large hand.

"Why?" The question more a moan than coherent word.

"Why this body? Surely you know the answer to that. You flaunted the power a female body holds. Made me listen as you rutted, but you showed me the inherent power not just because of the intercourse, but in how it can be overlooked. I saw the way the men in the building looked at you, daughter. When you were beautiful." The nurse slid her hands down over her breasts, her hips.

"There is more power in this form than in all the muscles of that male orderly you coveted. Ingvar is his name. How delightful it is to remember." Aldini flashed a toothy smile at Francesca. "Last night I had pizza with extra sauce, a vulgar meal, yet somehow entrancing, and because I left those memories with you, it was like tasting it for the first time. Intoxicating! I can't wait to find out what other surprises this body has in store for me."

"No! Don't leave us like this." *Us? Me?* Francesca didn't know what was right anymore. She reached out a hand toward the nurse. *My father.*

Francesca watched her father stare back at her as she struggled with the emotions, like a child abandoned at an amusement park.

"Don't worry, my sweet. I didn't mention the third gift yet. You have your dolls, but those old, misshapen hands were useless. Instead, I gave you the strong, supple limbs of Ingvar. A bit calloused perhaps, but still young and steady enough for the fine work. Indeed, you may even find some small comfort in wrapping those arms around you at night."

Aldini moved toward the door, and Francesca burned at how smooth, how easy her movements were. "As for me, you'll never see me again. I have other plans. Plans that do not include looking after a broken woman and a man in pieces."

She flicked off the light and closed the door behind her as she left.

And then, there was only the darkness.

IN THE TRADITION of Spy vs. Spy, Lennon and McCartney, Statler and Waldorf, or even the Odd Couple, Robert E. Walton and Tobin Elliott bring their own quirks to the table when writing. Walton evokes imagery and atmosphere reminiscent of classic horror mavens, Poe and Shelley, while Elliott brings a detail-focused grittiness, a visceral touch, fuelled by his literary idols, King and Lovecraft.

Together they create rich worlds inhabited by characters that will steal your heart and then stab you in the back. Then they'll likely eat your heart.

Pieces marks their first collaborative conjunction and launches their *Of Gods and Monsters* series of books, currently in the works. They've also taught a Masterclass on collaboration for both the Ontario Writers' Conference and the North Words Literary Festival.

ROLL CREDITS

The Inspiration
Writers' Community of Durham Region
Mark Leslie Lefebvre

The Editors
Kate Arms
Colum McKnight

Turning Dreams into Reality
Dale Long
Pat Flewwelling
Tobin Elliott
Connie Di Pietro

Task Master
Karen Richardson Elliott

Authors
Connie Di Pietro
Yvonne Hess
Kevin Craig
Samantha Banik
Kate Arms
Pat Flewwelling
Tobin Elliott
Dale Long
Mel E. Cober
A.L. Tompkins

Made in the USA
Columbia, SC
14 May 2017